By Jardine Libaire

White Fur

The Sober Lush (with Amanda Eyre Ward)

Here Kitty Kitty

You're an Animal

You're an Animal

You're an Animal

A Novel

Jardine Libaire

HOGARTH

New York

Copyright © 2023 by Jardine Raven Libaire

Published in the United States by Hogarth, an imprint of the Random House Publishing Group, a division of Penguin Random House LLC.

HOGARTH is a trademark of the Random House Group Limited, and the H colophon is a trademark of Penguin Random House LLC.

LIBRARY OF CONGRESS CATALOGING-IN-PUBLICATION DATA
Names: Libaire, Jardine, author.
Title: You're an animal : a novel / Jardine Libaire.
Description: First Edition. | New York : Hogarth, [2023]
Identifiers: LCCN 2022055638 (print) | LCCN 2022055639 (ebook) |
ISBN 9780593449431 (hardback) | ISBN 9780593449448 (ebook)
Classification: LCC PS3612.I23 Y68 2023 (print) | LCC PS3612.I23 (ebook) |
DDC 813/.6—dc23/20221121
LC record available at https://lccn.loc.gov/2022055638
LC ebook record available at https://lccn.loc.gov/2022055639

Printed in Canada on acid-free paper

randomhousebooks.com

9 8 7 6 5 4 3 2 1

First Edition

Book design by Sara Bereta

To my Texas family, with so much love

Contents

ONE: RIDING

Honey 3

Milk 23

Chicken 33

Tarantula 43

TWO: PLANTING

Peach 61

Meatball 75

Lime Cake 99

Pet 115

Egg 131

Lone Star 145

THREE: LOVING

Dr Pepper 155

Cocaine 163

Glue 173

Fish 181

Steakhouse 195

Tomato 205

Yogurt 217

FOUR: TELLING

Wild Strawberries 223

Feast 229

Vulture and Dove 241

FIVE: TAIL END 249

ONE

Riding

HONEY

THIS IS A love story, for what it's worth.

NO ONE ON the compound was expecting the girl, because her cousin hadn't told them she was coming. He was working with Ernie that day, and he might have been freaked out by the bees and forgot. Later Ernie would tease Vick at dinner, say he was a bad cousin.

That morning, life sizzled right out of the gate, hotter than usual this time of year. The square maze of buildings huddled under the red ash trees the way animals do during the Oklahoma springtime, slowly and lazily and naturally keeping shade. Most members of the compound were still sleeping, but four shirtless men in Carhartt shorts—Jared, Vick, and Carlos, with Ernie leading the operation—were moving the frantically buzzing hive from near Tim's personal barracks into the field.

Man, they're stirred up, Ernie said.

Ernie's face was worn like a rock in a stream, even though he was just thirty-four years old, and his long hair was bleached reddish by the sun. He was tall and skinny, a goofball, a character. His eyes were almond-shaped, his nose broken more than once. Chipped teeth, red arm hairs shining in the sun. Ernie looked like a hustler-Jesus from outer space, but chances are he was mostly white with a Mexican or Choctaw grandparent.

(He was found, at maybe a week old, in a gas-station bathroom, wrapped in a man's blue-and-black flannel shirt. He'd seen the newspaper article about it. Well, it wasn't an article, it was just two lines in the *El Reno Tribune* of January 16, 1962, and no one ever solved that mystery.)

Ernie felt Tim watching their progress from the screen door, muscular arms crossed and an unreadable look on his face. Tim said he'd had a dream the night before that it was bad luck to keep the hive so close to where he and his wife (heavy with their soon-to-be-born baby) were sleeping, and that's why he needed this done pronto.

Here's the thing: the dream was true. If only Tim was the type of guy to understand what it really meant, maybe everything would have gone down different, maybe everyone could have survived. But he wasn't that type of guy.

It's so loud, Tim said, unhelpful as usual. *Sure y'all are doing it right?*

They don't want to get moved, Ernie said, exasperated. *This is messing them up.*

Um, I don't really think you're going to ruin their mood, Tim said in his "bossman" tone, trying to catch someone's eye to laugh at Ernie with him. *They're bees.*

The group carefully balletically quietly pushed the hive over bumpy ground till it was about five hundred feet from the main buildings. They lowered the handcart and shifted the hive into the wild grass.

Now what? said Jared, wiping sweat from his lip.

We set them free, Ernie said, and removed the screen very slowly. *Here we go, easy now.* Then he got stung on the neck three times—bam bam bam—and he hop-danced in pain. *Well, fuck!*

You okay? Vick asked with concern.

Jared grimaced, looking at Ernie: *Man, looks like they got you three times.*

I'm fine, Ernie grumbled, and slunk back to the compound.

In the shadows of the doorway, Tim's white teeth glowed as he grinned, but he said: *What? It's not funny, I'm not laughing.*

Ernie walked by without saying anything and slammed open the screen door of the kitchen. Cupid, never without his lip ring and beanie, was peeling potatoes, and he cut raw onion for Ernie to press onto the red swelling bumps.

Thanks, brother, Ernie said.

No problem, said Cupid, straight-faced, but then he smiled: *Looks like a hickey.*

Whatever, Ernie said, smirking.

He checked himself out in the window glass and pretended it was a hickey. Ernie was in a state of familiar turmoil just then. He barely had one full thought—it was just loops and spirals and falling stars of anger, hatred, embarrassment, and desire. And it was all about Tim. Ernie had set out to do something helpful. As usual, it turned into Tim making fun of him. Who was Tim anyway? Tim's *uncles* owned this place, and their nephew just lived here, a freeloader.

But whenever Ernie truly considered this, he got moody, because in this world, real estate *did* put Tim in charge even if he hadn't earned it. Sometimes, when reality hit Ernie like it did now, he couldn't move. He just stared at the kitchen floor, knowing how weird he looked—like someone pulled the plug on him for a ten-minute spell. When it was done, he was about to drag his sorry ass, his sweaty, gleaming, tattooed chest, his long and knotted hair, his self, his body, to his bed. He had no energy for much else. But that's when she showed up.

Ernie saw the silver super-dented minivan bumping up the long driveway like a small-town hearse. Out popped an uptight couple. Or maybe they only seemed uptight because they were upset about what they were doing. Ernie would later find out this was a half sister who'd been taking care of the girl since the death of their grandma Inez (the girl lived with her grandmother for years). But the half sister was now getting married to a Mexican cowboy from Ojinaga— a very Catholic man, very strict, very boring—and there was no room for the girl in their double-wide. Which seemed to be an un-Christian idea, having no room for the girl, but here they were anyway, and they sure seemed steadfast in their decision to hand her over.

The cowboy had a big mustache and pleated jeans. The couple waited in the dirt drive until finally the back door of the van slid open and Coral came out. Everyone who lived on the compound was watching from their bedrooms, or from the garage, wherever they found themselves.

In fact, Holiday Ray was smoking at his window, and he said to Staci, still lounging in their bed: *Incoming.* The couple would rehash that moment years later, trying to understand everything. But while it was happening, Ray didn't think for one hot second this teenager could affect their lives—sure, maybe other lives, just not the lives of Ray and Staci. He was more interested in lighting another cigarette. *Come here, baby,* Staci said, more interested in Ray.

The girl held her late grandma's white valise, the case gone creamy yellow in spots, the handle tarnished, as well as a Discman with giant headphones and a trash bag that looked stuffed full of clothes. The couple talked to Tim, who put on his welcome-to-my-world face, but the girl didn't speak. She didn't say one word. The foursome stood under the live oak, arms folded, rocking back and forth on heels, and the cowboy handed Tim an envelope.

From where Ernie was standing, spying from the kitchen door, the girl didn't look like the kids who landed here after binges or stints on the streets in Albuquerque or Dallas, or after they were booted from their group home or got out on bond. With her not-short not-long greasy blond hair, and her black socks in the middle of summer, those blue eyes, her Hanes T-shirt and cutoff black jeans shorts, she could have been twelve and really big for her age, or twenty-two and she simply hadn't gotten wrecked by life yet. In reality she was seventeen. She wasn't a clump of mud. Light pulsated through her the way it did through a yucca blossom or a spider's egg sac. Through the cellulose material. Maybe Ernie wanted her to look afraid, and she didn't, and that was what sparked his original disdain.

The half sister said: *This is Coral, and um, she's a good girl, for the most part, not a bad girl, not exactly. She had an accident when she was little and her hearing's messed up, but she can still tell what you're saying, usually. And, also, she sort of doesn't talk. But she's good at cleaning and weeding and folding, those type of chores.*

Tim nodded. *Hey all right. Welcome.*

Coral didn't shake his hand or hold up her fingers to say hi. She smiled with her mouth, not her eyes. Her two front teeth were tilted toward each other, which signaled mischief or lightheartedness in a way that was maybe false advertising.

Tim kept nodding as if he was assessing her. *We got a bunch of weirdos living here,* he said in his goofy-but-in-charge voice. *They're decent people, though. Some really nice loonies.*

They talked a bit more, then the half sister sighed and moved to hug Coral goodbye. The girl let herself be embraced. Both the half sister and the cowboy reddened as they took a long last look at the girl, guilty like they were leaving a grand piano on the side of a highway in the rain. The couple drove away, and Ernie tried to read all their Jesus bumper stickers.

He lost sight of Tim and Coral as they stepped into the blue barracks where Tim showed Coral to a bedroom; he waited while she put worn-to-translucence sheets on the stained mattress and threw her trash bag in the corner.

Okey dokey, let's get you oriented, Tim said.

As he took Coral on a short tour of the place, he gestured at the hundred acres with grandeur but didn't take her out into the woods or anything. Everyone knew Tim wasn't a nature lover like Ernie; Tim spent his time proselytizing about the Illuminati to whoever was sitting around the picnic table, and watching TV with his wife. He showed Coral the kitchen, the bathrooms and showers, the laundry shed and clothesline. She looked hard at it all, the rims around her blue eyes a bit red, not like she'd been crying exactly, like maybe she was tired, maybe she wanted to lie down and be alone.

Honestly, I exhaust myself running this place, it's a labor of love, he told her, holding a door open. The fact was that everyone else cooked and cleaned while he listened to talk radio all day and lifted barbells on the porch but anyway.

Howdy! Ernie came around the corner and pretended to be surprised. *My name's Ernie.*

Tim told Coral: *And this guy can be your own personal servant.*

Oh, wow, so funny, Ernie said sarcastically.

What? Tim said. *You'd be good at it.*

He's kidding, Ernie told the girl.

But Coral was looking down the porch.

Guess we gotta keep moving, Ernie, Tim said with fake politeness, capitalizing on how the girl had dismissed Ernie already.

Ernie sat at the picnic table and lit a smoke while Tim displayed his riches, pointing out the garden to Coral, thick with collard greens and zucchini vines, and the chicken coop of hens. *I always dreamed of communal living, you know? I'm proud as hell of this place.* Tim didn't tell her that Uncle Axe and Uncle Jay were doing time for selling guns, which was why Tim had run of the land. Those guys had just used it for target shooting and hunting when they were free men living in Fort Smith. They'd laugh if they saw this compound their nephew had rigged up because they were fairly antisocial human beings. Tim never told them his plans, he'd just started inviting a friend or two a few years ago, and it became a crew of people, growing food and collecting rain, collaborating with local bikers to make a living, canning fruit, saying fuck you to the government by holing up here, and discussing various manifesto ideas. No one had really locked down a good philosophy, so ideas floated in the air like ash from a campfire. They all liked the idea of having ideas but did not quite agree on the ideas themselves.

This system of rickety buildings, which could hardly be seen from the highway or the sky, was a kids' camp years ago, in the seventies and early eighties. Firepit outside, long skinny cabins with a few bedrooms in each, an industrial stove in the common building with a table to seat twenty, and faded corduroy couches. Linoleum floors and open closets. When Tim's family inherited the place, there was still a chalkboard left over from the camp era in one of the buildings, with horses drawn on it.

Ghosts of horses.

Those camp kids must be grown, the horses old or dead, the counselors barely in touch with one another anymore and living different lives. It had been an evangelical outfit, and God was still in the light that came through the trees at a certain hour, reaching like a hand into a box to get you.

Tim named people as they passed, walking on the grass back to her room, and then he pointed at the girl, tapping his ear for them: *This is Coral, she's a bit deaf.*

Everyone waved, flashed a jagged dark grin, or winked. The population was like a bunch of students who weren't friends really, they just ended up in the same afternoon detention. It was a roster that wouldn't last much longer, but no one knew that on this blue-sky day. The delusion was that they were there for a reason and the reason would keep them together. Up to today, it was sixteen residents who made their beds here.

Shayna, Tim, and the baby-to-be were the royal family, obviously.

Holiday Ray and his lady, Staci, just got here a couple months ago, because Ray vaguely knew Jared from Michigan and tracked him down when they needed a place to rest. Ray and Staci were coming from Florida, but really they were coming from anywhere and everywhere. They'd always stayed too long when they should have left a place, left a place too fast when they could have stayed. Ray and Staci often stood with a hand in the other's back pocket. Staci was tan, bleached blond, burned out, with scars and classically fake tits. Ray was roughed up too from hard living and riding. A magnetic couple.

Ernie had bounced here on his lifelong tour of Texas and Oklahoma, from home to institution to home. He was an avid reader, a lone wolf without meaning to be, a quasi-biker, capable of extremely complex ornate concertos of manic joy then depression, up for weeks or months then down, and no exhausted, underpaid doctor at any of the low-grade clinics he'd been to in the course of his life had ever been able to help much. What a shocker.

Cupid was a part-time tweaker, an asexual baby-faced runaway from Louisiana.

There was white-dreads Brandy and her girlfriend, Trick. They'd battle every full moon, and someone would get a bloody lip. Brandy did homeopathic tinctures and homemade tattoos and I Ching readings.

The three guys, Vick and Jared and Carlos, were all felons. They worked for a cellular phone company, installing satellites, eating ham sandwiches while suspended on a telephone pole.

Lynn and Judy, a flimsy pair, had arrived last year from Arizona—or Houston? No one could remember because their story made no impression. The couple pretended to be in love, but why pretend?

Mister Plenty often wore an oxblood suit, which looked good in his white Caddie with calligraphic lines painted down its flanks. He'd done enough LSD to have established some lord in the sky who was a constant audience, who never blinked, who admired and purred at the fantastic performance, the theater, that was the labor of Mister Plenty. *That's my stripper name,* he'd say, crunching a carrot he ate whole and unwashed.

Cousin Sherry-Ann, 350 pounds and diabetic, and her four-year-old, Ashleigh, who was scared of demons and also the dark and also mountain lions and also grown-ups and also lakes and also bats and also aliens.

Coral brought the population to seventeen people. Was seventeen simply too many? Did she tip the cosmic scale, or had the upheaval been triggered decades ago, when a butterfly closed its wings somewhere? Tim finished the tour, led her back to her bedroom, and saluted from the threshold.

Make yourself at home, he said.

THE GIRL MUST have slept through dinner, so the next morning, Ernie saw Brandy knock on her door to deliver a welcome breakfast:

porridge with fermented garlic or something like that, and yerba
maté, and wild blackberries canned last summer

Coral, Brandy said, *I want to Honor your Presence here, and Provide you
with Nourishment.* Even when she was speaking, Brandy capitalized
some words.

The new girl sat on her single bed and picked her nose a little—
not self-consciously but not grotesquely. Today she wore a Slayer
shirt.

Brandy went on, with her Zen smile and sense of seniority, *I don't
want to imply a Response from you, I give this to you with a Free heart, to enjoy
at your will, Coral.*

But Brandy did seem to wait for a thank-you. Coral looked out the
window and eventually Brandy left, making a namaste motion, her
harem pants stuck in her ass crack.

So began the wooing of Coral, which wasn't a massive effort and
didn't last long. Because Tim talked about everything in life as trans-
actional, each member wanted to see if a newcomer could be an
asset. Is this someone I can save and look good doing so? Can they
save me instead? Will we fall in love? Will we bond and become
cooler than the others? Will we become cooler and thus more powerful than the others? Will everyone envy us? None of this was conscious, it was just an undertow.

They all watched her chew a peanut butter sandwich at dinner,
refusing the stew everyone else ate. Coral would occasionally look
up and scan their faces. Her eyes were not shallow or dumb, they
were infinite—but infinite with what? Everyone looked down
when she got to them, jolted. They didn't mean to flinch, it just
happened.

Sherry-Ann whispered to Trick: *She's a kid, I bet she doesn't like being
away from home, doesn't like new food.*

That or she's picky, Trick said.

Do you know if she's staying awhile? Sherry-Ann said under her breath.

Trick shook her head. *No idea.*

They watched her like they were waiting to see if a transplanted tree takes root or dies.

She's sort of hard to read, Trick said.

I mean—almost impossible, really, said Sherry-Ann.

Coral licked peanut butter off her hand, her tongue pink and quick.

The compound watched as Coral crept around in the early morning, found the shower, changed inside the stall, and came out wet-haired, the Slayer T-shirt damp already. The story circulated about her "childhood accident" (which was not a childhood accident but something worse), because Vick told a couple people who told a couple others. While rumors often flew around the compound, this one was just a little too sad, too icky, and it lost steam before most of them heard it.

Tim heard it. And when they were alone at the picnic table, Tim interrogated Vick—even though Coral barely acknowledged her cousin.

I'm just curious, Tim said. *What exactly's wrong with her? I mean—what happened to her after—everything?*

Vick said: *Honestly, man, I don't know that much, but I did live out by Grams's farm right when she got custody and the girl was already quiet on arrival.*

Quiet, huh, Tim said. *Like, just didn't talk?*

Well. She was maybe four, when she showed up? Hair was, like, matted with lice, skeleton body, kept shitting her pants. Nobody wanted to take her in because they were scared she wouldn't make it, and they didn't want that happening on their watch. Right? But Grams wasn't scared. Gave her a bath, shaved her head. Fed her. She'd bring the kid along to house-painting jobs, kept her nearby on a blanket in the sun while she worked, that was that. Grams let nature take its course, it was just her way of doing things.

A cloud blocked the sun, flattening the grass and trees.

Coral go to school? Tim asked after a minute.

She lasted like a week and bit a teacher. But Grams didn't give a shit about school.

Right on, Tim said as if he too knew all about not doing things by the book. *Sounds like a hoot, your granny.*

Vick laughed, and when Tim kept staring at him, Vick filled the silence. *Yeah, she was. Shot her neighbor in the leg one day because she was sick of him beating his horse. Then she took the horse and kept it! They did what they fucking wanted, her and Coral. Had their own law. Kind of spooky.* He shrugged. *She and the kid picked fruit and raised goats, and they salvaged cars, and the girl roamed around otherwise. Grams didn't like talking so they made a good pair.*

Birds fought on the lawn, and the men watched.

What do I know, Vick said, stroking his mustache down with thumb and forefinger. *I moved to Tulsa when she was around-about ten and haven't seen her since. Her half sister who you met tracked me down.*

Tim nodded like a wise man processing new wisdom, but he'd most likely already gotten bored with the topic and was thinking about dinner.

Brandy showed Coral how Tim liked the laundry done, hanging it to dry in the sun. After chores, Coral would lie on her bed with her Discman turned up loud. Curled like a snail in a shell, she picked at her lip and stared out the window. No one interrupted her.

After dinner, she sat by the bonfire and watched the fire instead of watching people and went to bed before anyone else. Staci had taken stock of the girl, her eyes widening at those black socks and that blunt haircut. Coral wasn't competition. A zero on a scale of one to ten. Staci was one of the few to hear the girl's story from Vick, and she mused now that childhood trauma either made someone grow up to be extra-hot or the polar opposite, and this was clearly a case of the latter.

On her fourth night, though, there was a big moon, no clouds, and the girl seemed drawn to walk in its light. She slipped out of the house and meandered, soaked it up like milk into a thick slice of bread. Her eyes were glassy with the world's reflection. Things might have taken shape now that were invisible in the daylight. Even if anyone at the compound could get to her thoughts, would they know how to decipher them?

When Ernie watched her disappear into the woods from his window, he assumed he'd never lay eyes on her again. This happened all the time. Someone dropped off a kid, they lasted a few days, awkward and resentful, and eventually the kid scrounged up enough loose change to jump on a bus.

But Coral came back, before dawn, in the same unrushed way she'd left.

He wondered that morning, as he drank coffee and finished reading his book about honey, what role she could play: some bees were born to be workers, others the queen, and there were security guards. And a tiny percentage of any hive was born with little bitty brains wired to be undertakers, to spend their lives getting dead bees out of the house. He found all of this just fascinating.

When he himself had arrived at the compound a few years ago, at the end of 1993, Ernie had a very clear role—he learned to be a good meth cook in prison, and that's how Tim paid the bills here. It's not like Ernie was glorified, he just added value to Team Tim, that's all.

But a few months ago, they'd been cut off from the Mexico supply of ephedrine, which used to be delivered by a girl named Thelma, and now Tim had this rookie Lynn cooking from cold medicine. Just over-the-counter stuff, it was so laborious and stupid, but Tim was convinced Lynn knew what he was doing. The guy spouted equations and chemical names, but he really just used some mutant recipe from someone who had learned from someone who had learned from someone who had learned from Bob Paillet. And Ernie didn't know what role that left him to play.

It was at the end of her first week. Ernie was chopping wood for the oven, and he saw Tim and Mister Plenty walk over to sit with Coral for fuck's sake, sipping coffee at the picnic table by the magnolia trees. Granted, she was staring at the sky and not paying attention, but still. God*damn*, Ernie'd been here for three-plus years and those guys never came to sit with him. Whatever, shut up, who cares, he thought, in the kitchen now, eating oatmeal, looking out the window at a world exploding into green and blossom. He knew the truth at that moment: the girl was going to stay.

THE NEXT DAY, Vick drove the truck up the compound's drive followed by Tim on a tricked-out 1963 panhead chopper they'd just picked up from a high-dollar bike shop. Tim spent the compound's money on his own toys, didn't even try to hide it. Ray was sitting on a decrepit lawn chair, smoking a cigarette, and he watched. Tim grinned like a juvenile and overrevved the machine before coming to a halt.

Jesus, Ray said under his breath, but he knew not to roll his eyes.

In a way, Tim was handsome, with a little dent in his chin like the one a great-aunt would make along the edge of the piecrust. He was 5'5" and came off as the cheap plastic action figure made of a real-life hero. His tight white T-shirt was always tucked in. He gripped the handlebars over and over like milking a cow.

Bro, come check this bitch out, Tim said.

Ray took a last drag and ground the butt under his bootheel. He pushed his body out of the chair and walked over, wallet chain jangling. *Stellar work. I like the bars, and the custom wheels, those are nice. Hey—you ever want to ride her, let me know—but you're the only one.*

True, Ray was the sole resident who'd ever earned a patch from a real club, but mainly Tim said he might loan the bike to Ray because he loved giving Ray a reason to ask him for something. If Ray wasn't down on his luck, running from various stupid warrants, he'd punch Tim in the face for fun. The guy was just so annoying.

But Ray was used to living in the kingdoms of other men, he knew how it worked. The upside being that it was low overhead, for starters, to be part of the pack and not the boss. But he knew submission was the tradeoff to letting someone like Tim do the organizing and leading that Ray was way too lazy to do. He'd noticed lately, though, that his will to yield was decreasing.

Jailbait, Tim said quietly, half-kidding, and jutted his chin to the left.

Fifty feet away, Coral was splayed on the ground against a tree, eyes closed in the dappled light, like she'd been shot from a cannon and that's where she landed. Occasionally she'd scratch her nose and that was how they knew she was awake.

Ray had nothing against teenage girls, but still. *If you say so.*

I'm just kidding. Seriously though—she gets so nervous around me, she stares at me, Tim said. *It's sort of endearing.*

Right. Ray hadn't exactly seen the girl staring at Tim, but whatever made him happy to believe.

Tim got Ray to sit on the bike, its leather seat hand-stenciled with skulls.

You should take the girl around the block, Tim said.

I don't know. Another time. She looks sort of wiped out.

They both watched Coral turn on her side in the grass, and then they looked away simultaneously and started talking about the hike again, as if they'd seen something they shouldn't have.

RAY SAT AT the end of their bed and bounced on the mattress gently, enough to wake Staci up without her knowing he did it. There was no reason for her to get up, he just wanted to hang out.

Huh? she said, barely conscious.

Tree shadows sifted through the rusty screen, and Staci woke up sober for the forty-third day in a row. (When they fled the shitshow in Miami, it made sense to get clean for a minute.) She was like, What's wrong? Because it was still so weird to feel everything, pinpricks of time and emotions.

Ugh, here she is, with herself, on some compound, but wait, someone else is here, she looked around—drum roll—it's Ray! So she wasn't by herself or even with herself; she was with the self of hers that she was when she was with Ray. Thank fucking heavens.

Morning, sunshine, he said with devilish affection.

Mmmmh, she managed.

She sat at her makeshift vanity table, a mirror propped on a couple milkcrates, and licked a brow pencil. After six years of being with this man, a bare face in the morning still made her squirm.

Can't you get us coffee, she said, in her hard New Jersey accent.

He groaned, stood, and did the roll-strut for which he was very famous out of the bedroom door. When he came back, she was powdering her chin.

Ray said: *We're having wild rabbits for dinner.*

She stared at him with what-the-fuck eyes. *Why would you tell me that,* she complained.

Because the look on your face right now is worth it.

Where the fuck did you bring me, she asked, her eyes suddenly filling with tears. *This place is stupid.*

Christ, don't get upset, Ray said. *I was just messing around. Let's take our coffee outside and watch the birdies.*

No, now I'm totally backwards, thank you. I woke up, got my heart and mind straight, and now I have to fucking start all over. The getting-her-heart-and-mind-straight part was kind of a lie.

Aw, come on, quit the bullshit, he tried out. He hovered, always. Enticing her, provoking her. He couldn't stop himself, like a puppy who wanted to play forever.

She stared him down. *Let's not talk, okay? Let's just be quiet.*

But then it was too quiet, so she started talking again. *All right, it's been two months. Plus. What's next, babe?*

What's wrong with staying here?

You said two months, though.

You've got shit to do somewhere else?

What if I wanted to go to cosmetology school, she told him, trying to think of anything. *It's not like I'm going to find one in the middle of nowhere, Oklahoma.*

It's not like you've been looking either.

She rolled her eyes. Staci was a city girl, a lioness of numbered blocks, nightclub strobe lights, parking garages, stilettos, elevators, garbage, traffic, extravagance, exhaust fumes, glitter. She loved how her reflection was fractured and elusive in the mirrored exteriors of office buildings, broken into pieces, filtered through the urban labyrinth. Here, in the countryside, she felt exposed, too obvious against the silence and the grass and the sky.

When she got up, he held her back from leaving the bedroom and kissed her. It was when he looked right into her eyes that she tasted something, felt something, and distrusted him violently. Her blood turned cold.

Why are you pretending to be so present in the moment with me these days?
You're beautiful, Staci, do you know that? Even though you're crazy
Shut up, she said, trying to get his arm off her.

He let her go when he wanted to. Their latest breakup-and-get-back-together had propelled them this far, but its force was fading. It took a bigger badder drama to spark the fight, then the reckoning was shorter and not as hot as in the beginning. But that was how they knew to keep the love lamp lit. Jealousy was their number-one hobby.

That night, at dinner, she realized he'd been lying about rabbits, and they ate white beans, bread, and salad from the garden. Everyone had a chore, washing dishes or whatever, listed on a notepad. To Staci this place felt like a rustic treatment center, or some alternative freaky college in upstate New York that she never could have gotten into. (When she was sixteen, her older boyfriend sometimes sold heroin at a place called Vassar, and she'd stare from the car at these girls with their plaid coats and heavy eyes and braids—what the fuck!—who were they?—where'd those girls come from anyway?)

While Staci swept the kitchen, Vick tried not to stare at her ass as he dried plates. Judy twirled her perm, reading a tattoo magazine, while Coral sat wedged into the corner, occasionally picking up a saltshaker or napkin and smelling it.

Did you finish your chores? Staci asked Judy, annoyed at both girls but not sure she could call out the kid.

Judy rolled her eyes. *Yes, Mom.*

Ouch, Vick said and laughed. *Gloves are off.*

Staci glared at her until Judy closed the magazine, suddenly aware of her crime.

Judy said: *Wait, did that sound mean?*

Staci kept glaring, which she was so good at doing.

Her mouth dry, Judy laughed and put a hand on one cheek, and became earnest. *Aren't we the same age, Stace? That wasn't like an age joke. You know full well we're not the same fucking age, Judy,* Staci said. *I honestly didn't know. I thought—like—are you like thirty-two?* Staci sneered, but her heart was softening. *Not exactly. You cannot be over thirty-three,* Judy said. *There's no way. I would bet my life on that.*

Staci sighed. She took a moment. But then she said: *I've always looked younger than I am. My whole life.*

I can imagine, Judy said, as if talking to a celebrity.

Both Staci and Judy tried to ignore how Coral had been watching them talk like some people watch a tennis match, her blue eyes candidly tracking whatever was being hit back and forth. What horrified Staci, without her knowing why, was not being able to tell if Coral was friend or foe. If someone had asked Staci what she thought about Coral, though, she would have said, *Hold on a sec,* then searched and searched, like looking for a lighter in a handbag heavy with cigarettes and lipsticks and sunglasses and gum and parking tickets and coke vials and keychains and a wallet and pamphlets and loose change and pencils and Polaroids and a candy wrapper; she really thought there was an opinion in her mind but she couldn't find it.

MILK

NOT LONG AFTER, on a late-March night, it was warm in the Kiamichi Valley, and a few of the crew were going to ride into Tuskahoma for a beer. Vick knocked on Coral's door, said her name, waited, and knocked again. It's not that she would go, he probably just felt like he had to ask her. Behind the door where Vick couldn't see her, she sat on the floor, staring at the red sun out the window. Did Coral know what was on the horizon? Was she the only one who smelled blood that night?

No answer. So Vick moved on to Ernie's room. *Get up*, he said, standing in his friend's threshold in a Carhartt vest and violet bandanna, his handlebar mustache yellow against his eternally red face. He glared at Ernie like he caught him doing something sinful when Ernie was just lying in bed reading a library book. *Close that damn thing and have some fun, you never come along anymore.*

Ernie *always* used to pony up when the crew mobbed up and went out. And he'd black out. Nowadays he held back, an old man at thirty-four. He was in a phase, struggling to function. But he let himself be convinced tonight because Vick was a big lumpy doof who meant well. Ernie put on his own vest and pulled his long hair out of it. They crossed wet twilit grass to the garage, and a few others were milling in the dark space of machines. They walked their bikes out of the building and revved up the collective beast.

Leaving the compound always felt like coming out of a bomb shelter. Ernie entered into the world, wanting so much, full and blooming with desire—of what exact sort, god knows. Even while he was on his way, the road into town blurring by in all its telephone-pole-litter-fast-food-joint disappointingness, he was sullen, knowing he'd get nothing. Tim liked to call him a walking self-fulfilling prophecy. *You're doomed by your own hand, Ernie.*

At the Bullet Pub in Tuskahoma, they played pool and bought bison jerky in ziplock bags off Sad Wolf who was always there, and got loaded. The crew united in public in a way they never did back at the ranch. Ernie was the shyest, but he got high fast on the pack energy, like sucking nitrous from a whip-cream can. He postured around, jutting his chin to say hi to this person or that one, jacked up and jumping on flat feet like a battery-operated toy.

Vick gave Ernie a beer and said: *Man, it's good to get out of the house. Either I have spring fever or I don't know.*

I hear that, Ernie said.

Lucky for tequila, Vick said and handed out heavy-bottomed glasses brimming with deathly clear liquor.

Ernie pretended to down it. He didn't drink much anymore because he couldn't hold his liquor. It blew up his moods, and he'd start saying things he should keep to himself. He was also bad at flirting, so when two girls in black cowboy hats asked him to pick songs on the jukebox, he looked to see who put them up to it.

Don't be a pussy, Ernesto, said Ray, in his ear, materializing out of the crowd as if he'd been born by Ernie's side.

Did you give them a bunch of quarters, Ray? Ernie said, embarrassed.

Sure did, brother, and I told them to go ask the nervous tall guy to dance.

Thanks for the vote of confidence, man, Ernie said.

Ernie felt like Ray was putting a rubber band on a cat's tail just to fuck with it for laughs, but he went to the machine. And ended up having fun arguing over Johnny Cash hits with the ladies.

"I Walk the Line," trilled one of the cowgirls. *Let's put in a hundred quarters and keep playing it over and over?* As if she invented that game.

And then Lynn arrived, with Judy by his side. Ernie wanted Lynn to see him with the girls, so he started yelling *woo-hoo* as he danced, but Lynn got immediately involved in the Daytona arcade game in the corner. Lynn had a rich luxe mullet, but it was thinning on top and Ernie felt this fueled a lot of Lynn's behavior. He tried not to watch, but Lynn kept making these exaggerated moves as he played the game. Loser, Ernie thought.

Judy perched on a barstool like someone she wasn't and twirled a drink stirrer in her mouth and watched Lynn play. Ray cheered Lynn on, then heckled him when he fucked up. Staci had stayed home and Ray was bored. Even when Staci was there, though, Ray could become supernaturally bored, bored enough to light the woods on fire just by looking at the trees with that boredom in his eyes.

Did you just lose again? Ernie shouted toward Lynn at one point, but no one heard.

He went back to two-stepping.

Lynn won fourth place and Judy pumped her little fist, the limp gold bracelet stuck to her skin. Ernie's hackles went up. Lynn put his tongue in her mouth, and Ernie felt like puking. Were they having fun at all, or was this a show of being part of a crew, having a blast, wild night with my buddies, hahaha, lost track of time? Do they ever even talk to each other, say real things? Their insincerity was fat and greasy like cheap bacon.

Ernie, Ray said. *You got that look on your face.*

Time to hit the road before he got into a scrap. On his way out, Ernie got kisses on both cheeks from the cowgirls, their hat brims tilted back, and he had red-lipstick marks as he walked into the parking lot. He was leaving first and alone (as he often did), so he wasn't there when the phone call came into the bar just moments later, and didn't know what was waiting at the commune.

Ernie jumped on his bike and rode, and he opened his whole self to the world around him, felt the planet as the seething foaming life-extravaganza that it was. As he entered dense woodland, Ernie thought of those girls, and how they could all three fall in love, and the things they could do if given a motel room and a bottle of fancy pink wine and a couple days and nights. Ernie had the ingenuity of a god, a creator, and could devise romantic universes in a hot second. There was never sex in these stories, just formless shapeless soul-melding and joy.

Riding up the long driveway, he saw lights in the main room. He walked in to find Shayna on all fours in a blow-up kiddie pool of heated water, Brandy rubbing her back with oil. She was moaning, and Sherry-Ann was on hand with towels and pots of boiled herbs. Ernie didn't physically recoil, but he did get primordially anxious. *Oh my fucking lord,* he whispered to himself. *It's happening!*

Brandy made her way over to him while Shayna continued breathing and kneeling. *Cupid and Trick are in the kitchen, on deck. Wanna wait there, we'll let you know if we need help? Here, take these.* She handed him towels with red spots.

He looked at the cloths in his hands, horrified. Then at her with big eyes. *Is this—is she okay?*

She's doing Amazing, it's normal. Just throw them in the washing machine. Yeah, you got it, Bran. He backed away, thrilled to be released. And that was when he saw Coral sitting on the floor in the corner viewing the scene like she was watching primetime TV. *She's gonna stay?* he asked Brandy.

Brandy looked toward Coral. *Why not?*

Ernie put the hand towels gently into the washer, like he was handling the violence of miracles, and then spent the next few hours in the kitchen. Trick had called the bar so the crew raced back, and everyone drank beers and ate sunflower seeds, spitting out the shells, and waited. Tim stayed in the other room with Shayna, and Brandy, and Coral. Ernie kept dwelling on the girl being included.

Shayna was crying and cursing, and yet it was more frightening when they didn't hear her. No one said anything but they all looked at the floor. Around dawn, she screeched like nothing Ernie ever heard. Then Tim carried in a tiny little soul, red and veined, in a blanket smudged with stuff.

Tim was manic, his eyes blazing. *Luther. This is Luther.*

The baby's mouth was perfect, pink, sucking at the air already.

And Shayna is—she's . . . ? Vick asked.

She's great, just great.

Tears, hands over hearts, a silence as the room gazed on the prince.

SPRING RAIN, A downpour mornings afternoons and nights. Then a few days of leaden heat. Tim managed to hide it from most everyone that Shayna was going through a rough time. He and Brandy had a furtive talk after everyone finished breakfast one morning, Tim swirling the black coffee in his mug like cognac.

What is it? Motherhood isn't what she thought it would be? Tim said, apparently aggrieved. He was the kind of man to think his wife should be as thrilled and giddy as he was.

So many women go through this. It's like a mystical Sadness at being separated from her creation. She's a brave Warrior, Tim. She'll survive.

Should I try to force her out of the house, go get a steak dinner or something?

Brandy shook her dreads. *Naw, man. Not yet.*

I could make her start running five miles with me every morning?

Maybe not?

Tim licked his fingertip and picked up grains of sugar off the table. He ate them, and sighed. *She really doesn't like giving Luther formula, and neither do I, based on everything I've read.*

We have no option, Tim, it's just not happening. Formula is it for the moment. Let me brew another tea, we'll just keep trying different ways of healing and dealing, cool? She's a Goddess. The Universe will take care of her.

He went back to the bedroom where Shayna was lying in their bed. Her dark hair was unclean and gleaming; she was elegant the way depression could make a woman sometimes. Tim had given her silk pajamas as a present, but she had on his Hanes T-shirt and her old panties. He held Luther over her like displaying a work of art. The little creature was three weeks old today, and Tim kept saying he was still scrawny because he wasn't getting real milk.

He arranged Luther on her chest. Shayna pulled down the sheet, and his face was pressed near the 14 Celtic cross, double lightning bolts, and death's head tattoos on her sternum. Luther put his rosebud mouth on her nipple (which was cracked and sore), and turned his head, bumping her teat with his lips, angry, starting to cry, crying more now, and screaming. As usual.

Shayna met Tim's eyes with sorrow, a listless apology. The way Tim looked at her betrayed his infatuation: that noble face and long wavy lustrous chestnut hair, and her athletic shoulders, strong like Joan of Arc, she was curvy and beautiful as an Olympic high-jump champion, loyal, devoted, quiet, humorless. He took Luther away, and Shayna closed her eyes.

I'll be right back, he said, his voice casual to soften the departure.

Tim took Luther to the kitchen, which was warm with sun. Brandy was boiling herbs that smelled gross—Tim let go of his nonchalance and was clearly emotional. Because she happened to be there, Coral was asked to carry Luther from one end of the room to another, rocking him, kissing his skull, as Tim heated up a bottle of formula and talked fervently to Brandy.

And then—Coral's shirt was wet.

Brandy couldn't hide her surprise—and then gave a belly laugh. *Are you serious? Dude, I know this cross-feeding shit goes down with chimps. But this is dope.*

She sat Coral on the sofa to teach her the basics. His head had been hanging back, he could choke. Brandy repositioned Luther on Coral's big white tit. And so the baby drank from a different woman. Tim went and told Shayna bluntly, just to get it done, and then he tried to smooth her ego like you pet a wild goat.

I think it says a lot that our community loves you so much they're willing to do things like this for you, he said, desperation showing at the edges. *You're like a queen served by the court, you know?*

She didn't answer.

Shayna had never straight failed. The first time she bowled, she knocked over all the pins. She made her way down the highway like a NASCAR driver. Men knelt at her feet and sang country songs their mamas taught them. When she wanted to go outside, she opened the door and the storm stopped, the sun came out, the rainbow shimmered. Until now. The effortless run of excellence, which everyone thought was a sure thing forever, just ended. It ended. It was this that kept her in dirty sheets, unable to even turn over some hours.

And so it went.

Shayna stayed in bed, and someone else fed her child the cream of life. Maybe Coral never meant to parade her new role, but her face was glowing for the first time since she landed here.

Everyone clocked what was going down with the girl and the baby—it was elemental, like noticing a newly discovered moon orbit the planet. No one talked about it, though, which was interesting because they casually and regularly discussed things over scrambled eggs like anal sex and race wars. This was hushed, a forbidden topic.

They'd all settled on their own ideas about Coral; it was a guessing game. Some decided she was an idiot. Others saw a superiority complex. She flitted through one person's consciousness as a sacrificial-lamb figure. A lewd daydream or two might have crossed someone else's mind but they'd never admit it. One person worried that she was like a broken-legged fawn that would get too domesticated to ever be returned to her habitat. Brandy had even projected hardcore Buddha-ness on her. But no one—*nobody*—had foreseen the part she was playing.

Early morning, Coral was handwashing pillowcases, baby bibs, and sheets outside. The sun also seemed to be washing the day, giving the sky a good rinse, and the birds were rioting in the trees. Coral's breasts were full and heavy. When Tim finally came to get her, she grinned, acne around the jaw, blue eyes lit. She quickly and crookedly hung the rest of the linens, and walk-ran inside.

Shayna was sitting in bed, propped against pillows. In Tim's short, stocky arms was a stack of baby clothes he was putting away in the dresser. He looked to the crib and Coral went and took their kid. Shayna looked away. Back in the dark curtain-filtered sunlight of her own room, Coral wet-nursed Luther. Days and nights went by. Nothing changed except the baby getting pink-cheeked and chubby.

Afternoon. In the next room, Coral was curled on her bed,

plugged into Megadeth, headphones crackling with so much noise that her ears shivered and vibrated. Tim brought Luther in and she sat up quickly, her teenage face wide-open the second she laid eyes on the baby.

Thank you, Tim said, mouthing the words in a dramatic way.

She smiled and it seemed not aimed at him but accidentally grazing him while she held her arms open for the babe. Even though the girl seemed powerless, she was also dismissive, and threatening; Tim had a look on his face that could be described as exquisite discomfort.

When Tim walked out, she pulled up her shirt. As Luther gulped, and milk ran down his chin, she inhaled the soapy smell of his head, touched the hair growing in whorls, watched his eyes occasionally struggle to hers, glassily making contact. Luther fell asleep in her arms, and she held him, the weight of him in her arms, the breathing, smelling his sweet-sour breath, touching the fragile dumpling of a tummy rising and falling, and she finally padded barefoot to put him into the crib while Shayna watched in the dusk light, and the woman's dull unpainted eyes followed Coral as she left the room.

What's your story? Shayna blurted out.

Coral turned to look. Stood there.

Never mind, Shayna said, turning her head away on the pillow. *I don't care.*

CHICKEN

ERNIE LIKED TO walk the property's perimeter after dinner as a way to keep his spirits up, not that he expected to "catch" trespassers. Anyway, the only people in these parts who'd ever intrude were dangerous not because they were stealthy and brilliant, but because they were so desperate and fucked, they'd risk anything. Ernie had been that guy back in the day. No way to protect against madness like that.

On his mission, Ernie sometimes playacted being a Comanche warrior or a Texas Ranger, unleashing both stories in the dreamland of his body. Once in a while, he imagined he'd moved into his ex–foster mother Gloria's basement, and he was fiercely guarding her. Maybe she counted on him now that he was a grown man.

The clouds were thick, the moon a sliver. Walking by the kitchen, he was considering getting a pickle before he retired when he felt the vibrations of two people. He stopped, unnoticed, and saw their silhouettes under the live oak outside the main building.

He heard Shayna, who he'd barely seen since she had the baby. *I* hate you, she said. *I hate this life. I hate everyone who lives here. I hate myself. But mainly I hate this place.*

That's a little harsh, Tim said.

Even Ernie knew this wasn't the right thing to say.

Harsh? she asked. *Do you want me to be specific?? I hate the smell of the floors, the stink of the beds, the sulfur in the water. How even when you're alone here you're never alone, 'cause someone is always in the next room, right out the window, walking down the hall. I hate the way we pretend we're one big family but everyone's shit-talking everyone else. And I hate that CUNT who takes— our—baby—*

Here she started to cry. To sob, actually, like a pig. It tore Ernie's heart from his rib cage.

I just thought she could help— Tim said.

She's helping me feel like a piece of shit!

Tim sounded beseeching, which was unprecedented: *I've read all about it, these aren't your real emotions.*

Fuck you for telling me what's real, she said softly.

The sound of leaves pulled off a branch. Ernie waited for Tim to answer. But he didn't. There was just the silence of the night, and little crystal-bead molecules of light exhaled by the moon. I know Luther is a blessing, Ernie said in his head, as he quietly let himself into the kitchen. But the baby had driven the couple apart.

Ernie felt embarrassingly glad about this because he'd been so jealous. As Tim worshipped the pregnant Shayna, parading her around in tight sweaters when she was about to pop, Ernie used to think bitterly: The world doesn't revolve around y'all's majestic capacity to make life. But Ernie also knew the earth *did* revolve around Luther. It should, it did, to love a child was the right order of things, and Ernie fumed as he looked for the pickle jar on the shelf, ashamed of his soul's furnace.

Ernie straightened up when he realized he wasn't alone in the room.

The girl, the deaf one, the blonde, the misfit, the one and only, stood near the giant butterscotch-yellow 1950s fridge whose base was dirty like a skirt hem dragged in the mud. She was eating an orange by peeling away just enough of its skin to get her mouth into the fruit. Who did that? Everyone peels all the skin first. He gave her quite a look. She gazed back with blue eyes that glowed in this unelectric shadow. He left, head down, pickleless.

LIFE WENT ON at the compound, March coming to its conclusion cloud by cloud, leaf by leaf. The sun got stronger. Ernie would later realize that he knew what was happening, without processing it, that he knew life here was breaking apart. One week slipped by in a hot and sweaty manner. Another week was sliding out of their grasp, its hand too wet to hold.

It was early morning, Coral placed Luther back in his crib, his fists under his chin, a drop of blue milk still quivering on his lip, his eyes drowsily closed. Shayna was standing at her window, looking onto flowers among the rocks without registering them: the arrow-leaved violets, and the prairie trout lily, that white flare of petal hidden among crags. Coral looked at them, too, and might not have known their names—the flowers themselves were a language.

Thank you, Shayna said after all, but without looking at the girl.

And that was the last thing she'd ever get to say to Coral. Tim tapped on the window from the outside and beckoned the girl to come into the yard where he was talking to Ernie.

I need you to run into town, Tim said.

Sure thing, Ernie responded. *I could use a little road time anyways.*

Take Coral.

Ernie and Coral looked at each other. Honestly, he didn't know why he disliked her as much as he did, but it had to do with her look right now, there, that absence on her face. Like she didn't give a shit about any of them. That was how Ernie interpreted it. And Coral didn't seem to want to ride with him, he could sense that. Her pudgy hands hanging on the belt loops of her black shorts, T-shirt yellowed at the armpits.

I said take Coral, Tim stated.

I never said I wouldn't, Ernie answered. *Fine.*

You sound like a teenager who doesn't want to do his chores, Tim said, smiling.

I said okay, Ernie answered quietly, no fight in his voice.

And Dale will meet you at the Red Stone around two.

Dale handled transactions for the local clubhouse that sold and distributed for the compound, their biking channels dropping off yellow crust through the Southwest. No drama, just business, ordinary as truckers driving eggs or mangoes. It was very very very interesting how Tim respected other men in the commune and even a few women far more than he did Ernie, and yet he only trusted Ernie to pick up cash. But was it a compliment, that he could be trusted with the money? Or did it mean he was a dog, loyal and weak?

Now Tim told Coral the shopping list at high volume. *We need diapers and wipes. More pacifiers too, they keep disappearing, I don't know how.*

Coral nodded.

Don't get lost, Ernesto, Tim said.

How could I get lost? Ernie asked.

Tim had already started walking inside. *Holy shit, you got to learn to tell when someone's kidding.*

Ernie stared after the man, that wasn't even funny, *don't get lost?* How was that a joke? So pointless.

In the huge, dank garage, gleamingly jammed with tractors in various states of disrepair, wheelbarrows, rakes, Trick's 1986 Ford Escort plastered in Grateful Dead and Greenpeace stickers, and motorcycles, Ray and Staci were working on her ride, tools splayed on the cement floor. The tank was painted candy pink. She loved it, and Ray loved helping her fix it up. Ernie and Coral got on Ernie's bike, the army backpack strapped to Coral's shoulders. They were awkward with each other's bodies.

Are you guys going into town? asked Staci. *Me and Ray need a bunch of odds and ends, mind if we tag along?*

I mean, we've got specific errands we have to do, Ernie said.

Not a problem, she said, since they didn't need anything, she was just dying to get off this property for a few hours. *We won't be in the way.*

They hit the highway, two pairs on two bikes. Ray on his customized Harley, and Ernie on his 1976 Honda CB750, its four-cylinder engine spooned into a chopped frame, a coffin tank resting on its backbone. Staci held Ray out of love. Coral held Ernie so she didn't die.

They rode. The highway was a lean ribbon, the sky big and blue. Ernie's long reddish hair fluttered madly in the wind. Coral leaned when she had to, pressing against him as minimally as possible. Ray had a long braid, dark hair streaked with gray, and a party face— a short beard, big happy eyes, a kissable mouth, a joke waiting there, always, to be told to you or at your expense, or both. Staci's bleach-yellow bangs flew in the wind too.

They nudged up against the speed limit, but nobody wanted trouble, so they just appreciated the clean sweet tar under their wheels. Spring was in their nostrils, down their throats, pollen sticking to their eyelashes, the way the season gets inside you when you're riding.

They stopped first at a store called Needlemeyer's and bought fifteen boxes of Allegra for Lynn, cleaning out their inventory. Then they went to Red Stone, to the statue marking the hiking trailhead, and there sat Dale in his black big-wheel pickup, Confederate-flag decal meticulously positioned on the rear window. Dale handed Ernie a brown paper bag of cash, which got crammed into the backpack. The operation was smooth and sociable, like ladies selling makeup in their hometowns.

At Banner Pharmacy, Coral perused the baby aisle. Ernie thought Coral had an old-fashioned face like a Swiss shepherdess. He looked at the red spots on her jawline, the tomboy clothes. Even focused on her task, she had an elsewhereness. Ernie approached as she piled diapers into a basket.

Man, you're like the official babysitter already, aren't you? he asked.

Coral looked at him. He'd barely ever spoken directly to her.

You haven't even been here that long and Tim like trusts you with everything.

Coral waited as if she wanted him to make his point.

I can't tell if you're smart and quiet, or super-naïve, he added.

She went back to picking out diapers, but he didn't know if she was offended, or if she'd even understood. At the counter, Ernie put down eighteen Sudafed boxes with the baby stuff. As he got rung up, he threw a couple packs of Bubble Yum into the pile.

That too, please, ma'am.

They grabbed lunch at Whataburger, unwrapping burgers at an outdoor table. Ray slurped his strawberry milkshake from the cup, and it hung on his mustache. Staci made sure she was getting sun on both arms so her tan would be even. Ernie had ordered Coral a double patty melt and fries because that's what he got, and she seemed to be digging it. It was a funny quartet of human beings who didn't really know one another.

Staci was going through the stuff she'd bought, and noticed Coral looking. She enunciated dramatically to Coral: *I'm a gratitude-list person. I needed a new journal and some cute pens. So.*

I'll never understand why you need to write that stuff down, if you already feel it, Ray said. *But whatever works.*

Ernie, do you think it's silly? asked Staci.

Not at all, Ernie answered sincerely.

Ray was smoking and feeding his hamburger bun to the crows.

Not hungry, Ray? Ernie asked.

Nah, man. I'm just trying to stop eating when I'm full, you know? Instead of always having to finish everything.

Ernie didn't need to think that way because his metabolism worked at light speed, but he didn't say anything. They sat for a while in the shade, no one talking. The air felt good. Ernie would normally keep chatting out of anxiety, but Coral being deaf, it almost felt polite to be quiet. He tried to keep still and it was hard. Staci noticed that his long, tangled hair and impenetrable sunglasses made him look like a 1970s rock star just off a coast-to-coast tour. She rummaged through her new stickers and tinsel-tasseled pens with adolescent excitement. At a certain point, Staci realized Coral had finished her own fries and was now eating Staci's—Staci was done, but still.

Staci laughed throatily. *Okayyyyyyy.*

Ernie grinned. *That's bold.*

Coral wasn't doing it furtively, just steadily. She ate the last one and wiped ketchup off her mouth with the back of her hand. Then she looked at everyone, not flinching. Ernie and Staci made amused eye contact with each other, which was fun—they were briefly conspirators.

We should hit the road, Ray said, getting bored and never afraid to show it.

Staci gathered their wrappers and sauntered in her little denim cutoffs to the white-and-orange garbage bin.

Ray called to her: *I love how you can eat a cow no problem but can't handle rabbits.*

Don't start, Ray. Her voice was enough to keep him from continuing.

A couple moms and their tots at the next table froze in place when Ernie and Ray started their engines. Everyone watched the machines roar out of the drive, girls hanging on the backs, bodies all bumping over the seam of the road. Coral with Ernie, Staci with Ray. They rode helmetless but otherwise safely, signaling by hand. The sky was crystal, the highway sparse, a caravan of eighteen-wheelers in the right lane.

A half mile from the commune, Ray noticed smoke on the horizon above it. He swerved up to Ernie and pointed as they rode side by side. The bikes pulled onto the shoulder when they got closer, and they watched the fire raging. Tongues of flame erratically showed above the tree line, and loads of smoke churned. Their faces were taut, blanched.

Ernie's insides twisted. *We have to go see,* he said.

You know we can't, Ray said.

We have to, Ernie insisted.

Staci grabbed his forearm: *Tim would want us to get out of here.*

Sirens, faint, getting louder.

Ernie, Ray said, looking around him. *Me and Staci have to run, with or without you.*

But Coral got off the bike. They watched her walk slowly across the grass, as if drawn to the compound. A helicopter appeared in the sky, hovering.

Coral, we got to go, Ray said in a big-brother voice.

She didn't turn around. Ernie kickstanded his bike and walked to her, put a hand on her shoulder. She jerked away. She dropped to her hands and knees and started crawling in the direction of the flames.

She's being crazy! Ernie shouted.

It's the baby, Ernie, Staci explained, because it was clear to her.

Coral looked back at them, face blotchy over her shoulder.

Ernie squatted and yelled down at her: *You're heading into a fire and a mob of police?*

Staci was desperate for him to understand. *Ernie, it's the baby.*

Ernie tried to pick Coral up, grabbing under her armpits, and she violently pulled away.

Are you fucking serious? he said shrilly.

He made another attempt, and Coral turned on her back, ready to fight. Ray revved the engine and Staci clutched his waist, and Ernie remounted, staring as Coral went back to crawling, and both bikes tore off as more sirens screamed in the distance.

Coral stopped and kneeled in the tall grass like a zombie. She was shaking but didn't cry, her blue eyes fixed on the disaster in the distance. Suddenly, a chicken raced by, in a ragged cartoon gallop, its wing singed. Her eyes committed to the smoke. Tears welled up, and she smeared them away with a fist. She stayed there for a long, paralyzed moment.

A vicious buzzing behind her. It was a bike—Ernie had come back. The helicopter was turning in their direction, the insectlike body tilted forward, determined, and she stared at it, then stood up, tripped over to him, and got on the bike.

They rode away.

TARANTULA

RAY AND STACI had been going slow so Ernie and the girl could catch up, and they all traveled in a time warp of hours, heading west on 199 then 70 without a destination, running from the fire. Late afternoon, they finally stopped outside Waurika, at a defunct gas station under a stand of huge trees. They pulled their bikes behind the impotent tanks and the building whose glass door was smashed; nature was taking over inside, vines crawling through shelves that used to hold engine oil and potato chips. They caught their breath.

Where to? Ray eventually asked Ernie.

Staci and Coral stared at Ernie too. He never guessed they would look to him, he wanted to whimper, but they kept staring.

Go south? he said, pulling his hair in distress. *Leave Oklahoma?*

Silence as they looked at one another. No one objected so the foursome set off with military calm, in a silent and controlled dread. On one stretch of highway, Coral was leaning back, a deadly

move, and the bike wavered; Ernie signaled Ray to the shoulder
with him.

He turned to the girl, jaw tight, and spitting: *What the* hell. *Hold on,
lean* with *me.*

Coral looked away, her mouth trembling, and something made
Ernie look down. Breast milk had soaked her shirt. She'd missed a
feeding.

Sorry, he mumbled.

She didn't look at him, her eyes brimming.

They got on the road again. They were all devastated, frightened.

They were suddenly in Texas, taking 79 South to US-82. Where
were they going? They could spend tonight in Lubbock, or right outside town would be better, Ernie thought. He realized they were on
track to hit the desert sooner or later, and then Mexico. The desert
felt too open, nowhere to bunker down, and crossing the border was
unthinkable. But if they looped around tomorrow and went south
then east, they'd eventually hit the San Saba River. They could end
up in the vicinity of Gloria's house, where Ernie hadn't been in many
years. A house he couldn't imagine seeing again.

They rode, tilting in sync at long curves, taking back roads when
they could. They bought Twinkies and sodas at the most brokedown
market they passed, staying off the radar of the bigger gas-station
stores with cameras.

The glimmer of a half-moon, early in the turquoise evening sky.

The dark shapes of deer moving on the road.

Blinking red stoplights.

The white line, luminescent.

Ghostly buildings, then nothing, then black woods, then buildings, then nothing at all.

Ernie signaled to an abandoned shed and they rolled the bikes
into the rotted building. Their faces were road-grimy, bleak with

anxiety. Their eyes were jittering with lampposts and signs, post-ride strobe flashes. No one spoke. Staci and Coral stepped into the field, stamping for snakes, then squatted, and hot piss hit the dirt. Ray and Ernie made beds for everyone on the dirt floor using vests and a mildewed tarp they beat for spiders and scorpions, and they all lay down, staring at nothing.

We're just going to be hungry tonight, Ernie said.

THE GROUP WAS sitting up and blinking, mystified, starving, in the morning quiet of this foreign structure. Twenty-four hours ago, they'd belonged to a chaos of personalities. The four of them looked at one another. Who could have seen this coming?

Lynn—just—made a mistake? Staci said. *In the barn?*

Ray answered: *Must have.*

They let the sun coming through the broken ceiling warm them up.

Where do you think Tim and everyone went? Ernie asked uncertainly.

No way to know. Ray shrugged.

But definitely they all got away, right? Staci said. *I'm freaking out.* Flies buzzed around her slightly urine-sticky legs.

Well, freaking out's not helpful, Ray told her.

While Ernie rode to town to buy donuts and orange juice, Ray tinkered with his bike by the overgrowth of muscadine bushes outside. Staci and Coral sat in the sun, and Staci looked at the young girl, studying her pinched eyes until she figured out what was going on. Staci had a friend whose baby died. She knelt by Coral, and the girl tilted her wide and pained face to her.

Staci put both hands on Coral's thighs. *Picture the baby in your mind, and if you could massage a little, then you could squeeze it out.*

Coral just looked.

Staci sort of gestured what she meant on her own breast, through her shirt. *Like this, all right?*

After a few tries, her T-shirt raised and her engorged breast aimed down at a beer bottle whose label had been bleached by time and weather, Coral expressed the milk. She looked miserable.

Aw, you poor kid, Staci said, viscerally feeling the distress. *This is no fun, honey. No fun at all. But I'm here, okay?*

When Coral was done, Staci took the warm glass bottle and delicately set it upright in the wildflowers out of some kind of respect for its contents, even though they were forfeited. Coral curled up on the grass, eyes closed.

Staci was fully alarmed by what she felt. Like a pearly worm of maternal energy was waking up in her psyche and working to find its way outside. What would she do next, tie the girl's shoelaces? Braid her hair? She might if she wasn't careful. But it was easy to feel this way about someone like Coral, she was starting to see, especially in the vacuum of emergency.

THEY GOT ON the road. Boulders were shoved up out of fields tufted with green trees, and granite outcrops glittered. They passed a herd of longhorns, who looked at the bikes shining by. They stopped in a one-intersection town to get brisket and beer, ate with their heads down, and didn't talk at the table, Ernie never letting go of the backpack of cash.

At dusk, they neared the ruins of a school and pulled over to use the pay phone. Ernie called JD Hoggins in Willcox, Arizona, a point person, while Staci, Coral, and Ray sat on a log.

It's Ernie, from Oklahoma.

Ernie.

Have you heard from anyone?

Tim, and Shayna and the baby, called from the road. They're in one piece.

Ernie gave his crew a thumbs-up with dire eyes. *Was it Lynn cooking in the barn?*

Yes sir, it was. JD was wheezing, he must have gotten up out of his chair.

Ernie was silent.

Lynn's missing, JD said. *Everybody else is all spread out but got accounted for.*

Okay, I hear you.

Well. There's something else.

The sun was setting through the monkey bars, and squirrels chased one another on porcelain-berry vines. *Tell me.*

Judy.

The group watched as Ernie switched the phone to his other ear. *What about her?*

She's in the Tuskahoma hospital. Unconscious, in a coma or something like that.

Damn.

Both men were quiet.

Tim said to call Chris W. in a couple weeks, JD counseled, *he'll tell you how to get the money to Tim.*

But where is everyone supposed to meet up? We have no idea where we're going.

Just call Chris W. I wish I knew more but I don't.

Ernie put the phone in its cradle. He looked at the group. *Tim's okay, Shayna and the baby are fine.*

Staci said: *Thank god.*

Ernie said to Coral: *You got that? The baby's okay.*

Coral stared at him, then looked away, into the scrubby woods.

Her skin was cold as stone, but her eyes seemed hot, and she trembled. Everyone noticed but told themselves she didn't want comfort—from them, at least.

Ray asked: *I can tell there's more.*

Lynn is—well, missing for now.

No one spoke.

Ernie cleared his throat. *And Judy—is in a coma.*

Staci linked her arm through Ray's, and Ray clasped her hand.

Ray finally asked: *Where are we supposed to meet them all?*

They're figuring it out. Chris W. will tell us in two weeks or so, that's when we call him.

THEY RODE THROUGH a chain of towns, passing snub-nosed farm trucks painted the color of sherbet still driving after forty years of work, passing Kmarts, log-cabin-style tourism offices, bars with no name, tiny post offices. Ernie hadn't been near these parts in a long time but it was all familiar, like finding a childhood book whose pictures he recognized but the story itself didn't ring a bell.

Twilight ended. The bikes rolled into a parking lot off a service road, the motel a sad line of rooms, chalky with desert dust, standing out in the middle of nothingness, a rose of Sharon planted near the entrance. Called the Gold Cross Motel. The sky was starkly purple above the white quarters. In the lobby, Ernie handed over money.

Y'all here for the Against the Wind run? the clerk asked. *You're a little early.*

Figured we could make it a vacation, Ernie ad-libbed, *hang out a while before the rally.*

Which one's yours? The clerk was lewdly looking outside.

The Honda.

The clerk laughed and showed a missing front tooth. *I meant the girls.*

Ernie was startled and looked out there. Staci was smoking, her blond hair hiding most of her face, her arms lean and sun-spotted in the T-shirt and a denim vest. Coral was standing with bad posture, her Slayer shirt stinky, her blue eyes red.

The metalhead, Ernie said.

They unlocked the room to cheaply stuccoed walls, a pink sink in the bathroom. The blankets were cigarette-burned, and a Bible sat in the bedside-table drawer. A delicate sheer red curtain hung in the window.

Home sweet home, Ray said, and his voice sounded strange and empty in the room.

All four were beat and they crashed, Ernie lying on the floor so Coral could have the bed.

IN THE MORNING, Ernie came back from town with food, a white bag jammed with foil-wrapped egg tacos. *I got these grapefruit from a farmer on the roadside too.*

Ray was smoking outside the room. *All right!*

Inside, Staci and Coral were wet-haired and clean. Everyone descended on breakfast. Ray cut the grapefruit with a hunting knife and Ernie watched them all eat.

Well, I paid for the room till Friday, Ernie said. *We've got to figure things out. Stay here or keep moving till we can call Chris W.*

The room was quiet.

I mean, are we really waiting to talk to this guy, when we could split the money, evenly? Ray asked awkwardly. *And go where we want?*

Ernie got hot in the face. *Not give it back to Tim?*

Well, not yet, Ray said. *Obviously we'd pay him back in the future.*

No one spoke.

But I mean, is it the four of us? Staci asked. *Should we keep it that way?*

Coral, sitting in a chair in the corner, looked at the ceiling.

Ernie pointed at her with his thumb. *She doesn't even care, I bet.*

They all looked at Coral.

Staci tilted her head at Ernie and spoke softly. *She does care.*

Ray said: *How do you know? You reading her mind, Stace?*

I'm not suggesting we leave her, Ernie said.

You're not? Ray asked.

Staci put on a face. *Not even an option, guys.*

We can't stay in motel rooms forever, Ray said. *We'll kill each other.*

You know what? We should be turning this over to a higher power, Staci suggested.

Ray laughed. *Don't even.*

Well, someone needs to do something, Staci said angrily.

I went out and got y'all grapefruit! Ernie shouted. *I got us here, I found a place to sleep. What have you done?*

Seriously, man, thank you for everything, and the grapefruit, Ray said.

Staci agreed: *The grapefruit's amazing.*

Uneasy silence as Ernie calmed down.

Coral watched him.

Ray finally said what he'd been withholding. *Ernie, you do know Tim was about to shut everything down, right? Shayna wanted out of the compound, that's why Tim upped the quantity of sales so fast. To put a deposit on a good old-fashion family house in Fort Smith after he kicked us all out with no warning.*

Ernie's adrenaline spiked with heartbreak and rejection. *He wasn't actually going to evict us.*

He was, Ray said.

How do you know that? Ernie asked.

YOU'RE AN ANIMAL | 51

Tim told Lynn.

Lynn told you?

Well, Judy told me. Lynn told her.

Ernie stared into the distance, processing this.

Staci glared at Ray, mouth open. *Why didn't you tell me?*

Ray shrugged, exasperated. *No one was ever supposed to tell anyone.*

Flustered, Staci said: *I didn't even want to be at that retarded place, and I was getting kicked out? I would have left on my own will, thank you.*

We did leave, Ernie pointed out glumly.

Someone in the next room was listening to the Tejana radio station. They all started thinking about how no extended family anywhere, for any of them, was waiting for their return to the fold. They'd bounced from community to community over the years, making friends and making trouble, and while it wasn't impossible to go back to those spots, it wasn't like anyone would throw a welcome parade either.

I personally think we're stronger together for now, Staci started. *The four of us.*

Ernie hid his surprise. But the way Ray looked down, and kicked the bed's ruffle with his black boot, made Ernie think the couple might disagree.

I'm with you, Staci, Ernie said. *We're an odd lot. But we're better together than separated out.*

Ray met Ernie's eyes: *Yeah, that's true, right?*

Here Ernie'd thought Ray knew everything, but, removed from the population, the man lost some conviction.

Sure, Ernie said.

And I think we should keep all the money to get by too, Staci said. *How much is it?*

Ten grand, Ernie said.

Pay him back down the line, Staci said. *It's Tim being greedy and stupid*

that led to the fire, right? And he wasn't even telling us his plan, so fuck him.
The last part came out more bitter than she meant to sound.

They all nodded, weighing the seriousness of that decision.

We could rent a piece of farm? Short term? Ernie asked. *Even make it the next place where we all live, if some of those folks want to join up again.*

Staci looked at Coral. *Honey, what's your sense about sticking with us?*

Ray and Staci and Ernie looked to Coral, as if her decision, like an oracle's divination, would be the answer. The girl slumped, her pink mouth troubled, a zit near her nose, the eyes wet and sly like someone who understood the end of the story and wouldn't tell anyone out of sheer malevolence. But suddenly a shiver passed through her, and she lay down and squeezed her eyes shut.

The other three left quietly to smoke outside, silent as they passed the lighter, then exhaled.

We have a moral duty to take care of her, Staci said, surprisingly adamant.

She obviously can't take care of herself, Ray said. *Doesn't mean it's the most natural fit.* He looked from Ernie to Staci and back, trying to get a read, and saw that it was already decided. Aw for chrissakes. No way out of this one. It fell into the category of "You're a very bad man if you say no." *But I'm in.*

Well. That settles it. I'll scout a spot tomorrow. Ernie took a last deep drag between his broken teeth and crushed the butt with his boot. He felt a bit high on the agreement. They all went back inside.

There was a new feeling in the small space with its one window and scratchy towels and phone book: it was the harmony that happens at dusk when all the animals that like the daytime are getting ready to surrender, and the night animals have not yet taken over the empire. But they will.

———

MORNING LIGHT FILTERED luridly through the red curtain. Shirt-less, Ernie cut the ragged ends from his beard with the hunting knife, and he smoothed his hair in the mirror. Staci and Coral paged through magazines they took from the lobby; Ray was gazing out the window. Staci had already done her face with the bulging kit of mascara and eyeliner and lipstick she luckily always kept in her purse, and she handwashed some clothes and rigged a drying line on the shower rod.

Ernie put his clean T-shirt on. *I'll be back by sundown.*

He rode. The land was wide, oil drills stood like sci-fi flowers in the desert, and buzzards drifted in the white sky. He rode through areas that were not quite towns: random clusters of trailers, closed stores, a drained public pool, isolated train tracks. He saw For Sale signs here and there on houses close to the road, with no shade, but he wanted a long driveway, tall trees, scrubland with room to build. He stopped at a food cart and bought homemade tamales.

Are you aware of any properties for rent in this vicinity? he asked the seller.

No comprende, said the man.

¿Conoce alguna casas en venta?

The man took a respectful moment to think, his tongue probing the massive gap in his front teeth, but then shook his head. *No, señor.*

Outside Menard, a billboard read: *Land parcels for Lease. Short term or Long term. Call Jeremiah at 432-445-8887.* Something about the salesman leaving his last name off the poster was reassuring, and Ernie found a pay phone. Jeremiah listened to what Ernie wanted and gave him directions. The directions were convoluted, which intrigued Ernie. When he got to the unmarked gate on the back road, Jeremiah was idling in an old Ford pickup, a weather-beaten fellow with a beeper on his belt and a gin-blossom nose.

Jeremiah's nephew Jasper unlocked the cattle gate, nodded at

Ernie as he rode the bike over the metal bars, followed in a stately way by Jeremiah's truck. Jasper latched the gate and ran to catch up. As they met under the shade of a gigantic tree, Jeremiah reached out for Ernie's hand, and Ernie felt like he was shaking a ribeye.

Howdy.

How are you, sir, Ernie said.

Well, this house has been empty about six months. Family of eight was liv-ing here, not in any extravagant lifestyle, but they kept it tidy and had things growing. Once all the sulphur mines closed down, our little town got real small real fast. So. There's our story. I won't lie to you about it.

Jeremiah went on as they moved through the house and into the backyard. The house was aluminum-sided, with a barn and shed. A butterfly zigzagged through fruitless melon vines in the deteriorated garden. Bumblebees vanished into roses whose limbs grew up a makeshift gazebo, and the bees came out of the petals, legs thick with pollen. A snake slid from the yard, where it was sunning, into the barn.

Can we do month to month? Ernie looked at the man. *If so, I can give you cash today.*

Jeremiah was taken aback but southwestern etiquette kept him from prying. *Well, then. I hope y'all will be happy here.*

THAT NIGHT, IN the dark motel room, Ray snored while Coral fix-ated on something visible through the red curtain, something in the night sky. It must have been the motel sign, the neon crucifix, be-cause Coral's eyes reflected it: X marks the spot.

ERNIE'S BIKE LED the way, the air clean and bright, past mesquite meadows, a coyote corpse withered and strung up on a fence as a warning. Sparse azalea bushes bloomed outside a highway church that could fit maybe ten people if they crowded together. Farm machinery was for sale in a lot.

Nobody had done much talking this morning. The fear of being on the run had curdled into the great uneasiness of being strangers stuck with one another. They knew they were headed to what would be their home, even if it was just temporary, but a homelessness hung around them like black flies. The woods got denser and buildings fewer, and then Ernie turned onto a washboard road, and Coral clutched his middle as they bumped over rough parts, Ray and Staci following.

Ernie got off the bike with his new key.

Open sesame! he said as he pushed the gate wide.

They rode the long dirt drive, the sun coming through the live oaks in a watery, swirling way. The screen door banged behind them when they filed in. The floors were uneven, worn over decades, and the cupboards were definitely made by a self-taught carpenter.

I'd say it was built in the 1930s, Ray guessed.

Chipped turquoise tile in the bathroom, a sink with stains like bruises. They moved through the spaces. The bedrooms stank, and blankets hung over curtain rods. Staci screeched when she opened a closet and some varmint scrabbled into a corner. The family room looked onto the backyard. There was a couch sunken by time and by whoever once lived here, a dining table and chairs, one tarnished spoon on the lazy Susan, and a teacup with carnations painted onto its fragile translucent ceramic. Staci and Ray tried to seem cool, so Ernie didn't get his feelings hurt, and Coral just stood there, arms at her sides, with a blank look.

This whole place is ours, Ernie said, even as he realized they might hate it, hate living with him, this was a big mistake.

Wow, man, Ray said, but could think of nothing else to add.

They had to kick the back door open like a S.W.A.T. team because heat had melted the paint and sealed it. The grass was knee high, but garden rows were still visible. Wire fences gave out in places, vines covering them. The land itself was taken aback by their arrival; no one had bothered it in some time and it wasn't happy to have trespassers. Everyone was careful as they broke the wilderness, watching for thorns, cacti, snakes, spiders. A shed was covered in greenery, and a barn was crammed with metal, the ends or beginnings of machines.

We're month to month. I said it was me and my sister, and my brother and his wife. The place needs help, that's why it's so cheap, Ernie said, *but we can plant whatever we want. Lavender grows like wildfire here. Rosemary.*

Staci and Ray acted like they were trying to see it, smiling vacantly, while their brains figured out how long this situation had to last, where to next, and—maybe most urgent—would Oklahoma PD bother to look this far for them?

Rosemary, man, Ray said.

Coral still had no expression.

I don't know if we're going to be here long enough to plant stuff, Staci said, running a hand through feathered hair.

Yeah, we don't want to put down roots just to pull 'em up, Ray echoed.

Ernie hurried to agree. *I'm not saying put down roots.*

Staci was staring at the girl. *Cor, are you—are you doing okay?*

Coral wouldn't meet her eyes. She went into one of the rooms and curled up on the floor. Was the ghost of a baby hovering over her? She looked at the wall for hours, motionless, drained of spirit, or destroyed by grief, or plain old tired, or something.

NIGHT FELL HEAVILY, and while the others slept, Coral snuck out and walked in moon shadows, zigzagging through a valley cut behind lines of trees. When she found a creek, its ripples shining, it seemed to be the answer to some question. She took off her clothes and left them on the ground. Stepping into the water, she stumbled on stones, and crouched, then sat and lay on her back. The water was trickling and cold, and it didn't cover her body entirely. Her legs and arms were goose-bumped, her sore nipples pointed at the sky. She started panting, and then she made a noise that was mangled, a wailing of sorts, the sound thrown into the darkness. Then she stopped, and just looked at the sky with saucer eyes.

After an hour or so, she stood up from the creek, put her clothes on, and settled in the field, flattening the tall grass, and slept continuously for the first time since they'd left the compound. She woke up and headed to the house in damp clothes when everything was still black and starlit. Along the path, she saw the tarantula. It was moving over pebbles, one slow and elegant step at a time. She squatted, and occasionally crab-walked as she kept watch, hands clasped, elbows resting on her thighs. Her breathing was heavy and unselfconscious. The tarantula—its furry legs so intentional—vanished into the grass just as a gold-gray light suffused the woods. The girl yawned, went inside.

TWO

Planting

PEACH

RAY AND STACI went into town to try Chris W. from a pay phone, but they called, and called again, no answer. On the way back, they saw a beat-up white van with a For Sale sign on its windshield in the dusty yard of a house, and they knocked on the door. Every good biker household has a backup van. A dog snarled.

Sounds friendly, Ray said, and Staci smiled.

A chain was unlatched, and a face with white hair looked out. *I'm Myrtle, who are you?*

Good day, ma'am. My name's Ray and this is Staci. We were driving by and wanted to ask about the van.

Oh, come in, she said, and led the pit bull away with her bony, ancient, slender hand. *Rex, don't you bark at my friends,* she told the dog.

The house's interior was a geode in a dull scarred rock. There were rainbow afghans folded over the loveseat, a TV with antennae parted, a rose-pink lamp.

Will y'all have a slice of apricot cake?

They sat at her table, eating off plates with scratched gold rims.

My son Wally John is gone to Alaska working on some boat, he hasn't come back here for two years, so I just put that sign up a few days ago. All the papers are in the glove box.

It's perfect timing, Miss Myrtle, Staci said. *It's exactly what we need.*

Ray test-drove it while Staci stayed, chatting, and looked at old photos on the wall. She pointed at one black-and-white shot: a couple sitting on a brick wall, the young woman grinning, arm hanging loose around the man's shoulders, his around hers, their faces open, and real.

Wally John's daddy. Devoted to me like I was the Queen of Sheba. Who ever knew why I was the one got lucky like that, out of five sisters. I hit the jackpot of love.

Staci felt a flash of heat. Wow, you're envious of an elderly widow, aren't you something. While Myrtle washed the dishes in the kitchen, talking about Wally John over the running faucet and the forks clattering in the sink, Staci spied sherry on the bookshelf, the dust on its curved glass indicating it had gone untouched for years. She snatched the bottle, took a slug, and put it back with a shaking hand.

Wa-ha! she thought in her giddy evil voice. I did it. Her cheeks turned pink and her eyes got bright, as usual, not from the liquor but from the immediate fever of disobedience and regret. Myrtle didn't notice anything different when she returned to the room.

It was dusk by the time the van crunched up the rocky drive of their new place, Staci behind the wheel, Ray following on the bike. They walked in the front door.

Hey guys, dinner's here, Staci said into the hollow rooms.

Ray carried a striped paper bag heavy with fried chicken.

Ernie and Coral were sitting at the table, painfully silent, and Ernie made eyes of accusation at Ray and Staci as Ray pulled the food from the bag.

Thanks for being gone so long, Ernie said. *Coral and I have just been sitting here, you know, just . . . hanging out.*

Ray laughed from his gut because Coral was looking at Ernie, and probably had been for hours, and Ernie couldn't handle shit.

No answer from Chris, Ray said. *But we got a van.*

What? Man, we need to save that cash.

It wasn't much, we have at least two months of rent still, Ray said. *And we brought you dinner. Stop complaining.*

THE MORNING SKY was sticky, overcast. Staci woke up on the floor, sore, stretching her arms above her head, her hair flat on one side and a rat's nest on the other. She knew she'd pledged herself to a commitment-free life, and this was the sad and lonely half of that adventure. This was when she and Ray got upended, when they lost whatever they'd collected. But that was the deal! Looking around at the grimy walls, the streaked window, the moth carcasses, she clapped her hands.

Okay guys, if we're staying put for now, she yelled, *we need to fucking pull this place together.*

Ernie opened all the doors and windows. Staci swept out dust, and it swirled in the muted sunbeam. Ray went out and bought everything from Ivory soap to canned tuna, came back with six heavy plastic bags twisting from each hand, his fingers red and white from the handles. They dragged rugs into the yard, filled trash bins, washed cupboards and counters and the fridge.

Without Coral's help. She slouched from room to room, fidgeting, half-moons hanging under her eyes that accused whoever happened to be in sight. Everyone excused her because she couldn't hear, or because she was young, or something. The fact that she was slightly revived today made it worse because she didn't use the energy to lend a hand. Exhausted, they opened the sliding doors that evening and sat on the couch with a mint-green fan pointed at them. A bat fluttered to the threshold and away, more of a sensation than a fact. Coral took a piece of bread into a bedroom, and they heard the door lock.

They gazed into the deepening darkness of the yard.

Do you think, I mean, honestly, Staci asked, picking at a mole on her thigh and not looking at anyone, *the police would track us all the way here?*

Naw, Ray lied. *Fires like that happen all the time.*

Tim would go to jail, right? Staci said. *I mean, before us.*

An awkward hush.

We were all there, though, Ernie said finally.

Look, it's one less lab, Ray said. *Cops are happy when they burn down.*

One less cook, Ernie said in a flat voice, and the hair stood up on his arm.

Well, Ray said, implying police felt the same satisfaction.

You know that changes things, Ernie said to Ray.

No one spoke for a while, Staci grinding her teeth without knowing it, Ray almost lighting the wrong end of a cigarette. Dusk got darker and the moths got whiter. They were all listening for sounds beyond nature, consciously or not.

Maybe Judy—if she does talk—if she ever can talk—will say it was just her and Lynn, Staci said with a morbid hopefulness.

I don't remember her being the martyr type, Ernie said gently.

Ray was staring off at nothing when he shrugged, half-hearted, but then he said something he meant: *People change.*

Ernie got three more beers, shuffling to the fridge and back, handed them out, and no one could stop thinking about what had been left behind.

Do you think all our stuff is gone? Staci finally asked.

Their communal thoughts formed a blizzard of objects in the air:

jars of pickled okra and raspberry jelly and stewed rhubarb; Mister
Plenty's pastel polyester shirts; bottles of distilled eau-de-vie and tins
of dried calendula and valerian; Vick's collection of ashtrays from
casinos; Ashleigh's dolls and teddy bears; silverware, books on survival, underwear, guns.

I keep thinking we'll go back, Ray said, speaking what was on everyone's mind. *But it's just ruins, I bet.*

*Maybe Tim will have someone salvage what they can, and we can pick it up
someday,* Ernie said.

The silence was full of the fragrance of plants at dusk.

Some part of me feels liberated, Staci said, trying to be sincere.

Ray gave her a look: *Yeah right.*

I believe in leaning into, like, new chapters, she said, determined to convince herself. *I wouldn't even mind changing my name.*

Ray thought about that. *But you're such a Staci.*

Ernie nodded. *You are.*

Coral coughed on her side of the door.

I think she goes outside every night, Staci said quietly.

Ray said, *I noticed that, yeah.*

A sense of liability made them silent. One minute, Coral seemed
more competent to live on her own than all of them put together; the
next minute she was a newborn rabbit, see-through flesh, beyond
helpless. Back at the compound, there were always enough people
around that no one in particular had to feel responsible for anyone
or anything. These three missed that phenomenon a little right now.

What she does is up to her, right? Ernie said unsurely, crushing his
cigarette in a bottle cap. *I really don't see why you'd stay up all night but.*

Oh my god, like you never stayed up, Staci said.

The cicadas began their nocturnal cacophony and it was really
loud.

Ernie pulled his hair out of the ponytail he'd rubber-banded so he could work. *I don't know. She just seems so miserable or scared or—I don't know. Honestly? Maybe she'd rather be with Tim and Shayna and we're not good enough.*

Staci shook her head. *No, it's not Tim and Shayna she misses, it's the baby.*

Ernie grimaced and tilted his head. *Mmmmmn, pretty sure it's Tim and Shayna.*

It's fucking biology, Ernesto.

What is?

Coral, the baby, the—milk. Come on, you know what I mean. The bond.

Ernie looked like it was just dawning on him.

Ray asked: *Staci, can't you become friends with her or something?*

Staci was offended. *Hold on, are you saying I haven't been being nice?*

You're the other female, Ray said. *You two could hang out.*

I already tried to be friends with her, she's not interested.

When did you try to be friends with her? Ray asked skeptically.

She's pretty much deaf, Ernie said as if they didn't know. *Makes it hard.*

She can still hang out, Ray said. *What, you think she's intimidated by us?*

Ernie tried that on for size. *Huh. I hadn't thought of that.*

Staci lit a smoke, thinking. *I could take her shopping?*

Great idea, Ray said.

The trio relaxed, nodding. All girls love shopping!

STACI COAXED CORAL into the van as doves fluttered, loud and graceless, into the morning sky.

Thanks for keeping me company, Cor! Staci said, driving with one elbow out the window and her hand holding the van's top. *You psyched to do some shopping?*

Coral's sideways look could be interpreted as *yes.* Or *no.*

I'm going to get some basics myself, that's all we can do after this horrible event in our lives. Easy does it. Fake it till you make it. One day at a time. Throwing a little program-speak at you, Coral.

She glanced at the girl, who was squinting out the windshield, her hair too oily to move in the wind.

I need to find some meetings in town, Staci said. You know what's funny about meetings? I think everybody should go at some point, whether they have a substance problem or not, because the shit they tell you in those rooms is amazing. Maybe you could come with me sometime, if and when I go?

Once again, Staci couldn't decipher Coral's expression. They arrived at an outlet mall off the highway, a row of chrome signs and smoked-glass electric doors and almost violent air-conditioning within. They walked into a Gap Factory store.

What's your favorite color? Staci asked.

Coral stood with hands in pockets.

Color is like, so important. Long time ago I lived with this girl Lori who could read a person's aura by color, Staci said. I was orangey pink, she told me, with black spots, but I can't remember what it meant.

Staci held up a cotton dress that looked like a nurse uniform but not a sexy one. *What is the purpose of this? Who would even wear it?*

Being around someone with a story like Coral's made Staci sad, sick to her stomach that it happened, but also intrigued. It was too— too *important* not to discuss. I shouldn't, she told herself, biting her nail. But I have to!

So—I heard what happened to you as a kid, Staci blurted out, flipping through the rack. She turned to look meaningfully at Coral. And I'm so a-hundred-percent here for you. I'm not saying I'm a trauma expert, but I'm not not *a trauma expert. You know?*

Coral was eyeing the food court, but Staci bet the girl was just avoiding the painful topic.

I'm extremely sensitive to other people's trauma, Staci continued. I feel a lot of, and I mean a lot of, of feelings. And I'll give you space, if this isn't a good time. Everyone deserves space. Over the years I've come to really honor the idea of permission, okay, me of all people, and—I'm not Miss Boundary Lines. Staci picked up red leggings. *I probably should have had way more boundaries at your age. I'll leave it there.*

They moseyed through the mall, Staci thinking she'd done her job, no need to push it. She bought Coral a hot pretzel. They hit up a bodycon joint where Staci got little acid-washed cutoffs and a gold Lycra dress. Coral picked out black sneakers at a Payless. Then they tried an accessories shop with walls of made-in-China trinkets.

So did you have a boyfriend before you came to the compound? Staci asked, as she held a hoop to her earlobe in the mirror. *In case you're afraid of men, just know: they're totally needy, every one of them. All you got to do is smile, honey, and make him feel good.*

Coral put on a pleather cuff with studs, black like the sneakers.

Oh wow, we have a match, Staci said. *Yay!*

Back in the van, Staci used her thigh to steer while she unwrapped sugarless gum. Coral pointed at a Goodwill, and the van swerved into the lot. There the girl unearthed T-shirts from the bins that Staci couldn't have been paid to touch, corduroys that smelled like rancid popcorn, and a sweatshirt with a horse on it. She also landed a scuffed Discman and a few CDs. The girl's mood seemed better, and they drove in silence until Staci felt comfortable enough to ask.

Do we intimidate you? Me and Ray, and I guess Ernie? she said. *You can be straight with me.*

The girl turned and stared squarely at Staci. Coral's eyes touched every part of Staci's face, like fingers going through her thoughts, examining each thing with expertise but not respect, the way a thief rummages through a drawer. Staci felt hot, her neck was pink. It was sort of exciting, she realized she liked it.

RAY WAS COOKING chili on the electric stove while Ernie watched.

Ray tapped in red pepper flakes. *Wonder how they're doing, they've been gone a long time.*

Ernie fiddled with his grape soda can, uncomfortable being alone with Ray, not sure what to say. *Yeah, man, totally long.*

Ray nodded. *I think it's actually a good sign they've been gone this long.*

I do too, Ernie said, anxiously taking a last sip of nothing, having already finished the soda a few swallows ago.

My honest opinion, dude, about this whole thing, this whole escapade? We got lucky, to get away from that compound. It was going nowhere fast.

Ernie looked at the man, his braid hanging on the black T-shirt, the tanned, sinewy arms working over the big bubbling pot. Then Ernie looked out the window, checking to see how dusk crawled over the land here, how it touched the shrubbery, how it lay down on the grass, moving thickly on the horizon.

Ernie hesitated, then asked: *Do you think everything happens for a reason?*

Ray tasted his chili on the spoon. *Now you're getting a little deep for me, brother. Wanna taste?*

Ernie took a bite, and his eyes opened wide. *Whoa. Just realized I'm starving.*

Yeah, they better be back real soon 'cause I ain't waiting.

That girl's going to grab a bowl and hide in her bedroom. What's her deal?

Ray threw the dishcloth over his shoulder. *With a start like she got, she's doing good. Talk about batshit crazy.*

What do you mean?

Her story, Ray said, wiping sweat off his forehead.

What do you mean?

Aw, man, it made the rounds when she showed up.

No one tells me shit, Ernie complained.

Her parents were insane, they were like fifteen when they had her. They'd drive all over Louisiana and Texas, New Mexico. And feed her a spoon of hot sauce or sip of gasoline, so she would cry and scream. Or they'd prick her little eardrum with a pin. Then they'd haul her into the ER and get some meds, snag prescription pads. Pill junkies—she was the prop. It apparently worked for a couple years. But they're famous because they got taken down in a shootout on a peach farm in Fredericksburg. They went out blazing, Bonnie-and-Clyde style. Total morons.

Ernie was almost speechless. Why? He was embarrassed to be so affected and made himself talk. *A peach farm, huh.*

Yup. Driving a black Trans Am with the gold eagle. But somebody maybe added that part, who knows, Vick said it's a family legend.

Added the part about the peach farm?

No, the Trans Am. It was definitely a peach farm.

Ernie thought. *Is her deal that she's like, she doesn't hang out because of what happened? Is she even deaf, or is that a ruse to ignore us?*

Ray lit a smoke and leaned against the counter. *My personal opinion, she's just a nice regular little freak.*

Was she in the car when they got killed? Ernie asked in a hushed voice.

No, at an apartment. They left her alone for days at a time. Don't tell me you're obsessing now. You got a reputation for fixating.

I'm not. But it's a poignant story.

It's poignant as hell. No one's arguing with that.

THE GIRLS WALKED in a bit later, carrying bags.

We're home! Staci yodeled. *Something smells good.*

Ernie couldn't help staring at Coral, specifically at her ears, but she didn't meet his eyes. He was consumed by trying not to look, it was like she had a vagina on each side of her head, that's how personal it seemed. He blinked, disturbed by his thoughts.

Hope you're hungry, ladies, Ray said, and spooned chili into bowls, topping it with shredded cheese and sour cream.

Coral ate a spoonful standing, too hungry to wait. Ernie watched her, his mouth open, as if he'd never seen her before. As if she still had a giant sewing needle, glistening with light, sticking out of her ear, its point jammed into the gumdrop of her eardrum. His soul churned. He felt ill.

Ernie said loudly: *Why not eat at the table tonight, huh?*

But she took the chili to her bedroom, and a ginger ale too, kicked the door closed.

His compassion was boiling over and his skin got welts of—anger? Humiliation? Rejection? Concern? Why was this such a big deal for him? He didn't know, and the confusion added to his level of emotion, and Ernie could barely sleep that night.

THE NEXT DAY, Coral helped the others move junk out of the barn into the yard so they had space to work on the bikes and get them in good shape in case of an emergency departure. Ernie felt hyper with attention toward her but didn't know how to handle it, so he ignored the girl as they worked. The engines and tools, intricately destroyed by time, were sharp and difficult to carry. When no one was looking, Coral disappeared to her room again.

Ernie came out with a rusted tricycle. *Did she leave?*

She's a teenager, Ern, Staci said, rolling her eyes. *Quit taking it personally.*

But we'd fucking cheer her up if she didn't run away all the time. He was furious with empathy and who knows what else.

Later, Ernie, Ray, and Staci ate tacos at the dining table, faces touched with sunburn, backs sore. The sunset was dirty violet at the horizon and ethereal floaty pale pink above. There was a plate for Coral but she didn't come out of her room. Ernie could think of nothing but that.

Finally he asked: *Is she just going to starve herself?*

Staci shushed him. *She's going through a separation thing.*

That was so many days ago! he said, getting up and knocking on her door.

Ernie, don't, Staci beseeched. *Just leave her.*

I'm sick of this. He opened the door.

Coral was sitting on the bed, pillow on her lap.

Ernie enunciated: *Coral. We got to work together, take care of each other. Nobody can be separate from the rest. You can't hide in here.*

She made a face, then lay down. It was clear she had no intention of engaging with his sorry ass. Ernie couldn't hide his shock when she turned away.

And I find myself wondering, Ernie said in a threatening voice, *if you're really deaf! Or if you just don't want to talk to us. We're not good enough for you.*

Ray tried pulling him out of the room. *Come on, bro. Don't do this.*

Ernie kept shouting at her. *Where would you be if you weren't at this house? What happened to "thank you"?*

Ernie let Ray drag him away and outside. They stood in the grass, light from the house spilling on their feet. Staci ran in pursuit, knock-kneed, and got in Ernie's face.

How dare you, she said. *Why are you yelling at a kid?*

She's acting like a princess, Ernie said sullenly.

She's not acting like anything, Ern. Come on, jeez.

Ernie bit his lip for a second. *Too far?*

Staci gave him a long, blistering stare. *Um, yeah. Too far. And don't pretend you don't know that.*

Staci went inside, slammed the door, and ran a bath so she could calm down, leaving the men to ponder things in the backyard. Ernie sat quietly with Ray, both smoking, their legs spread in lawn chairs. Night birds rustled in the trees. They were silent for a long time.

Someday you got to learn to control yourself, Ray said.

Look who's fucking talking!

After another long moment, the screen door squeaked open. Coral came out, face bloated. She stood in front of them but stared at Ernie. Ernie stared back, at this girl in her cheap shorts that looked like a Mormon missionary had cut his slacks at the knee, her yellow socks, her Metallica shirt. Chewing on her lip.

I'm sorry, he mumbled. *I have a temper.*

She gave him a *yeah I noticed* look, and they almost laughed.

I just felt like you didn't want to be here. Ernie was exhausted, he was done.

Suddenly the girl sat cross-legged on the grass in front of him, her shins on his feet, and she looked up at his face. It was a super-weird moment, so Ray slowly crept away to smoke a cigarette. Then smoked another.

Her eyes had never truly met Ernie's till now—those little crystal-blue portholes became a flurry, a storm of dream and memory, pieces flung at him, a massacre, relentless, a million arrows. Ernie's sense of self got dislodged, like in an alien abduction or near-death experience, so intense. His own eyes jittered—it was too much—then her lashes blinked. It was over.

Finally Ray cleared his throat, came back, and pulled over another chair for Coral without looking at her, and she sat. They watched the moon, Ernie's long noble dirty fingers over his mouth, the trio bristling with cosmic gawkiness.

Ernie remembered she still hadn't eaten. *You want food? We got tacos left in there?*

Coral stood to get a plate.

I got it. Stay put. You need to start eating from now on, okay? He heard Gloria in his voice, and so he went inside (like Gloria would) to fix the girl dinner.

MEATBALL

THE NEXT MORNING, Ernie woke to an unfamiliar noise outside, metal clanging against a rock now and then. He stared around his room, which he'd already hyper-organized, nails aligned on the wall so he could hang his scissors, a John Deere hat, and a towel. Lying side by side on the windowsill were his knife and a mauve comb. He got up, and as he braided his long reddish hair, Ernie looked into the yard.

Coral was hand-tilling ground like a pro.

Well, I'll be goddamned, he said, pressing a cigarette into his mouth and cupping his hands to light it. He stood, shirtless in sweatpants, and watched her work. She was using a shovel and a digging fork to break it all open, since they didn't have a rototiller. Lots of people work like they're punishing the earth, but she looked kind, even tender, as she ripped things up. What if she wasn't a nihilistic wasteland inside after all? She was stronger than he'd given her credit for, handling the tools with the confidence that came from knowing how to parcel strength and energy over hours of labor. She'd done this before.

EVERYTHING CHANGED. NO more hiding away. She worked in the yard most mornings, turning the soil, trimming shrubs, pulling weeds, and then, once the sun got to noon's height in the sky, Coral hit the kitchen for a tuna sandwich, knocked back some iced water. The sun being too hot to go back to work, she wandered.

Following a deer path behind the barn, the girl entered a dark, scrappy woods that opened into an abandoned apple orchard. A few knobby trees. She touched the bark, put her hand in the crevice between branches like she was finding something out. She squatted and pissed in a meadow.

She walked through scrub brush, then stopped, looking down— a small bleached shit, probably coyote. A creek ran under live oaks. She took off her sneakers and stepped in, picked watercress to taste. Her body might have been generating new cells as stems and petals do. She grew from the earth. She stood still and closed her eyes and it could have been a dull lavalike orange-red inside. Maybe it was her own sun, inside her mind, a kind of photosynthesis, every hour. When she came into range of mountain laurel on the way back, its smell traveled through her without having a name, without a comparison to anything else, free of an idea, the fruity flamboyant perfume in charge, not her.

The sky, too, in its original state, did not exist in relation to her. She wasn't the dominant force. But relations between her and her surroundings happened like the slow merging of two trees, or wet leaves rotting in a stone's cleft until they become its dark seam. She didn't look passive—she seemed to be foraging for something, or hunting something down, violently learning every little thing. Coral walked to the house, sun baking her wet hair into a shell, a stone in hand. She tossed it away before opening the back door.

She started sitting at the table for dinner, pushing food around her plate, eating some of it. Color was coming back to her eyes, which had faded the day of the fire. Staci, Ray, and Ernie all looked at one another like delinquent babysitters with good intentions who'd finally made the kid happy. They shrugged when Coral wasn't looking, like, *Not so bad, hey? We did all right!*

Droplets of light scattered all over the deep satin galaxy. She stared out her bedroom window a long time. Her body didn't look like it was dragging anymore, it was getting strung up to each star, threads in the night. Relocation.

WHOEVER WENT INTO town would try Chris W., but never with any luck, and it was Ray's turn today. Before he went in to go shopping, he used the phone outside the grocery store. He was surprised when someone answered.

Yeah? said the voice.

Hi, I'm a friend of Tim's, we got told to call you.

Did JD give you the number?

Yup, Ray said.

Right on. Well, I have an address and time for you.

Is this—are we supposed to meet them? Because we also have a place where everyone can stay.

Oh—this is just to meet a guy who will pick up the money. Jay Crowley will be in Santa Fe next week, on the ninth at—

Tim didn't say where we all should meet up? I mean, everything I own was at his compound.

The guy didn't say anything, and the call was getting uncomfortable.

And we have this girl with us, Ray said.

Don't know about any girl

A girl who can't talk. Didn't Tim ask about her?

Sorry, man. Never heard about a girl.

So he's not meeting us, and he's not taking the girl, Ray confirmed.

Chris W. hesitated, then said: *I got the impression everyone was going their own way.*

Got it. Then you can tell Tim that's exactly what we did and he can fucking fuck himself, he won't see a penny.

Ray smashed the phone into its cradle, and a couple shoppers gave him space as they rolled carts by in the lot. After standing there, wondering if he should call back and fix things, Ray got on his bike. Too mad to buy food, which said a lot. He felt rage as he rode through dappled streets, passing bakeries and churches and feedstores.

He started to calm down as he turned onto their own road, which was long and lonely and without personality. Almost no houses for a few miles, and scrappy weeds of bushes and trees along it. A busted-up mailbox now and again for what looked like deserted spots where a trailer might have lived. But then he saw a car deep in the brush, only a quarter mile from their place. It had gone up a dirt road that dwindled into nothing, and no car should be there, and no local would make the mistake of going up there to get somewhere. Ray knew because he had turned onto it once by accident.

From what he could see, it was a Chevy Caprice, maybe, a metallic maple-brown, unexceptional and forgettable like undercover cars tend to be, professional or otherwise. The car waited, like a dog growling in a subsonic way, too low to hear. Well, that's not good, Ray thought sourly, not looking directly at it, afraid to meet someone's eye.

As he walked onto their porch, he felt something else, a convergence. The smell of morning coffee in the kitchen, the dewy sparkly grass in the yard, the age-stained fabric ruffled around the kitchen windows, the Texas sage bush with its tiny purple flowers—these random particles had all started to combine into a new and undeniable reality. Was it because he suddenly thought it was threatened that he now gave a shit about the place?

He didn't tell anyone about the car. He had plenty to tell them as it was, which would make them nervous enough, and it took him all day to spill the beans. They were playing cards that evening. They'd started a game, and Coral pulled up a chair, so Ernie dealt her a hand. After she watched their first moves, she joined in, a decent hearts player. She must have played with her grandmother. Ray was worried, almost wishing he could redo the conversation on the phone, but who was he kidding, pretty much nothing could have gotten him to pay Tim back. There was a time when Ray would have at least given him half so they could both save face. He no longer had that in him.

Ray cleared his throat. *I got through to Chris today.*

Everyone stopped playing and waited. They were reflected in the door, a dark and thorny evening beyond its glass.

Tim, he said, *wants nothing to do with us except collecting his money. So I said fuck off.*

Cicadas made noise. No one spoke for a moment.

You told him to fuck off? Staci said as if she might have misheard.

Ray nodded.

Ernie threw down his hand, picked up the local newspaper, and unfolded it to the want ads.

Ray aggressively asked: *What are you doing?*

Ernie was upset. *Looking for jobs.*

Um, jobs? Ray asked.

We're not going back to being a compound, apparently, Ernie said, *and now we also owe Tim a bunch of money. So yeah, jobs.*

They all were quiet, the air crackling. Ernie wasn't even reading the ads, he was just furiously acting out a job search because he didn't know how to deal. It was embarrassing to watch.

Ray sighed deeply and took the paper away from Ernie and folded it. *Why would we do shit jobs? If we don't have to? I vote that we do what we were doing at the compound, and then we don't need social security numbers, we don't have to punch a clock for pennies,* Ray said. *It's easy.*

Easy because you're not doing it, Ernie said.

I'll handle the sales part, Ray said. *That's my job. I'll be just as involved as you.*

What about like, have you guys ever thought of—Ernie's heart was pounding—*I don't know, doing something different, like*—*setting up beehives, and selling honey?*

Staci broke the bad news, a hand on his forearm. *Babe. That's for rich hippie housewives pretending to have a business. You do know that, right?*

Yeah, Ernie lied. Why was it for rich hippie housewives? *What about opening a bookstore? Or like a breakfast place, nothing but eggs and coffee and pancakes.*

All that takes more investment money than you ever earn back realistically, Ray told him, impatient and ready to move on.

That doesn't make sense, Ernie said.

Exactly, Ray said. *And the bank will never give your ass a loan, trust me.*

Staci said: *You could go back to bouncing, Ray.*

And you could dance, he added.

Dancing! Those days are over, please, are you kidding? Staci slyly looked to see if he meant that at *all* seriously, because it would be flattering if he did.

The problem is that—*I don't want to test my luck,* Ernie said. *Are you forgetting what just happened?*

So then tell me how we're going to come up with rent and buy food, Ray said.

Staci stared gloomily at the floor, arms crossed. *I'm mainly concerned with not paying Tim back. He's nice until he's not nice.*

Tim seemed like a run-of-the-mill insecure person. Harmless, at first glance. He was embarrassed he couldn't spell for shit, for example, never felt like the best kisser, was sure his mom liked his sister better. But a superiority had been growing in him for years, picked up like a virus somewhere. It gave him meaning, and the meaning was made of hate. He didn't get angry. He hated. Hatred was his project in life, he worked on it any spare moment he had. Building it, trying it out. Such a mystery of an American man, and there were more like him.

I guess he worries me too, Ernie said. *To be honest.*

Jay will be in Santa Fe on the ninth, Ray snapped. *Call Chris if you want to deliver our imaginary money.*

They decided nothing. And Coral as usual loitered on the edge of everything that was happening, like a kid eternally smoking around the back of an apartment complex, and yet she was also at the core of it. Because although she never weighed in, and although they rarely asked her opinion, she was what mattered. They all tried reading her moods, interpreting her posture, without knowing that's what they were doing. None of them looked her in the eye for fear of being decimated somehow. She was the center of gravity.

IN THEIR BEDROOM, Staci floated a bandanna over the light. She could tell Ray was shook up by the phone call today, guilty he spoke his mind to Chris. He was dwelling on the possible, if not likely, consequences. She didn't even know he was also stressing about the car in the woods. What she *had* learned, from many years of practice, was that distraction was good medicine. They got to it.

It felt lonely, but neither was willing to admit that out loud. They used to get off on the attention she attracted at a beer garden or the girls he flirted with at a rally, but the couple was now in this bizarrely domestic situation with no one to use for ignition.

For being in his early fifties, Ray was keeping up. He gave her a series of spanks at the end, and she squealed. The hour was technically satisfactory for both but nothing to write home about. Their warm bodies breathed against each other, and they stared out the empty window, eyes glittering.

Have you ever thought maybe we could be happy here? Staci whispered.

Ray sat up and reached to his shirt, hanging on the chair, and got cigarettes from the pocket. *I miss my partners in crime.*

Name one person you really miss.

It took him a second too long. Silence as he smoked.

We've never lived on our own, Staci said. She didn't want to betray their code, which was to stay in flux, to chase and catch with the pack, to run away and turn back. But she couldn't stop the pillow talk coming out of her mouth.

Ray sighed. *Not this.*

Maybe it's interesting to be separated from your buddies. For just a little while.

We're stranded with a couple cuckooheads. In Nowhere, Texas. I can hear the grass grow.

But you're stranded with me, she said in a baby voice.

He knew where this was going. Staci got up to grab a T-shirt to sleep in. He watched her slip it over her head, and he looked at those hips, her grapefruit breasts, the fake tan line.

Yeah, correct, Ray said. *I'm with you, so why are we discussing it?*

I can't ever figure out what you want, Raymond Aggatello. She sighed.

I want to go for a ride, alone, he said flatly. *That's what I want.*

She sat in the sheets and watched him pull on jeans and boots, and if she had felt beautiful, that was over. Ray left the house and got on his bike. He vaguely knew what Staci wanted: for him to say she was enough. But that was a stupid thing to want from someone, and a *ludicrous* thing to want from him. He could love her, and still need the world. That's how he was made, and so was every real man he knew.

He ended up at the Bluebell Saloon, and one beer became six. The girl behind the bar was slightly cross-eyed, with a high ponytail that she flipped around because she had nothing much else to do.

You remind me of someone, he told her on his seventh beer. Her eyes freaked him out so he addressed this to the cocktail-napkin dispenser.

Is that right? she asked.

Mnnh. Yes.

She waited for him to say something else. *Was she nice at least?*

I can't remember.

He couldn't remember who she reminded him of, was the problem. This happened all the time nowadays. People got combined, or lost, in his mental library. Memories trucked through his brain on their own accord, disobeying him.

What time you get off? he asked, giving her a diamond-sparkle smile.

Midnight.

She seemed to blush, taking the cloth from her back pocket to shine steins, but he decided to go home, leaving a three-dollar tip, which, for Ray, was a fortune. Getting on his bike, he thought of the jokes he would make to his buddies, his brothers, if they were all stumbling out together, after a long, drenched night, and were roaring now into the darkness, kings on a nihilistic mission, grim reapers, a band of men. But it was just him, and he revved his bike, and the noise echoed through the foreign wilderness.

Almost home, and there it was, a light exactly where he'd seen that car. Buzz. Kill. He couldn't tell much, it wasn't headlights, just the interior. A fuzz of glow deep in the branches and vines, no one would notice unless they were looking for it. But there was nothing he could do about it on his own, not right now.

THE NEXT MORNING, he got up late. Ernie and Staci were eating Pop-Tarts, and they looked drained.

What, he said. *Am I in trouble?*

It's not fucking about you, Staci answered. *Lynn's dead for sure. And Judy woke up.*

Ray couldn't move. He wanted to put his mug on the table, he wanted to go sit down, but he was not able to. He just stood, open mouth and wide eyes, like a kid smacked across the face. Finally he came to sit with them. He broke off some tart for himself. Strawberry jam stuck in his beard.

You've got to be fucking kidding me. She woke up?

Staci felt a chill. *Yeah, and Lynn's in heaven, babe. Did you not hear the first part?*

All of it, it's horrible, I can't believe it. How'd you even find out?

Ernie leaned forward. *I've been riding to a shop off 522 that's got all the newspapers. The* Kiamichi Herald *says they found Lynn's, you know, enough to identify him, and that Judy's in a hospital.*

Staci asked Ray: *Are you worried about Judy talking to somebody?*

Ray looked at Staci for a long second. *I mean, yeah, I guess.*

I feel horrible that she's alone, Staci said. *I mean, that would just suck. I would be so scared if I was her.*

Fuck, Ernie said sadly.

We could pay her hospital bills, at the very least, Staci said.

With what? Ray said.

They were quiet.

Ernie said: *It's hard too because none of us were close to her. I don't think she'd want to see me, you know, if I showed up?*

The silence was odd. Staci said: *Ray. Are you even listening?*

Yeah, he said, *definitely.* He drifted off to take a shit. He called back down the hall: *That's so fucked up about Lynn.*

Staci and Ernie looked at each other.

Later, Ernie watched Coral wolf down her noontime sandwich. He saw blisters on both her hands from pruning the brush, and the shears were standing on the tip of their blades by the door, so he assumed she wasn't done yet today. The girl barely bathed or brushed her teeth and she stank, but Ernie didn't mind. She worked the yard and roamed the woods and nested in the greasy sheets on her mattress. So was he supposed to tell her about Lynn? Did she care? What about Judy? He didn't know if she understood Ray's phone call to Chris and how they were on their own now. Should Ernie tell the girl they planned to "keep" her? That sounded horrible in his head.

Hey, Coral, he started.

She wiped crumbs from her lips and waited.

I like what you've done outside, he said after a moment, smiling crooked.

STACI WENT BACK to bed for hours, lying in the sheets but not sleeping, just smoking and looking at the wall. Lynn was an odd guy who showed up with his lady out of the blue. His chain of friends of friends led to Tim, which is how everyone arrived at that place. Judy tried to bond with Staci and then Brandy yet didn't pull it off. No one believed the couple was really in love but guessed they'd both been lonely and bad at romance so they teamed up to fit into society.

Judy. She hadn't been important till now. She was just a girl with an underbite and a bunch of annoying stories about waitressing at a biker bar in Arizona with a posse of other unimportant girls who at that time felt important but didn't realize it wouldn't last. Judy would say the name of the bar as if everyone would know it and be so impressed, which just made it clear that Judy's world was as big as a shoebox. Or she'd talk about this guy at her gym one year who was obsessed with her. She'd brag about restraining orders, and the details always shifted.

Staci hadn't been mean to her face but she sure as hell talked behind her back; she even did a Judy impression, jutting her lower jaw out and twirling her hair and talking to the air about a really busy Saturday night at the bar in 1991—*it was so crazy, we ran out of Budweiser!* Now Judy was crucial, front and center. All because she was widowed, stuck in a hospital, and she could tell the police anything she wanted. Well, you're finally important, Judy, thought Staci, and her body shuddered. Something about Judy that was impossible to name frightened her.

Stubbing out her smoke, she decided to meditate lying down.

Ray busted in. *You seen my silver lighter, babe?*

Ray, I'm in the middle of something, she said, eyes closed.

Well, real quick then, you seen it?

No, she said, closing her eyes tight.

He left the room, the door not shutting. She decided not to be annoyed and whispered her gratitude list. From experience she knew that gratitude led to confidence, which made Ray instantly more attracted to her. *Thank you for saving us from the fire. Thank you for Ray. Thank you for the flowers outside, the butterflies . . .* She racked her brain.

When Ernie knocked to go grocery shopping, she was pumped because she'd told herself she'd do yoga for an hour after meditating, and she totally didn't want to. Yoga also made her somehow hotter but it was boring. As they walked to the van, they passed Coral sitting cross-legged in the front yard, picking weeds, letting them fall from her hands.

Sweetie, do you want to come to HEB? Staci asked.

Coral seemed to shake her head, the sun highlighting a fuzz of blond split ends.

Halfway to town, droplets hit the van.

Think she took cover? Ernie said in the tone they'd developed for talking about the girl: partly flippant, partly genuine, partly bewildered.

Ha! Probably still out there, soaking wet.

They passed a church and Staci realized it must be Sunday because of the cars and people. A mother had hold of her teenage daughter's elbow in this way that made Staci smile with recognition. The girl was trudging up the steps, in her Chuck Taylors, nose ring shining, and her mother was grim-faced. She thought: Oh Mama, you can drag your baby to mass, but you can't make her believe. The windshield streamed with water.

This is like Florida, she said. *All summer, monsoon every afternoon.*

Think you'll go back there someday? Ernie asked.

Hmmmmm. Not sure.

You didn't dig it?

Oh no I did. There were literally turtles everywhere, and parrots. Like—zoo-type animals, but out in the wild. Hot tubs. Nightclubs. It was my shit. People in Florida, no offense, are fucking crazy, though.

Ernie nodded, the car ahead spraying a massive wake.

I mean, we're crazy too, she said. *I know that. And I did cause trouble down there. For one hot second, I totally thought I was in love with this dude Dwayne. In no way was that a good idea. But it's hard when you suddenly feel that strongly about somebody and you don't want to be unloyal to your heart. And then, you know, Ray beat Dwayne half to death, which sucked.*

That why you left?

Oh hell yeah, left that night. New Year's Eve. But that's Holiday Ray. You know that's how he got his name, right? Always getting into it on the holidays.

They parked and ran through the puddled lot, shook dry inside, both feeling a trace of shame from being so bothered by rain. Because the girl was probably still sitting in the grass as the water rose an inch, the earth refusing to absorb the downpour. The girl was delighted, for all they knew, which seemed demented—but perhaps *they* were demented to fear something as pure as rain. *Anyway.*

The pair walked the aisles in silence and filled a cart with spaghetti and Froot Loops and hot dogs. Then Ernie stopped in front of the cold medicine. There it was.

Should we, I guess? Staci said.

We could at least get it, so we have it, Ernie answered.

They'd done the math, and then redone it, and the math blew. Any other way to make enough money became less and less realistic, or appealing, the way it always did. When he couldn't sleep the night before, in fact, Ernie made a decision to look the other way in his heart. Soon, soon, after this round, he'd really—this time—truly—investigate alternatives. God, he felt deflated, but they put twenty Sudafed boxes in the cart.

Then Staci grabbed a few bottles of white zinfandel—totally not as harmful and dangerous as hard alcohol. They added Sour Patch Kids as they waited in line for the register. Loading bags into the van, Ernie politely didn't say anything about the wine. She felt defensive though.

Look, I know you think of me as sober, she said as they drove home. *Drink definitely used to be my demon. Well, and cocaine. And pills, I guess. But I learned all about my brain in meetings and books, and I have rewired myself. I sort of reset to zero, to where I could drink again. I love my new clarity. You know?*

Sure, Ernie said in a soothing voice. *Let Ray deal with it.*

She cranked the radio, driving careful on the black slick roads, and singing aloud to "Candy Rain" by Soul for Real. A hologram of Judy hovered in the backseat, meeting their eyes now and then in the rearview mirror.

RAY HAD CHECKED for that car every sunrise, every afternoon, making up reasons to go for a ride, get milk at the grocer, pick up cigarettes. Nothing for three days. No fresh tracks in the dirt either. It ended up being Staci and Ernie who pushed things, who dropped hints about getting to work, they were the impatient ones now. The cookie jar of cash was dwindling.

Yeah, you're right, what are we waiting for, Ray muttered, picking his teeth with a matchbook, unconvincing to anyone, but it was good enough.

The next morning, Ernie closed the barn door but the chemical stink came out. At noon he emerged, wearing an apron and rubber gloves, whistling. He picked up a plastic bucket and went back inside. The door revealed a glimpse of coffee grinders and battery packaging.

Ernie finished for the day. He leaned against the house afterward, letting the sun sort him out. His power was stringy, his masculinity narrowed in long bones and quick movements. He stood tall, head and shoulders up. Something about how his long dark hair and beard were tinged red, almost strawberry, said he was close to the sun, he knew his way around a meadow. It was like a beautiful stain.

RAY AND ERNIE and Staci talked over baloney sandwiches and agreed not to contact the old Okie connections since they were probably still in touch with Tim. The house had a landline now but

Ray drove to a strip-mall pay phone. He beeped Ugly Sid who he hadn't seen in five years, an old ally, and then studied his boots in the tall wildflowers. When Ray was a young man, this kind of risk was fun, sent adrenaline through his blood. Not so much now.

Sid Sid Sid, he said when the phone rang. *It's Holiday Ray.*

I'll be blasted, she said.

Long time, darling, he said.

Few years ago, I heard they were hunting you down in Shreveport.

Oh yeah. That blew over a little. Hey listen. I got a favor. Are you still in El Paso? He explained in code and she said yes but he wouldn't get fully paid up front.

Long as we get paid eventually.

That's how it works, she said.

When they hung up, he snapped a cornflower off its stem and pinned it behind his ear.

RAY AND STACI got ready to ride west, the goods under the motorcycle seat in an insulated compartment. Ernie was nervous as he saw them off, pulling his red beard in the driveway, white blossoms twirling off trees in the sunrise light. Coral stood like a shadow behind him.

We'll be back tonight, Ray said, grinning as if he wasn't nervous too.

Don't let anything happen, Ernie said.

You're crazy, what could happen, Ray shouted as they rolled away.

Of course, as luck would have it, the spot gleamed with a car nested in its brambles today. He had the sensation of the seat between his legs being X-rayed. Was it the same Chevy? He tried not to look but he couldn't stop himself from glancing as they rode past; he thought he saw beige, a sedan. What the fuck. He kept looking in his mirrors. He waited for them to follow, and when they didn't, he waited to be pulled over by a cop alerted by the sedan in the woods. But when his bike hit the open road, where bluebonnets and lupine made the highway look like a path to Wonderland, Ray stuffed the threat away for the time being. Nothing else to do.

What more could you want? Ray shouted to Staci. *Huh?*

They rode past foothills, past rest-stop windows with handwritten signs for burritos, and past motionless livestock in fields. Vultures wheeled in the sky, their wings so ragged and uneven, they looked corrupt. Closer to El Paso, the sky turned ominously bright. They slowed down as they entered the city, absorbing the noise, the smog. Wild dogs. Food carts. Staci grinned at the chaos, the streets frantic but laid-back, smoky, shimmering with bumpers and windows and lights.

This is us, Ray shouted to her.

They pulled up to the clubhouse and a man named Maggot popped into the front yard, with two Dobermans, one on each side. He grinned and he had silver front teeth. He was high. His T-shirt had a pink ribbon and said MARATHON FOR BREAST CANCER, EL PASO, 1993. His jeans were black. The dogs were really old and sweet. Ray rarely did business with people this high during the day.

What's the story? Ray asked.

There's no story, Maggot said, jittering.

But Ray didn't feel like driving back without getting this transaction done. They ended up in the main room, two girls playing pool behind them. Staci drank a Diet 7UP while the men talked, and she could tell she was supposed to play pool too, but she wasn't going to play a game with children, because those girls were young enough to be kids, honestly. She glared as Ray got comfortable here, in his old environment of brothers, dudes coming and going, and business at hand. He sat with his legs extended and his thick gnarled fingers laced behind his head, totally at ease.

This had been part of Ray's value to Tim, since every person had a specific value: Tim idolized the bikers from other clubs, but Ray actually communed with them. So Ray became Tim's surrogate in socializing. On his own, Tim would get spotted as an imposter and scammed. Ray in general got men in a way Tim didn't; he'd grown up in swarms of boys and bullies and uncles, assholes and brothers and buddies. He knew the importance of being free, *regulate this, motherfucker!* and he also knew that any motorcycle club, for example, had a thousand rules for eating a hamburger. The protocol was to pretend there was no protocol while mastering the protocol.

Ray told Maggot they just moved to Texas from Florida. They talked about a person they both knew called Gayne, who recently stole a crop duster plane and crashed it on a football field. They talked about a gang riot in the Huntsville prison. They talked about the best places nearby to get a fajita. Maggot revealed that he loved fajitas but did not love when he walked out of the joint smelling like meat smoke and burnt onions, so he preferred outdoor venues.

Staci watched one of the girls rack the balls and break. She had a blond pompadour, smooth plump young arms, chipped yellow nail polish. Maybe fifteen, or sixteen? As Staci watched, the girl flickered like a vision because it was impossible to know if this girl, preying like a shark on billiard balls, moving around with slit eyes, laughing from the gut, was miserable and being exploited (of course she was!) or free and ditching school and living the life and being wild (of course she was!). Staci's judgment went off and on, a broken light.

Hey, yo. A man with a backward trucker hat and no shirt came out and the girls straightened up, their energy shifted. *Bobby.*

I'm Ray.

The man shook Ray's hand and they went into another room to do the deal. Bobby was the Tim, Staci realized, the one who everyone loved and hated, who kept them in discord and also kept them bonded. Bobby made this house a club. So interesting that Ray yearned to be back in a place like this, in a bigger crew, because it made him feel bigger—but why did he look smaller right now? This was too clear suddenly when it wasn't clear before. She was afraid someone might hear her thoughts and kick her out.

Staci turned to the girls. *You two spend a lot of time here?*

They stared at her. *Yeah?*

I mean, do you still go to school?

They looked at her, disgusted. *Why?*

Never mind, ignore me. Staci's hands shook as she paged through a magazine without seeing it. What on earth was she doing? Acting like a truancy officer. Jesus. She knew this room backward and forward, she'd been here or someplace exactly like it a million times. The bar fridge. The sticky bottle caps on the counter. The ashtray. The Confederate flag. The plaid couch. The ceiling fan. Stickers on the door. The sense of who was in charge, a ladder of men, the energy throughout the house constantly shifting depending on who was where and what mood they were in. A particular flavor of power and glory. She was sure she missed it.

So why didn't it feel quite right, now? And then she thought of their own misfit house, the dandelions Ernie stuck in a mayonnaise jar, the gold light through the windows, the smell of earth. No one in charge. The hours slipping loosely through the halls, running out the screen door, stretching across the yard like a breeze. Space and blue sky and stars.

Did you hear me? Ray said, hands on hips.

He and the other two men were looking at her from the threshold.

Sorry—what? she said.

These guys asked us to stay. Gonna grill up some T-bones in an hour or so.

Staci smiled, closed the magazine, putting up her tits, stalling, desperately thinking of an excuse because she really really wanted to leave. But none came in time. She used to have so much energy for this kind of night. She'd suddenly become a charm-machine, a fountain of innuendos and baby laughs. But now she felt like she'd taken a bunch of sedatives. Her body was just as heavy as her heart, not willing to play.

The guys seemed to have a blast. They took the night in stages: sunset spliff, grilling, tequila, getting-to-know-you stories told too loud and with frantic laughter. *Right? Right?* someone kept saying. Then some blow and they were outside looking at bikes. Then a pool game that got a little too real at one point. Like visiting stations of the cross, they moved from one to the next in a holy order. And then the night hit that place where the order reversed and became pure and brutal disorder. Shrieking music, an assault rifle fired from the roof.

For hours, she did the bare minimum to convince them she was thrilled to be here. Her greatest sin would be to come off as uptight. But when a scrawny dude with no shirt, pink like a pale sickly person straight out of a hot tub, ugly, with stupid tattoos randomly placed, started speaking antagonistic gibberish, she knew to vanish. He was the canary in the coal mine.

She asked a girl where she could catch some shuteye, and when she made it into the bedroom, she locked the door and stood there. High alert. She almost fell asleep on top of the covers, clothes on, boots on, until someone quietly started to work the doorknob from the other side; she just knew it wasn't Ray, and she held her breath. They wiggled it, stopped, and she could almost hear breathing. Then they tapped quietly on the door and tried the knob again. Her heart was racing.

Who in this house scared her the most?

Herself. Oh, the doors she'd opened over the years. Please don't, she thought, but she could feel her body getting ready, she sat up like a sleepwalker. In these moments, she was torn in half. Part of her heard her best friend in eighth grade, Kelly, teaching Staci to gaze at a boy's mouth as he talked and lick her own lips. The girl was like a military general in love with war. *We're on a mission, to seduce every single one of them, or die.*

The other half of her mind heard Savannah, an ex-dancer she knew in Vegas. Savannah and her girlfriend would spend hours by the pool, and Savannah told Staci she hated men, then laughed viciously. *Even the ones who seem good will annihilate you.* She'd become an amateur bodybuilder, and always looked above a man's head if he talked to her. Including her brother, the mailman, the owner of the gym. *You're a sucker if you believe a word they say.*

Hey babe, whispered the stranger now. *Hey sweetie, whatcha doing?*

Her body stood up and walked to the door. She didn't move, stuck in the dark, and she listened. Her hands quivered—all she had to do was untwist the lock.

You lonely in there? he whispered with a smile.

Somehow, she delayed things long enough that he gave up, even though, as he whispered in parting, he could smell her through the door. She could finally breathe again, and let her shoulders fall, let her head drop. Staggered back to the bed and crashed, dozed for an hour or two. At dawn, she peeked out. Ray was on the couch with Bobby and Maggot, drinking coffee, no one having slept. They waved at her, and she put on her swimsuit-edition smile.

We better hit the road, babe, she said to Ray, as if she was wistful about it.

Yeah, he groaned, *I guess you're right, now or never.*

She moved her hips as she crossed the room, denim shorts and high-heel booties, distract distract distract and jet. She linked her arm through Ray's and dragged him to the door, and almost cried with joy when they hit the highway.

—

THAT AFTERNOON WHEN they got back, Staci thought about her need to escape the motorcycle club. It had been so intense. So melodramatic and disloyal, not just to Ray but to the whole universe of bikers, clubs—hell, to men in general. Was that it? Should she feel this guilty just for wanting to come home? But she did. She wanted Ray to be happy and forget that she'd been a sourpuss, so she lured him into bed for the day.

They had fun, there was some tickling, pillow-fighting. They felt like buddies, best friends, which happened sometimes. Staci believed she'd made up for her bad attitude in El Paso, and Ray didn't even have to tell her he ended up hating those guys and was just as happy to leave as her. They were the wrong people, he regretted being put in touch, but it was kind of too late now.

Later, Coral was filling a glass at the sink when Staci wandered into the kitchen, wearing a lavender negligee, her hair in knots.

We're just having a little boudoir date in there, Cor. Oh my god, he still wears me out! Staci made another round of margaritas in the blender. *You want one?*

Coral shook her head.

I'm making mine virgin and Ray gets some tequila. Staci made a show of pouring tequila into only one, even though Coral had already left the room. Then she looked into the fridge. *I mean fuckin' A. I'm starving.*

She ate leftover meatballs with her fingers and called into the bedroom: *Ray, you want meatballs?*

She waited to hear.

Ray. You want meatballs, honey?

Sure, he called out hoarsely.

Ernie walked into the kitchen and looked wide-eyed at her, two icy glasses full of neon-yellow slush in her hands, cum drizzle on her negligee, a shadow around her eyes where the makeup was sweating.

You're back, he mumbled. *Finally.*

Did you and Coral have a party while we were gone?

No, he said as if it was a real question.

I was joking. She put the glasses down and hugged him. *We're back*, she said sincerely into his ear, *we got paid, more on the way.* She pulled away to hold his face and look him in the eyes. *Everything's going to be okay, right?*

Yeah, everything's okay. He was blushing from the close contact.

She smiled, and took her picnic to Ray.

THE NEXT AFTERNOON, as Ray did the routine check, a car was in the spot yet again. This time he was pissed enough to ride home and come back on foot, sticking his wallet chain in his pocket so it didn't jangle, his armpits sweating in the sun as he walked.

He stood behind a scraggly tree, barely able to see the car from there. But still, it only took a second for his brain to identify what he was seeing, the head bobbing up and down under the steering wheel, and the driver's chin up. Classic. Ray turned away, he even laughed out loud, and it was only as he walked into the house that he put two and two together and knew the carrottop doing all the work was a boy, maybe seventeen, who Ray had seen strolling the road now and then, talking to himself, shooting invisible basketballs, wistful, aimless, maybe in love, maybe for hire. Ha!

Some muscle in his chest relaxed. The place in the woods was just a hiding place, a spot to hook up, to buy pot, who knows, who cares. He simmered in relief, he waded through it, he glowed with it. His wave of optimism surely wouldn't last, but Ray was good at pushing forward, screw the little voices in his head saying this alarm might have been false but the next could be real.

ONE NIGHT, IT was 3 a.m., they all woke up to a full moon and the perfume of smoke. Ernie met Ray and Staci in the living room to watch through the window as Coral burned something in the firepit. Her face was bronzed by the flames.

Should we . . . ? Staci said, biting her nail.

Ernie shrugged.

Ray coughed and scratched his balls through his boxers, poured himself tomato juice in the dark. They stayed until she was done, to make sure she didn't hurt herself and also didn't torch the house.

Her eyes glittered out there in the yard. She had set fire to the clothes she'd been wearing when they left the compound and made the big ride, the clothes she'd last held Luther in. Gone, all gone. The pale flakes of nothing drifted on the wind.

LIME CAKE

THE NINTH OF May—the day when Jay would be somewhere in Santa Fe, the window for payback—came and went. No one called Chris W. for details. No one even brought it up. Fuck Tim. No one said it out loud and no one needed to. No one mentioned what the repercussions could be either.

Instead, they spent what they had on a big fat TV, a dartboard, and a trampoline. Cases of beer, fancy soap, fluffy towels like you get in hotels. Ernie insisted on buying Coral some Beanie Babies and took forever picking them out, yet the girl didn't seem to care about the Beanie Babies, or the dartboard or the trampoline for that matter.

Even after Ernie got up on the trampoline and bounced, his long hair rising and falling, his shirt coming up, laughing. She watched without an expression then went back to her room, leaving the three of them in the yard, feeling like they were deserted. The girl didn't seem dead like when they first got to the house. Now she seemed alive and impatient—for what?

Maybe she's one of those people, Staci said, *who's never happy? But I guess Luther made her happy.*

They all thought on this for a moment.

Is there an arcade nearby? Ray asked. *We could take her to play pinball.*

Or a public pool? Ernie suggested. *Does she swim?*

What about a movie? Staci asked. *She understands us, she can like, read lips.*

They called the movie line, and there was a matinee of *From Dusk Till Dawn* at the Havens Movie Magick Center. Ernie put his hands on his knees to ask Coral, like she was ten, if she wanted to go for a ride and check out a flick. She did her shrugging thing.

Excellent, he said, clapping his hands. *We're all in.*

They showed up early, buying extra-buttered popcorn, Milk Duds, and soda, and took the center of the giant room. People glanced at their wallet chains and leather vests and neck tats, and gave them plenty of space. Ray put his boots on the worn velvet seat in front of him.

Enough preview shit! he yelled at the screen.

Staci punched his arm. *Previews are my favorite part.*

Ernie popped candy methodically as the movie began. He was there—at the hotel, in the shoot-out, at the bloody strip joint. The film flickered on his face, his hand stroking his red beard when he got nervous, laughing when someone was rude.

Yeah, get that loser! he egged on the star.

Coral lounged with knees spread, popcorn butter making her lips shine, and looked around the room as much as she watched the screen. Staci meanwhile sat upright, vaguely positioned like a Barbie, elbows crocked at a nasty angle and little feet arched eternally. When it was over, they skipped down the psychedelic hallway carpet, pretending to shoot guns.

Coral, did you like it? Ernie asked.

She gave a thumbs-up, but everyone was so invigorated, they forgot she was the reason they came here. They walked with post-movie pep through the dreary parking lot, and crossed paths with a flock of burnouts wearing drainpipe jeans, sleeveless cutoff flannels, their long hair wavy, and each group eyed the other.

Ray turned back. *Hey.*

What? snarled a guy.

Your sister called. She wants her pants back.

Ray was in a great mood. He stopped in front of a Range Rover. *Let's fuck it up.*

Ernie and Staci stood with hands on hips. Ray wasn't even drunk! Usually this side didn't emerge until he was four whiskeys and a hit of acid and a sniff of coke into a night.

They think they're hunting in the English countryside or something, Ray said, kicking the bumper.

How about we drive by Dairy Queen instead? Staci said, handling the crisis.

Ray contemplated this, and they got on their bikes. They rolled up to the drive-through and ordered shakes, and then floated home, borne on the dusk. This world could burn in a day, be bombed, get struck by a meteor. Everyone could die but them, and they would ride over the Earth, disobeying stoplights, looting, breaking into mansions and drinking wine cellars dry and draping themselves in jewels, and ride into the sunset, a rich woman's lingerie tied around their necks.

Back at the ranch, all four sat in the kitchen, calming down.

Tim believed he was ready for anything, Ray said, thinking about the movie.

No one can be, Ernie protested. *Besides, we were never gonna survive on canned peaches.*

True, Ray said.

It's interesting, Ernie said. *I felt safe when I first got to that compound, and the longer I stayed, the more dangerous everything felt.*

It's 'cause this outlaw named Coral showed up, Ray said, trying to be funny and smirking at the girl.

Ernie said quietly, *And then we finally ruined it. Not the government. Not some outsider.*

The Judy apparition peeked in the window.

Lynn ruined it, Staci said, uncorking a bottle of wine. *We didn't.*

Ray looked at her. *What's that you got?*

White zin.

I thought no drinking in the house.

Things are different now. In a good way.

Ray narrowed his eyes at her.

I've changed, Ray. I did hard work to get here, and you aren't appreciating that. Staci's eyes welled up, and she sipped her pink drink.

It's just that you told me to hold you to it.

Well, it's not fair of me to ask you that, Ray. I should never have put you in that position.

Staci was *mystified* as to why liquor had always been her enemy in the past. Why are you so mean to me, she used to scowl at the Absolut bottle. I never did anything to you. And yet—and yet—back in the day, there she'd go, four doubles on the rocks, and she suddenly felt quite moved to tell some girl at the other end of the bar to climb off her high horse and get the fuck out of her sight—*why?* said the nameless girl—because you're *stupid,* Staci would tell her, and then— blank spot—suddenly Staci was tripping and skinning a knee at Whataburger, mustard on her cheek mascara running *fuck off officer* and they laughed but it wasn't the nice laugh no it was the other laugh *come on sweetie* said the cop, *we'll just go out to the parking lot and talk about this, don't be afraid.*

Trust me, Staci said now to Ray.

Ernie had a sudden craving for a chili-cheese hot dog—where did that come from? Some long-ago carnival, must be, that just set up for a brief moment in the empty dead-grass field of his left cortex and lit up. He grinned at the machines of memory.

Anyone want a hot dog? he asked carefully, always bracing for rejection.

Nah, I'm good, Ray said.

Staci declined too but they stayed put, which gave Ernie a flush of comfort. Ernie showed the bratwurst to Coral, not expecting her to want one but she nodded, so he boiled them in an inch or two of water in the skillet then browned them for two minutes. He pointed to the coffeepot and raised his eyebrows—when the girl nodded, he poured a mug, and held up the cream. She nodded again. He did the same thing with ketchup and relish, and Ray growled.

Just give her the stuff, for godsake, you're not a waiter.

Ernie could hardly believe it when she tipped her head for Ernie to come outside. Coral took her hot dog and coffee to sit on the weather-disintegrating chair, and he followed, elated. The light was the kind that formed a white membrane on everything, shined through every single blade of grass so that the eye was seeing too much. Every insect was intensely visible as it floated and looped in the air. It was that sort of almost-summer evening. She ate, rubbing her eyes with the heel of her hand, and wow, her round face, the plump cheeks, the complex jewels of her eyes—no other girl compared to this cherubic metalhead who Ernie was proud to call his friend. His friend. We're just friends, he thought and stopped staring at her because he realized that's what he'd been doing, and he sipped his coffee and pointed at a butterfly.

Look, a butterfly, he said, trying to sound Zen.

ERNIE SURGED WITH energy. He couldn't sleep that night. He turned over, and turned back, tried different positions on the mattress but nothing worked. His body was golden with moonshadow. He slept in skivvies, his thighs lean and strong. Parts of him were wildly perfect—his hands, his calves, his long and graceful neck—paired with the broken nose, his black-cracked toenails, the scars on the insides of both wrists.

He made himself stay in bed till 5 a.m., when he got up to brush his teeth, ready—so ready—to plant that backyard. Out of his imagination came this cartoonish ideal—he'd wear a straw hat and tilt his watering can down the rows, and big juicy drops of water would pop out the spout and dance onto the leaf and darken the soil. He could picture himself sunburned and tired, with a bowl of figs or cherry tomatoes, offering them around, a humble emptiness on his face as everyone's eyes twinkled, they tasted what he'd grown, and realized what a decent man he'd always been, even when they hadn't noticed.

Ernie got Ray to come with him to a nearby nursery, listening to talk radio on the way because it still felt odd to be alone together. At the nursery, Ernie stared, hands on skinny hips, at the racks of seed packets.

Oh man, he mused. *How to choose.*

Simple. Whatcha want to eat in a month? Ray asked.

If only it were that easy. Ray, I wish you were right about things more often, Ernie said, scanning the row of packets for lettuces and watermelon and larkspur and chives.

Ray rolled his eyes. *Are we spending our whole day here or what?*

A white-haired man with tiny bandages on his face, maybe from skin cancer, came up. He was hunched, slim, but spoke with hard work and authority. *What are you looking for?*

Trying to plant a bunch of stuff that will actually grow around here, you know? Ernie said.

Irrigation at your place?

Basic.

Soil?

Um, we've started composting but need to catch up.

Let's get you a cart.

Ray and Ernie pushed their shopping cart of fertilizer, lime tree saplings, mulch, seeds, and seedlings to the car. Their wallet chains clanking, long hair shining in the sun.

They got lunch at Bonnie J's BBQ, which they'd driven past many times but had yet to try. They walked in, stomp stomp, arms crossed, surveyed, and immediately could smell it was the right spot. The ceiling was high because of the flames in the pits and the walls were stained black from smoke.

A lady with powder-blue-enamel eyelids, and JEREL sewn in script on her shirt pocket, greeted them: *Don't just stand there, boys.*

Good afternoon, ma'am, Ernie said. He chided himself because he was already thinking about that lime cake behind the glass. But first: brisket.

They headed to the counter with orange plastic trays, and Ray ordered for them: jalapeño sausage, brisket, beef rib, pit ham. Then they slid down the line for cold macaroni, coleslaw, beans, onions and pickles, a half loaf of Wonder Bread, and two freezing-cold cans of Big Red.

Look out, I'm getting ready to make a mess, Ray said, with pleasure and aggression.

The only other person in there at this early hour was a guy sitting in the corner, his body the size of two men, but not fat—just solid. His head was shaved, with curlicued sideburns, hands wet with meat, a turquoise stud in one ear. What looked like flower tattoos covered both his arms.

They squirted hot sauce and dug into the gleaming, pink-rimmed, fatty brisket. Outside, boys on bikes pulled a kid on a skateboard with a rope, and his wheels rumbled, chunky and squeaky, over the ground.

No place for a skateboard, said Ray.

Ernie agreed. *Did I ever tell you about my friend Jesse?*

Ray shook his head.

Jesse had hit his head skateboarding down a bank's metal banister at midnight—it was caught on videotape—and knocked a piece of brain loose—the camera light shining in his bloody face as he drunkenly laughed—and he couldn't smell from then on. He went from consuming a fucking *pair* of chicken buckets every day to having to eat protein milkshakes to keep his weight above 120.

Why didn't he eat more? Ray asked.

Because if you can't smell, you can't taste, and if you can't taste, you just don't want food.

Even if you're hungry though?

Yeah. You have no appetite, Ernie said, licking sauce off his thumb. *It's scientific.*

That reminds me of this other fucked-up story, wanna hear?

Why not.

Girl named Sara Boyd, holy shit. Ray destroyed the last of the beans by tipping the Styrofoam cup to his mouth. *This was years ago, back in the day, I still lived up in Michigan. Up north, people'll bring you a casserole if someone dies, and pull over if you got a flat. Except when they're not nice, then they're some of the coldest motherfuckers.*

Including you, right?

Ray laughed, coleslaw milk on his lips. *Yeah, including me. So, she was in love with Kevin, they were together, I mean, all the ladies loved him. He didn't talk much. He didn't treat her that nice—not bad, just not nice. So this band comes to town, right? They play at the Python, everyone's on speed. Sara—seemed like a good girl—but she was mischievous at heart.*

You know that firsthand? Ernie blushed because whenever he tried to sound worldly and tough, he sounded the opposite.

Ray didn't stop to answer this rookie question. *So apparently she spends the night at the motel with the bass player. Who cares. But Kevin finds out, and the whole town was like—quiet—waiting. She'd never cheated on him. No one had. A day a week a month go by, and Kevin blows off steam, a trip into Cincinnati, partying, then he goes to her house.*

How do you know? Ernie asked.

The entire town knows this story. They get pizza, go drinking, and he's got her in the backseat of his '62 Mustang, right? Going down on her—

Ernie was aware of how loud Ray was talking, and the silence otherwise.

And he pulls her panties down, pushes up her skirt, so he could spread them—and—CHOMP! He bites out her clit!

Ray went into paroxysms of hoarse bark-wheezing—*You follow? An eye for an eye! Tooth for a tooth!* Ray was laughing so hard, his eyes were wet before he could talk again.

Ernie was half-laughing sort of slanted, making an are-you-serious! face with his eyebrows crumpled. Ernie was trying to please both Ray and the man in the corner who Ernie feared was disapproving.

What does this have to do with skateboarding? Ernie said quietly.

You know, if she can't want it anymore, will she ever get it? Ray said with deliriousness.

The man in the corner suddenly got up and banged his tray into the garbage. Ernie cringed. He walked toward them, pulling a key ring from his back pocket. He looked at these two misfits, and he threw and caught the keys in one palm, and they waited for judgment, for sentencing, but he strolled by, shoulders wide, in silence. The screen door slapped shut behind him.

He didn't like that, Ernie said, worried.

Nobody gives a shit, Ernie. You overthink this stuff.

The man came back in, and they both jumped. He looked at them.

Then he said, with a lisp: *That your van? It's sort of blocking me in. Don't want to risk scratching it.*

They went outside and read the script on his truck. He must be Baton Rufus! They recognized him from billboards now. Rufus owned a psychedelic tire-shop franchise, with locations all through Texas and Louisiana. The garages had speakers blasting Frank Zappa and Captain Beefheart and Bootsy Collins as your car got jacked up and then serviced, and the buildings were painted like tie-dye. Staff wore neon headbands, and kids could get fifty-cent toys from a machine, like candy rings, plastic race cars, or tiny baby dolls, while their parents waited.

As Ray moved the van, Ernie stood in the hot dirt lot and wanted to ask this entrepreneurial god to invest in his dream bookstore, or at least give him some tips. He wanted to tell Rufus that ever since he was little, he'd had the "businessman drive." (He'd also fucked up every venture, starting with the pecan stand he built at the age of eight; a sudden rain soaked all the nuts when he went inside for a soda.)

Rufus was the miracle, he started his company from scratch, he'd taped the dollar bill above the cash register. But before he even asked, Ernie became convinced the man looked down on him. This happened with no logic, like the wind changing direction. He just watched Rufus work his toothpick, and Ernie was mute.

Rufus got up into his own truck and waved. *Appreciate y'all.*

Ernie waved like a kid left behind. They went inside and ate lime cake.

BACK AT THE ranch, Coral was doing her afternoon meandering. She slid up and down the land like a tide. If a stranger was looking, they might miss her as she slipped through the catclaw trees and the ragweed. She ate some honeysuckle, pinching the back of the flower and pulling it onto her tongue. Rolled an owl pellet between her fingers to break loose the tiny bones. Fell asleep on pine needles. When she woke up, a Chihuahua with no collar was rooting around in the myrtle; his owner didn't keep him in the yard. He had a happy-go-lucky walk.

At the barn, she checked on the swallow's nest. Four black-feathered babies, with yellow beaks opening and closing to the sky. The mother had stopped feeding the smallest one a few days ago, and it got weaker, quieter but desperate, and finally, maybe today, it was pushed from the mud-shaped bowl in the rafters; Coral looked at the body on the ground.

Maybe she heard the van, maybe not, but either way, Coral was standing in the driveway when they pulled in. She helped unload everything, and Ernie monitored her reaction.

Coral, think we got enough? Ernie joked as they carried mulch bags on their shoulders.

She seemed to be in a good mood, and he laughed out loud, not because anything was funny, he was just so happy. Ray popped a beer and hauled out some tools, and Coral started to arrange seed packets in lines on the ground. Even Staci ambled out to join the fun.

What's the story? she asked, surveying things. *Are we going to—like— have a whole row of that basil there?*

This kind of work was a novelty to her. As she pointed a long red fingernail at the herbs, she snatched glimpses of her reflection in the window, straw hat and terry-cloth shorts, like a pastoral *Playboy* shoot. Farmgirl centerfold. She loved pointing at the plants, being serious. Bending over.

That's actually cilantro, Ernie said.

They spent the afternoon digging and watering, and Ray added

vertically to the fence so deer couldn't jump it. Ernie watched everyone turn and shovel and stretch, watched them move how people
move around gardens, focused on what's underfoot, lost in the hour.
It was a meditative way of being, and also dumb in the way intimate
work with dirt and plants was dumb.

How'd you become such a pro, by the way? Staci asked.

I used to help Brandy in the garden, Ernie said. *And when I was a kid, I
learned a lot at Gloria's house.*

Where was that again? Staci asked.

Not far, actually, it was in Menard, about twenty miles as the crow flies.

Staci smacked a mosquito on her cheek. *And when were you there?*

Age eight to thirteen, I guess.

And she was your—aunt or something? I can't remember.

*No, she took in foster kids. And she grew up on a big, industrial farm herself
so she knew a lot. We had a little vegetable garden but she didn't want to be in
agriculture, so she sold mail-order vitamins for a living.*

What'd she teach you?

I dunno, Ernie said shyly, grinning crooked.

Come on.

*Well. Let's see. Horses and dogs are natural enemies. But the eggplant and
the marigold are friends, you know? One keeps away bugs that eat the other
one.*

Okay.

You can live without a truck but not without a hat.

She laughed at that.

He continued: *Hose-water keeps things alive but rain makes them grow.
Um. Don't fight the weather. Don't fight the flies. Don't let foxes guard the
henhouse.*

Even I know the fox-henhouse one. She sounds cool, this lady.

A bumblebee reeled drunkenly through the air between them.

Ernie seemed pensive. *She used to say it was strange to live in a world where kids and animals don't get any guarantees. But she was still really*—he searched for the word—*positive. Like*—*she had the best smile.* For no concrete reason, he felt he'd said too much about a sacred subject. *What'd your parents do?*

Staci leaned on her shovel and wiped sweat from her forehead and looked at her fingers to see how much concealer came off. *My mom worked at JCPenney in the mall, and then also at this eyeglass place for a while. My stepdad did HVAC, started at the bottom, made it up to where he just like fielded calls and sent people on jobs.*

Coral was staking popsicle sticks wherever a row had been planted. Her hair hung in her face. They knew what her parents had done.

Staci thought about how not a single person at the Oklahoma compound had asked about *real* life, her parents, her childhood. And she had never asked anyone anything that mattered either. All they did was talk smack, and she was one of the worst. Tim acted like a mediator, even though he set the feuds in motion. Or he talked about *his* compound, his wife, his baby, roping people into his life since it was simply more important than theirs and worthier of discussion. Staci used to pity Brandy, who spent days working through Tim's issues and desires with him. Her own dreams and fears pushed to the corner. But didn't he do that to everyone? And didn't we, Staci thought, let him, even invite it?

Meanwhile, Ernie returned from the kitchen with lemonades. Sitting on a stump, Staci finished hers in one glug. She watched as he handed one to Coral then knocked his own back, his neck gleaming with sweat. The sun shined like an open cantaloupe, pouring out light. There was nowhere to be but here—what an exotic feeling.

That hit the spot, she said, smiling. *It's fucking hot out here.*

Yeah, got to stay hydrated.

So—how long till we have tomatoes?

Well, a good minute.

In New Jersey, tomatoes were like the one thing we could brag about.

Texas tomatoes can be damn tasty, Ernie said, licking his lips. *Ever had a Texas tomato, Coral?*

She nodded but he had a feeling she didn't know what he said. He looked at her dirty hands, the wet armpits of her T-shirt—and felt pure accountability. Those turned front teeth like a bluegrass twang that comes out of nowhere at the start of the song. Her pink earlobe. Freckles on her thighs.

He never told anyone, he barely admitted it to himself, but he'd snuck into Coral's room at the compound and rummaged through her stuff. The white valise's name tag was tied to its handle, with old-fashioned handwriting that said Inez Harris and a phone number whose first digits were letters. The suitcase had very few things in it. Maybe ten photographs, worn at the edges. He guessed the top one was Inez, must have been, with a granny-mullet of white hair, a gut, mega-biceps. She stood grinning—not in a humble, sugary way like a regular grandmother, more like a redneck gangster—at a pink-cheeked plump Coral (maybe six, or seven?) sitting on a Harley, Inez holding the bike up. Coral grinned back at Inez, not the camera. One of a young Coral, shotgun broken over her arm, a half circle of dead wildfowl in the grass. A photo of a raccoon playing on a couch, one of a blurry field of flowers, and Inez cooking at a grill hand-built on bricks, and Coral splashing in underpants in a lake.

It didn't feel like luggage as much as a tiny museum. There was a Milky Way whose wrapper was almost disintegrating. And those wrappers do not disintegrate. A piece of rough rose quartz. And a $10 bill folded in half. All of it left behind at the blazing compound.

Maybe the garden, he realized now, was for Coral. Maybe this whole place, this project, was not to show Tim that he wasn't needed, or to impress anyone at all, but to give the girl a home. Holy shit.

Could that be it? Had he finally found his calling? His body, from head to toe, vibrated with this news.

THE SUN, THE labor, and this monumental revelation exhausted him, and Ernie lay down on his bed before dinner, sweat turning to salt on his blanket. He was entering a phase where he had energy even while napping, and he could sort of steer his dreams. He'd been here before, he loved it.

He went from consciousness right into a secret chamber in the shed where wild strawberries were taking root. Ray pointed his burly tough hand, with its skull ring and scars, at the tiny jewels. Ernie opened his mouth, but no words came out. Then they watched a vine of zucchini blossoms grow through the spokes of their motorcycle wheels, locking the bikes into the garage. Ray got confused, and Ernie tried to reason with him, then backed away. He ended up alone and tending to a trellis of sweet-pea plants, their stems winding and twirling, the pink bonnets opening. Inside the bloom was a red bead, and when he touched it, the bead punctured and ran down his hand. When he rubbed his fingertips together, the smear could be nothing else but blood. This vision kept evolving over an hour.

He remembered some of it waking up, but forgot the details berry by berry. He couldn't hold on, he never could.

PET

AND THEN CAME days of heavy, relentless rain. It drummed the roof as they slept, pounded the wet earth all morning, and each time it seemed to be done, the sky darkened, and pellets would start banging again. On the third night, Ernie stood with a cigarette at the window.

Well, this will be good for the garden, he said. *If it doesn't wash everything away.*

He wanted them to see the rain as a benefit so this claustrophobic week didn't make them think about disbanding. At this point, Ernie was obsessed, whether he knew it or not, with getting everyone to stay here forever. Coral was mooning out the window, which made him panic. Ah, dear girl, he thought, maybe you don't know yet. Half of life is about being stuck where you are, certain you're supposed to be somewhere else, but it's not worth setting out in a storm when you don't have a destination.

Cor, he couldn't resist saying. *You need anything?*

She shook her head.

Sure? Ernie asked, *Iced tea?*

Ray threw up his hands and scowled. *Again, with the concierge act.*

Staci kept catching Ray look out the window too, but he wasn't looking at the rain, he was trying to see past it. So often now, he seemed gone. She'd been trying to ignore it, but she couldn't. Somewhere else, a place with no name, a land she'd never visited, that's where he wanted to be. How did she know this? The knowledge came to her like chills. When they first got to this house, she could say it was the upheaval, but they'd been here awhile. Maybe he was keeping watch for blue lights on a cop car, or someone Tim sent, she thought, and Ray *was* doing that—yet all his life he'd known someone could knock on the door at any minute with handcuffs, and that never made him disappear like this.

ERNIE'D BOUGHT T-BONE steaks in town today as a ploy to make everyone happy.

Well-done for me, Ernie told Ray, who was pan-searing the meat.

Ernie, I'm not giving you any if you insist on well-done, okay? There's no point in eating meat then.

But I don't like it red in the middle, Ernie whined.

Well I don't care, Ray answered. *I'll do medium but that's it. Staci and Coral are getting rare because they know what's good.*

When he finally tasted it, Ernie reluctantly admitted it was better this way. Staci did dishes. Before he cut up and served the cherry pie, Ernie put wet clothes into the dryer. They played Monopoly. Ray wore mirrored sunglasses on top of his turned-backward hat, even in the darkness of the monsoon, as they battled for Park Avenue, moving plastic markers and counting paper money. They might as well have been a family in some suburb outside Philly or Los Angeles or Lexington. Ernie tried not to check Coral's expression every couple minutes, but it was hard.

Ray started the donkey-in-the-well tale, which Staci had heard too many times.

Please just don't, she said.

But it happened so long ago, he said. *Nobody's in pain anymore.*

It doesn't matter. I can't handle hearing it, she said dramatically but sincerely.

Ray loved that she couldn't handle it. *The donkey deserved it, he was stupid and fell in a well.*

La-la-la-la! Staci yelled, hands over her ears.

Ray waited for her to finally take her hands off her ears. *That's life!* Ray said, because he had to have the last word.

Smartass, she said. But at least he seems happy when he's telling stories, she thought.

Then he launched into a different direction. *Did I ever tell you about Chester? He could kick my ass in ten flat, unarmed—and he fucked guys. Chester High was his actual name, which sounds like a school. Dressed like a straight dude, talked like a straight dude.*

There's no dress code, Staci said. *Duh.*

He always had someone, like a little blue-eyed teenager who stared at him longingly while he worked in the garage, like a girl looks at a guy, and he'd give them presents, a key chain or a tiny bottle of cologne. Ray coughed merrily. *Live and let live. Am I right, Ernie?*

Ernie wrestled with libertarian ideas, since it worked until it didn't. *I mean—*

I'm cutting you off, Ernie, before you start lecturing. Anyway. Chester souped up this Ford, installed red-leather seats and everything, and he was driving to Indiana to see his uncle, and he ran into a moose, going seventy-five.

Silence for a moment.

Why does everyone die in your stories? Staci complained.

He looked at her so dearly, so lovingly, that she almost got creeped out. *Because my stories are true.*

ON THE FOURTH morning of bad weather—gray and steaming heat but no rain—Coral and the van were gone, which no one noticed until the phone rang and someone delivered the news.

It was a stranger. *Heyyyy, um.*

Who is this? Ray asked.

I'm Doug, I work at the 7-Eleven on Platters Road, near the highway. This—I'm sorry, this is awkward, I think it's a girl? They, um—they—gave me a piece of paper with your number.

Ernie had scribbled it down for her when they got the landline.

Metalhead? Ray asked.

A pause. *I mean, I guess. With a white van outside? Ran out of gas but they don't seem to have any money.*

Ray and Staci tore off on a bike, and when they walked into the 7-Eleven, the girl looked at them. Ray and Staci both had their hands on their hips, like parents at a principal's office, at once feeling apologetic for their child and angry at their child and defensive of their child.

Coral, Ray said in a tone that held all those things.

She stood there, arms crossed loosely, unlaced sneakers, and behind her were the bright lights of the refrigerated shelves. Everything glowed: the beer cans and Sunkists and milk. There should have been an organ playing and a spiral of doves circling her, the birds suspended in a mystical design. But this kid was not a prophet! Was she? If anything, it more and more felt like she'd come to destroy the message.

Not understanding her used to be funny, but it was becoming serious. Did she run away for attention, or was it a game? What was happening behind that baby face? Algebra equations? Song lyrics? Ethical arguments? Nothing? Gibberish?

On the way home, Coral picked at the torn pleather of the passenger-side door.

I didn't even know you could drive, Staci said, shocked to hear her own voice catch. Was she furious? She didn't know.

Coral looked at Staci and half smiled. Was that good, or fucked up, that she smiled? Then Staci noticed Coral's pockets were stuffed with chocolate bars. The girl opened one and took a bite. Staci tried to drive in a straight line because she felt turned around, made fun of, or tricked.

When they arrived, Coral jumped from the van, full of energy, and fell into bed with her Discman and candy. Ray signaled to Ernie and Staci to follow him to the barn. No one knew what to think, and they didn't want to believe they'd just been humiliated.

Ray finally spoke: *Well. That was bizarre.*

I thought she was a little bit happier lately, Ernie admitted.

You want the truth? Ray asked. *I never fucking have a clue what she's thinking.*

It's the trauma from her childhood, Staci said. *I can see it a million miles away, trauma ripples through your life, over the years.*

They pictured ripples.

I guess, Ernie said, wavering.

But then—it's like, Staci hesitated, afraid of being a snitch. *She stole some chocolate. When nobody was watching.*

Maybe she wasn't sneaking, maybe she doesn't know any better, Ernie said. They all knew she knew better.

Suddenly Ray laughed. *Dude, that guy on the phone, he was confused. You got to admit, it was funny. I mean, she doesn't always come off as a girl. Right?*

Yeah, but it's not like she comes off as a boy, Staci said. *She just generally doesn't fit in,*

We don't fit in either, Ernie reminded her.

No, I know, Staci said fast. *I don't think she has to fit in with everyone, it's just like she could try to fit in with us.*

They all pondered this.

No matter what, Ray said, *we can't throw her to the wolves. I mean, if she jumps ship again, that will be—not cool. But.*

Ernie snorted. *But what, should we ground her? She's not twelve.*

And we're not her parents. Ray kept repacking an unlit cigarette on the back of his hand. *Did she just want the chocolate?*

Want to hear something crazy? Ernie said. *For a minute, I thought she got kidnapped.*

Normally they would have teased him, but the idea of her out in the world, with no protection, made them queasy. Why had they never worried about that? They just expected her to stay put. The 7-Eleven guy made them grateful like any parent whose teenager goes missing then shows up unharmed. They were stupid grateful.

The one thing I truly deep-down believe, Staci said, without conviction, *is that her leaving doesn't mean she's trying to get away from us.*

Yeah, we can't give up, Ernie said.

On what? Ray asked.

On her, Ernie said.

No one said anything about giving up, Ray said.

And that was how they left things. But Ray had gotten a whiff of something, of an exotic deviance. What was it exactly? During his life, he'd seen a lot of people break the rules, and he could always smell the reasons: revenge on a childhood priest, or just getting carried away, or daddy issues, or addiction, or a tiny dick, or crossed wires, or sadism. But this one here was a rare case. Behind the high-school-dropout DIY-haircut unlaced-sneakers front—she was something else. He was sure now. It wasn't that she was missing a piece or two. It was more complex, it was radical.

ERNIE TRIED TO hide his feelings, but he was hurt Coral had taken off. When she came into the kitchen for a soda the next morning, he crept into his room, wounded. When the sun broke later, Ray decided to get his buddy's mind off things. On a whim, he took Ernie to Walmart and they bought a couple guns and a six-pack of Lone Stars.

They walked a deer trail into the woods east of town, and suddenly ran into some scraggly guys at the bottom of the rockface. A dog raced up to Ray as if it was going to attack, and Ray attacked the dog instead. They fell to the ground, Ray on his knees, wrestling and laughing hysterically, and it became playtime for them both. But that's how it went when Ray ran into other humans and animals. It was a party or a fight, nothing in between.

Ernie was stroking his beard, eyeing the operation. *What are you people doing?*

What the fuck does it look like they're doing? Ray asked. *They're smoking weed and skipping school!*

The guys, who had been glancing skeptically at each other, smiled. *You want a hit?* said the gingerhead, offered a joint.

So everyone smoked together in the shade, and one kid with a filthy bandanna and unselfconscious pimples dug peanut butter out of the jar with his finger and let the dog lick it off. Two guys had belts attached to rope, and everyone's hands were pale with chalk. It appeared they were living out of a baby-blue van in the shadows.

Y'all are crazy, Ernie said.

It's not that scary, one said.

Ernie smirked. *I didn't mean it's scary. It's just that you don't need fucking ropes to do it.*

Ray fell apart laughing because Ernie was being the provoker, usually Ray's job. Ernie was untethered today, out for blood, and Ray had known this part of Ernie would show eventually—the part that really didn't mind dying. Some people kept this at their core, others just went there when they got high and drunk. Ernie was the rare type whose revolving mindsets couldn't be predicted or controlled, they couldn't be integrated into one man's soul, they just took turns. Nothing to be done but try and catch him if he falls.

The climber smirked back. *You can't do it without ropes, my friend.*

Ray and Ernie gave each other that I-dare-you look they both learned in first grade.

Ray laughed, phlegmy, and said: *The question is, what kind of chips you boys putting on the table here?*

The guys were newly high, their faces puffy, and they looked at one another. Did they royally fuck up by asking these two strangers to smoke with them?

Ray said, *Okay okay how's this, Ernie hits the top with none of your bullshit equipment, we keep your dog.*

One guy laughed until he realized Ray was serious. *We're not putting Ralph up as a bet, and that's kind of not cool you even asked.*

I was just kidding, Ray said in a voice that was not kidding at all. *And Ralph is a stupid name for a dog. What else you got of value?*

When did we agree to a bet? said one of the guys, but the other three looked at him like: Shut up.

Got any candy? Ernie asked.

One dude grabbed a dark chocolate bar from his backpack. *You really going to climb that route for this?*

What do we get, asked another guy, *if you don't make it?*

Ray slipped his hand in his jeans pocket and showed them a sterling silver lighter with a naked woman hand-etched onto it, and Ernie had to hide his surprise that Ray would put that up.

Who's the leader here? Ernie asked.

Um, why would we have a leader, the gingerhead said under his breath.

One pushed another, stifling a grin, and mumbled: *How about you're the leader, Brendan?*

Ernie reached out his hand. *Let's shake, man.*

After they shook, Ernie took the gun from his waistband and handed it to Ray. *Hang on to this, would you?*

The crew all watched, murky from cannabis, as Ernie took off his boots, tested his fingers in the cracks, pulling himself up for a second, letting himself back down. Then his eyes got eerily focused. It wasn't pretty, his bony toes jammed into crevices, hands turning white and magenta as he pulled himself up, inch by inch, his body hunched in a very unbeautiful yet powerful way.

Ray was cheering him on in a coarse wrecked voice. *You're a fucking champ, my man, just don't look down.*

Up and up. Suddenly, at about forty feet, there didn't seem to be a hold, and Ernie was shaking, hyper-vulnerability on display.

Fuuucccck, Ernie cried out.

Brendan shouted up: *Left foot, crack by your knee, lift and get it in there. . . .*

Shhhiiittttt, Ernie said, about to fall.

You got this, man, Brendan said, kind and even. *Deep breath, center in your belly, and get that left foot to the crack by your knee, okay?*

Ernie swept his leg up a couple times before landing it. He was back. He catapulted himself up, grabbed a hold, and worked like a madman to climb the rest. Everyone whistled and shouted. He threw a leg onto the grassy plateau and hauled himself to it then screamed in primal victory.

That's when he looked at everyone. *How do I get down?*

Same way you went up, Ray yelled.

Ernie scowled.

The guys took mercy. *Follow the trail behind you through those bushes, just keep descending and it will wind out here.*

Hurry up, ya freak, Ray said, lighting a cigarette.

Ernie high-fived them all, Brendan told him he was awesome and an idiot, Ernie grinned and took their chocolate, and he and Ray walked a half mile into the dense brush. They knocked back two beers each, thirsty, and then put the bottles on a boulder and shot a few rounds until there was nothing but crystals of brown glass in the weeds. They both forgot to think or worry about anything but the target and its glittering destruction.

In the van, Ernie inspected his cuts and scrapes with a crooked smile, fucked teeth. *That was dumb.*

Ray let out a booming laugh, an eleven, volume-wise, and Ernie raised an eyebrow. He never heard Ray laugh quite that loud so he waited, slightly apprehensive.

Man, you're all right, Ray said, swerving as he raised his hand.

Ernie flinched, thinking he was about to get cuffed, but Ray roughly tousled Ernie's hair. This put him on cloud nine. The rest of the ride was breezy, indigo-blue with deep Texas shadows and pale with summer light, and songs on the radio that just marching-band-paraded through his heart because Ernie felt respected. Tim would have said something like what Ray said—he might have even tousled his hair too—but he would have added: *How hilarious if you fell.* In that tone he had.

Ernie looked sidelong at Ray playing air guitar to Guns N' Roses's "Patience" with his forearms on the wheel, and let himself join Ray for the chorus, howling. When they pulled up to their house, it felt like coming home. And it was true that Ray really liked Ernie. He was comparing him in his mind right now to Mister Plenty, who he also liked, but whose insanity was noble and reliable, very self-contained. Mister Plenty calmly enjoyed his own madness, sitting on the roof some days back in Oklahoma, shirtless and barefoot in mauve slacks. He'd gaze out at the property, not as a sentry, but a modest witness. Never bothered anyone, never imploded, never did much for anyone either. But Ernie was, in this freaky way, so *generous*, he let it all flow and hang out, sharing what he could of his bonkers bananas spirit, even though it would never end well, not for him.

Ray put the van in park, and they looked at their house.

Home again, home again, Ray said.

Ray got out but looked back when Ernie stayed in the van. Ernie was overwhelmed by everything he'd managed to forget in the last few hours—Coral leaving them, how cold she'd been when she got back, how little he understood about what she wanted. Fuck. What could they do? He was stressing and staring at the house when he remembered—out of the blue—Gloria's ten cats back in the day who would pile up on one another, entwined in her bay window, in a pool of sunshine. Then he thought of the dog at the rock and bolted upright.

Dude, he said to Ray, climbing out and slamming the van door. *We should get Coral a pet.*

We could find her a rottweiler, man, Ray suggested, going along with it, as they walked into the house.

Yeah, Ernie said. *Hey, Stace, we're back. Where's Coral?*

Staci was sitting on the couch with the fan blowing her hair, reading a magazine. *Taking a walk.*

Ray said: *Me and Ernie were just thinking, why don't we fucking get her a pet?*

Right? Ernie added.

Staci stared at them and closed her mag. *When my grandmother passed,* Staci said with fervor, *we bought my gramps a little Yorkie. Belmont. It, you know, didn't save him a hundred percent from his grief and all that, but Belmont definitely definitely helped him.*

Should we get her a Yorkie? Ernie said.

Ray lit a smoke. *Or a pony could be cool.*

I had a python at her age, Staci said. *I loved that thing. Oh my god, loved.*

Ray nodded for a while. *Look. Why don't we take her to the pound.*

I totally dig this plan, Staci said. *What took us so long to think of it?*

THE ANIMAL SHELTER was closed over the weekend, so they planned to go Monday, but that Sunday, Ernie and Ray hit a Tex-Mex joint for lunch, a totally random choice. They parked the van in the shade. Grackles dive-bombed for tortilla chips on the patio and the men went inside.

I need a cold one, Ray said to the waiter.

Two, Ernie said.

There was a buzz in the corner, where two unsturdy tables were pushed together and a small crew was doing shots. Ernie did a double-take.

I know that guy, he said.

When they approached the table, the group went silent, but then Manny smiled weakly. *Hey long time, man,* he said. *Ernesto. You heard the news?*

Ernie shook his head. *What happened?*

Manny did look run-down and pale. *Diego got locked up,* he said.

Whoa. When's the trial?

No trial, brother. No bail. Nothing. He's gone, kicking him out of the country.

Sorry to hear that, Ray said.

We're liquidating the ranch. We got two boats and a prop plane if you know somebody.

Yard sale, huh? Ernie said.

For real, Manny said. *Come see. Me and Roger are heading back now.*

They caravanned to the mansion, the van bumbling behind the jacked-up Lexus with gold rims and smoked windows, its white paint covered in red Texas dust. They got out and stretched in the driveway.

Well, here we are, Roger said.

The house had three arches on its grand stucco face, and cameras in every nook and cranny.

Was Diego in Dallas when they got him? Ernie asked.

Yeah, but they're gonna come here. It's a matter of time.

You should sell the Lexus pronto, Ray said.

Tell me about it. There's no title is all. We even got a white Ferrari in the garage here. But it won't start. It's like only Diego could start the machine.

He was the captain of the ship, Ray said, smelling a jacaranda flower hanging off a tree near his face. *The ship hath run aground.*

Those flowers don't have a smell, Ray, Ernie said quietly to set things straight.

Manny played with his one earring. *It's not like I couldn't see this coming. That doesn't mean I prepared for it.*

Ray said, *You just described my whole life.*

They all watched a grackle put up his oily wings and go buckwild crazy at another grackle, shining violet-black in disarray, a mess of aggression, in the sun.

So you're just gonna let this place go? Ernie asked.

We don't have a choice, man.

Ray said: *Well, I hope you had parties galore while you were here. I hope you tore it up. This is a party palace.* His shiny arms crossed. *You should have a going-away party.*

The men looked at Ray with dull matte expressions, not quite done, but not alive either.

Ernie said for them: *I doubt they're in the mood, Ray.*

I would have a party, Ray said. *I'm just saying.*

A monster cloud covered the sun and the grackles chilled out.

Want to buy some furniture? Roger asked. *Come have a look.*

They walked into a house missing its authority. The mold the lichen the rot—it wanted in, it needed to take over. They looked up at a baby-pink chandelier in the foyer; if crystals could smell like vanilla, these would. They walked by room after room, seeing a crib with a bare mattress in one, a jacuzzi in another. The floor was cool terra-cotta, glazed over, and a statue of the Virgin Mary bent her head in an alcove in the wall.

Then they heard a deep, guttural, unhealthy noise that almost didn't sound human. Coming from a closed door at the end of the hall. They all stopped.

Who the fuck is that? Ray said quietly.

You met Slash, didn't you, Ern? Manny asked. *You did, I remember.*

Holy shit. Diego must be dying without him, Ernie said.

And vice versa, Slash is like depressed, Manny said.

What's going to happen? Ernie said.

Manny shrugged. *Your guess is good as mine.*

Ernie's eyes lit up. *Can I use your phone? Ray, come with me.*

They used a lavender telephone in a room that was empty except for a cheap mirrored armoire. Ernie called Staci, and it took a moment before she understood, but then she started laughing, and shrieked *YES* through the line.

Destiny, right? Ernie said to her.

Destiny all the way, she said without hesitating.

A COUPLE HOURS later, Staci and Coral were playing cards, even though Staci could hardly focus because she was too excited, and the van came up the drive.

Don't look don't look! Staci said as she herself peeked through the curtains. *Here comes your surprise, babe.*

Outside, Ernie and Ray stood at the back of the van, trying to figure out how to do this. Ernie was actually shaking.

Jeez, you're tripping, Ray said.

Ernie waved him away, like *shut up,* but he couldn't stop trembling—the adrenaline! Ray called into the house for Staci and Coral to help, and Coral wrinkled her nose, and her posture changed, as she got close. The four of them hefted the huge kennel covered in a tarp and moved it slowly to the shed, Ray yelling out to step over roots and mind the branches. They looked like pallbearers, but the thing in the cage wasn't dead—a living body was shifting around in the box, making a low moan that gave them all chills.

They got it through the doorway of the shed, where the space smelled of mushroom and shadow, and when they placed the kennel on the ground, Ernie caught his breath and put his hands together in prayer.

Are you ready, Coral? he asked.

She looked at him.

You sure? Ernie said.

Staci squealed. *Do it! I can't take it!*

He and Ray looked at each other, beaming, then ripped off the tarp like magicians.

EGG

AND THERE HE was: Slash. A 132-pound male cheetah, slouching against the back bars, trying to disappear. Golden fur, with black spots against whiteness. His eyes were cloudy and wary; he was skinny, filthy, with scabbed cuts on his face and chest.

Well!? Ernie said. *What do you think?*

The girl looked at the animal. What did she see? Her eyes roved over his body, her retinas fast to inventory the thing in front of her. The animal wouldn't look at her. He looked all around, everywhere else, at anyone else, instead, not necessarily with shyness but maybe desperate awareness. He whined, a sound that pierced the dank musty shack.

Ho. Lee. Fuck, said Ray. *Fuck. Me. He looks a whole lot different in our backyard.*

Staci was reminded of meeting her sister's toddler for the first time on a New Jersey backyard patio. Granted, Staci was on an afternoon-gin-and-blow high, her pockets hanging below the cutoff jean shorts. The toddler's face showed such terror, Staci dropped her arms, which were out for embrace, and her sister had rushed to say: *Oh stranger danger, it's a thing,* blushing as the little boy started to wail. Staci popped a Diet Pepsi and laughed as if "stranger danger" was a darling little happenstance and not a serrated knife in the heart.

Manny'd left a metal bowl in the cage, but when Ernie dragged the garden hose to it, Slash lashed out, hitting the bars, screaming, his teeth bared and eyes wild. They all ran out of the shed, Ernie running back to close the shed door and put a rock in front of it, even though Slash was still locked in the crate. They regrouped in the yard. Ernie, shaken, finally cleared his throat and tried to smile.

He said to Coral: *We got him for you as a present.*

It was really Ernie who picked him out, Staci said.

Yeah, but we all had the idea, Ernie insisted.

Sort of, Ray said. *It was your idea and we went along with it.*

How can you guys say that? Ernie said.

Coral seemed to be in shock.

Listen, Ernie said to the group. *Slash is easygoing, but the last few weeks, without his owner, Manny said he got depressed. He'll recover. Just gonna take a minute.*

There was a roar from the shed; no one moved.

You know what that is? Ernie said. *He's hungry.*

He pulled the five bone-in steaks from the packed cooler Manny had given them. He tried to walk casually back toward the shed, as if he did this every day, and he showed the meat to Coral on his way.

Do you want to help feed him first, so he gets, you know, imprinted? Ernie said.

Coral looked at him like he was crazy. Ernie nodded, pink juice dripping over his hands, stalling, and finally entered the shed where he held his breath and mashed the steak between the bars. Slash glared and Ernie walked backward, trying not to run, hiding his fear.

Through the door, everyone watched nothing happen, even though the cat must have been hungry.

He probably wants privacy, Ray said.

Ernie closed the door without meeting the cheetah's eyes.

THERE WAS COLLECTIVE insomnia that night. Slash's round head, his giant teeth, his spots, gleamed in their minds and haunted them as they tried to sleep. The cat had cuddle-baby ears, which were somehow the saddest thing right now.

Pitch-black. Coral lay awake in bed, as if listening. Slash was making a noise between growling and crying. She stared at her ceiling. For hours, she didn't stay still, as if she'd taken speed and had to keep rearranging her body; she got up, moved around the dark room, and sat on the bed, then did it again. She wore Hanes underwear and a ribbed undershirt, and she kept scratching her head so her hair ended up in knots.

She couldn't see him, but the cheetah was pacing too.

THE NEXT DAY, Ernie and Ray went to Home Depot and bought a shit-ton of galvanized-steel fencing, rebar, hog rings, wire cutters, string, and latches. They unloaded the materials from the van into the backyard.

Before they even started, they were drenched in sweat, and took off their shirts.

Manny had drawn an elaborate diagram of what to build, and they set out to make it in one day. They reinforced the existing shed itself, which was about 15 by 15, so Slash could use it as a den, and built an outdoor cage *around* it that was 50 by 60, so the cat would have 3,000 square feet to roam. The cat cowered in the crate as they banged and sawed, and they pretended he wasn't there because they felt so lame.

We're giving him a headache, I bet, Ernie said.

Well, Ray said inconclusively.

They constructed a food and water hatch. And the last thing they did was attach a string to the guillotine entrance of the crate so that from outside the cage, they could lift the crate door and let him out. When they were done, they left the cage and latched it behind them.

Let's hope we didn't screw up something major here, Ray said, wiping his face with his shirt.

High stakes, Ernie agreed.

Staci brought them cold beers, and they stood in that late-day orange light and looked at their work.

She back yet? Ernie asked, trying to seem cool.

Nope, Staci said.

They'd wanted Coral to be here for this but she'd headed into the woods earlier. Ray lifted the door to the kennel by pulling the string, and then tied the string to a nail they'd hammered into the tree. Slash stayed in his crate, though, a cage within a cage, and his giant amber eyes avoided theirs.

He hates us, Staci said glumly.

No one argued with her.

She tossed ice cubes into Slash's dish and filled it with water by pushing the hose through the fence. Crouching on the other side of the wire, she made kissing noises, like coaxing a kitten.

Hey li'l Slashie, don't be afraid. Come get some water, it's nice and cold.

He studied her, then sauntered over and lapped at it with a scummy tongue. Staci couldn't help but move away, even though she knew there was a barrier between them, and she felt bad, like she was making Slash feel unloved. But the bottom line, she knew, was that he wanted to kill them all.

CORAL SPENT THAT day like she spent most days, roaming and idling, athletic socks pulled to her scabby chubby knees. She moved through every little cove in the woods, turning over rocks with a stick, staring at the potato bugs and centipedes carving out dirt under the stone. She stood stock-still near a trumpet flower until a hummingbird zoomed up to spike the blossom. She crept, as if hunting for one lizard, one egg, as if restoring her beliefs stone by stone, fern by fern.

Photons and radiant particles were spinning around her skull. She walked and surveyed, and her whole body seemed to be part of it. Foraging, she looked alive. How did the birdsong and insect-frenzy register on the screen of her consciousness, the webs and droppings, the down, the seedpod, the thistle, all of it catching on her? The dank-woods morning gave way to a smoldering afternoon. Millions of smells, the threads of life and decay, all of the things that were here and missing and morphing. She walked, stepping high through the brush, burrs and vines connecting like Velcro to the blond fuzz on her legs, her knees. She looked at a small muddy pond for a long time. Clouds tumbled along.

Back at dusk, she hurried by the cage without checking out what the guys built, head tucked. Ernie was messing with the tomato plants, and he gave her a smile and a wave like a clown and immediately regretted it. She looked at him and disappeared inside.

THEY ATE DINNER, knowing who sulked in the dark shadows a hundred feet from their table.

Ernie cleared his throat and tried humor. *Ray, want to be a man and do the deed of feeding the beast?*

Sure, I guess. Who wants to help? Ray asked.

Coral didn't look up.

What about you, Stace?

Nuh-uh, honey. That kitty cat is too hungry for my liking.

Guess you're it, Ern, Ray said.

Ray held a baking sheet heavy with beef while Ernie opened the feeding hatch of the pen. The caramel prisms of the cat's eyes glowed in the shadows of the shed, but a stink carried through the air, an unhealthy smell, like the sweat of fear.

Ernie said: *With each feeding, Manny said, he'll like us better.*

Ray threw in the meat, whispering to the cheetah. *Dinnertime, buddy.*

Slash suddenly launched himself out of the darkness screaming, and both men cowered. His round face tilted this way and that as he hissed, and they retreated. Once the men were thirty feet away, Slash crouched. Attacking the beef with his teeth, his small head jerked from his long neck, the lean body coiled, the cheetah gulping back protein.

The men lit smokes with nervous hands in the yard, unable to face the ladies yet.

Not real sure he likes it here, Ray noted quietly.

It will take time, right?

Ray said: *I got to be honest with you. He seems more wild than like a pet, man.*

Look. When I met that cat, couple years ago, he had full run of Diego's house. They also had his brother Axl then, don't know what happened to him, but yeah—they would both lounge by the hot tub. He slept in a bed, he even played with Diego's kids, I swear to god.

They listened to the chewing.

I guess he might get comfortable here. Maybe.

The girl doesn't seem to care though, which sucks, Ernie said, hoping Ray would say something reassuring back, like: Oh, she'll come around, or She's interested and just hiding it, I can tell.

Definitely not, Ray said instead.

In the kitchen they ate ice cream with maraschino cherries, but Coral was already under the sheets, lights out. The cheetah's sadness spread like ink in a pool, fast, and no one could escape it.

I bet Tim could get that creature under control, Ray said to provoke Ernie.

How? Ernie said.

Same way he did all of us, Ray said. *Manipulate. Spoil. Humiliate here and there, offer free shit, pit us against one another.*

Ernie was shocked. They'd never openly talked about this. It had always been the elephant in the room, and he'd thought he was the only one who got so played by Tim. *You two think he used us all?*

Staci laughed at Ernie. *Of course.*

Why did you stay then?

Ray shrugged. *He gave us a place to crash, food, a little family of freaks to hang with, and all we had to do was pretend he was king. And wash dishes.*

Why didn't these guys hate treating Tim like a king? They even went along with it! Whereas it practically killed me, Ernie thought.

I guarantee Tim found a new set of people to do his laundry and kiss his ass wherever he landed, Staci said, licking the back of her spoon.

A moth got into the kitchen, so Ernie turned out the light.

Ray shouted in the dark: *What are you doing, doofus, I'm eating!*

I want the moth to go outside, Ernie said, holding the screen door open, *to the moon.*

Just kill it.

The moth flew out and straight into the sky.

See? How hard was that? said Ernie, flipping the switch on.

Okay, Mother Teresa, Ray said.

It's not like I idolized Tim, said Ernie, unable to let the topic go.

Sure you did, Ray said. *Meanwhile you were especially low on his totem polo.*

Ray! Staci said.

I'm helping Ernie understand that Tim doesn't rule the world was his answer.

I know he doesn't, Ernie said, but even as he said this out loud, Tim occupied his heart, whispering insults.

I mean, he ruled the compound to a degree, Ray said. *But then the overall game is to see him for what he is and see what he needs, and then use him back. That's human society in a nutshell, kids.*

Not all society, Staci said doubtfully.

Sure, all society, Ray said. *Not everyone gets to play, is the only thing. Ironically, it's strong powerful folks who can get used and use back, and the weak just get crushed by being used. But no one escapes the system.*

Staci felt dizzy, she didn't like this conversation.

Ray continued: *For the record, I don't owe Tim a dime, not in my mind. There is no debt.*

You can make that true by saying it? Ernie said. *What the fuck kind of thinking.*

No debt! Ray grinned like the Joker.

I just don't know, Ernie said, lost.

Ray then looked serious. *I assure you he's dreaming up ways to punish us. Losers have tunnel vision when it comes to revenge.*

No one laughed at that.

The boys finally turned in, but Staci stayed up at the kitchen table and chugged wine. Ugh, why did she keep thinking about Judy? It did no one any good to obsess. The same details kept coming up, like clues to the disaster, but they weren't remotely related to what happened. The poor girl kept orange Tic Tacs in her pocket but no one ever wanted any. It was always while someone was cooking or cleaning that Judy cornered them to tell a story. For some reason, Judy thought seeing bra straps outside a tank top was sexy, but it just looked sloppy.

Why, though, Staci wondered, did the whole compound shun Judy so harshly when the woman never hurt anyone? Meanwhile Tim was a genuine prick who lied, took everyone's money, used people, preyed on folks like Ernie, but he was treated like a great guy, a best friend. Tim used to put his hand around Staci's waist and pull her to him whenever Ray was in the next room, and Staci let him. They all let him do whatever. At the same time, Judy's greatest sins were being a blundering mall rat, a grown-up adolescent who chewed her food wrong and laughed too loud, and she was hated like someone who murdered children.

In her bedroom, Staci dabbed lotion on her legs, changed into a chartreuse slip, turned off the lights, and rubbed against Ray under the sheets. When he didn't take the bait, she fell into a funk. He snored while she panicked silently. She kept thinking about the cat outside, and Coral in her room, and Ernie all alone. Why did she feel alone too?

The dark shadows of her many selves were chasing her, and she'd avoided them for months, years even. Seems they'd finally caught up. Why now, she didn't know. Up to a point, avoiding offspring, giving the finger to a ranch house with a satellite dish, saying no to stability and a 401(k), had all seemed glamorous and outlaw. Didn't it? Fuck, she's not even sure it did—maybe she'd been putting a spin on things from day one.

No, it *was* slick, it was vicious, it was good. She was a star, she was on fire. It was real, the glittering black galaxy that had no walls, the way she walked through deep space with a straight face, and even when she was scared, she never let on. There was that night in the yellow Mercedes, there was that week in the dude's crazy palace in Cabo with Laney and Amber. There was her run as a dancer in Dallas, she got a huge bouquet from this Saudi Arabian prince-type, the whole apartment complex saw it delivered on her doorstep . . . they saw it. . . .

That blazing trail of petals led to another scene: that same apartment building, a bathroom, a lighter under a spoon next to a tub filled with Sheena's kids' rubber ducks. Where did that memory come from, why was it necessary? Why couldn't she just catalog the nights of laughing hysterically, the guy infatuated with her in Atlantic City, the lounge, the purple martinis, her and Gemma trading dresses in the limousine and then laughing forever, everyone in love with each other and with the night, with life itself, with white stilettos? She'd looked so good, her nipples burning red like cigarette lighters in a car. A fantasy to everyone who saw her, a walking calendar girl, tinsel-strewn like a Christmas tree . . . Right? It was worth it, right? They laughed all night. . . . In Phoenix, in Atlanta . . . There were dawn pancakes and bacon at IHOP with the two Air Force guys, it was hilarious, coming down after a fucking insane binge, never saw them again, but it was worth it. A life of fun and mad adventure, a life like hers, people could probably still see it in the way she holds herself, in her eyes—that she'd been a fearless explorer, a wild child. So she might not have a real home now, no children of her own, she might be on the road, at forty-two, maybe scared of what's happening, she might have lost her last belongings in a fire.

The cold wind of all this could keep her awake on the hottest night; it was a meat locker of truth. No one could sleep in here. When Ray got up to piss, which he had to do ten times a night these days, she snuggled into him as he got back in bed.

Baby, she whispered.

He didn't answer.

Baby?

He grunted.

I'm asking you something!

What, Stace?

You think that cat's going to die?

He rolled over and didn't answer.

WHY AM I thinking too much? Staci wondered the next day. The hangover anxiety pushed her to go shopping. Driving around, she found a stationery store, and a bell jingled as she opened the door to fetid carpet and Windex smells. Objects stacked everywhere triggering that purchase hormone: maybe a journal, some candy, or burgundy pantyhose would give her a ten-minute high.

So what if I'm fucking materialistic, she thought defensively, nobody's watching except that fat bitch at the counter. The girl was recently pregnant, Staci could tell, and her bottom teeth were browned like she smoked cigars all day. Sometimes Staci let herself go on internal rampages, little festivals of hate. When she was growing up, the people in charge told her to be a nice girl, be polite, behave, treat others right—meanwhile none of *them* behaved, so why should Staci?

She brought colored pencils, guava face cream, and a big "diamond" key chain to the register. The girl studied Staci, and Staci braced herself with slit eyes for some passive-aggressive comment.

The cashier finally said shyly: *You look like a movie star.*

Wow, really? Who? Staci asked.

No, just like you could be, like famous.

Staci managed to say: *Oh that's super-nice, thank you.*

The girl's eyes were turquoise as a Jamaican bay among the zits and studs and scars and pits as she gave Staci change.

Staci blurted: *And you* have *gorgeous eyes! Thanks for making my day, babe.*

The girl smiled and looked down. Walking across the parking lot, Staci swung her bag and laughed out loud. What happened in there? It's like Staci had locked the front door but left a window open and the cashier threw a little Molotov cocktail of kindness inside. She hefted herself into the front seat of the van and checked her face in the rearview. Her lids were caked in silver, and the curved lashes were lumpy with black, like strange pollen on a stamen. These were supposed to be the eyes of a coldhearted power witch. A nightlife monster of love. A hard woman.

Staci giggled instead. What is *wrong* with you? You're getting soft. But this was the best mood she'd known for a while, and nothing really went down, nothing was traded. It was just a honey droplet, that was all, an itty-bitty sweetness with a stranger. Maybe she'd been looking for happiness in exclusive and expensive places, and there it was, at the dime store this whole time.

At dawn, Ernie stood outside the cage, where a golden cloud of sadness hung in the atmosphere, germs of depression. Coral watched out her window as Ernie whispered to the unseen animal, trying to lure him out of darkness into fresh air. Slash wouldn't budge. Ernie sagged in defeat as he trudged back to the house; he didn't know he was being watched or he would have stood up straight like all was good.

That day, Coral lay diagonally across the bed, music pressed to her head for hours. In her hands, the Kiss CD, Gene Simmons's long tongue and the black flared ink around his eyes like the dragon wings in a storybook that another kid would have read a hundred times. She didn't come out of her room except to pee, and everyone assumed she was locked in for the night.

At sunset, Ernie, Staci, and Ray ate eggplant parmigiana outside, looking at the spider webs born during this hour, glistening and infinite in the tall grass. These big-bellied spiders were embroidered with colors, each leg long and pointed like a protractor, and they moved with intelligence. Everyone avoided looking in the direction of the shed. No noise, no sign of life.

I mean, how do you even sell an illegal pet, if you need to? Ray asked.

No idea, Ernie said.

Just put the word out, I guess, through people you know, Staci offered.

A sound behind them, they all flinched, and it took a moment to believe what they were seeing: Coral stood there with the night's meat.

Ernie held his chest, then laughed. *Jesus, you scared me. Wait—do you—want to do the feeding?*

She shrugged.

She walked with him to the cage while Ray and Staci traded looks with each other, and Ernie pulled up the food vent.

Get how this works? he asked, showing her the string.

Coral dumped in the meat, and Slash stood, painfully, and lumbered toward them. His torso was too lean, the ribs sharp, the fur unclean. And then there was his face: he had a white under-chin of super-soft fur, and those rounded ears. His eyes seemed distrustful, and his distrust seemed significant. His upper and lower eyeteeth fit like a puzzle, yin and yang fangs. Black dots on the golden coat, and then long long black lines from the inner corner of each eye down around his mouth.

They were like scars from tears. An onyx map of sadness.

Coral didn't look away.

LONE STAR

ERNIE HAD BEEN up since 4 a.m., sitting in the living room, smoking Staci's disgustingly thin menthol cigarettes because he'd run out, and he'd eaten four plums already, he was jacked up. When Ray finally came into the kitchen to make coffee, Ernie cleared his throat and suggested a field trip.

It's time to read up, he said.

The foursome rode the two bikes under a cloudy sky. The small library was adobe, with a scrubby lawn, and its patrons looked out the windows at the bikes' roar. Ernie and Staci and Ray and Coral strutted into the building, and even though this was their first visit, Ernie acted like he owned the place. Ernie had a thing for the Dewey decimal numbers taped on book spines, and he loved the cards in the back of books, those handwritten names—his brothers and sisters. Once he found a pressed cactus flower in a library book's pages, another time it was a train ticket to Birmingham, Alabama.

All righty, let's find the nature section, Ernie whispered.

Ray sat on an upholstered chair under a skylight while the others looked.

Here, Staci said, and touched her red nail to a shelf. *Exotic cats.*

Yes, indeed, Ernie said. *Good eye.*

As they took books off the shelf, Coral's eyes flicked to Ernie, and he looked away. She wasn't a pageant queen, she wasn't capable of those flaunting, destructive looks a woman would give out a truck window sometimes. But Coral wasn't the girl sitting in the front row at church either.

They set their stack on the checkout desk, and the librarian handed Ernie a new card.

He said to the lady: *I was just telling my friends a library is one of the greatest unused resources. It's a free education.*

Free if you don't get any late fees, the librarian corrected him kindly.

Ernie agreed, turning to the crew. *Exactly. No late fees.*

Back at home, they checked on Slash, napping in the shed, and then leafed through their haul at the kitchen table while Ray smoked out the window. Staci read a children's book out loud.

So, says here that cheetahs are endangered, she informed them. *And they're the fastest land animal in the world!* She turned pages. *But a gazelle, if it kicks the cheetah*—Staci karate-chopped her neck—*can kill it. That's fucked up. . . . They have litters of one to four cubs—oh my god, look at these little babes!*

She held the book open to a picture of cubs doing somersaults in front of their mom.

Right? she said. *Beyond cute?*

Ray didn't look, Ray didn't care about books. Sometimes he read *Penthouse* or biker magazines. Even his hands looked too beefy to handle paper. But that's not why he was so distant, Staci thought now, it was something else. Was he daydreaming about the renegades he'd finally rejoin, the band of faceless merrymen with one-syllable names who made him feel alive? He let his cigarette burn into a long ash. He got up after finally stubbing out his smoke. *Where you going?* she said, knowing it would irritate him, and it did. *Nowhere,* he said, and went to lie down in their shadowy bedroom. Ernie and Coral loitered outside the cage, the cat just visible as a silhouette. He was licking his fur, rubbing his ear with his paw. But flies buzzed all over his rejected breakfast.

THE NEXT MORNING, Coral wore her Motorhead shirt and green shorts to go running with Staci. At the shady end of their drive, Staci led stretches before they set out, Coral grinning as she mirrored Staci, hands on hips, leaning to the leffffft, then to the riiiiiight.

Girls need to move their bodies, Staci said. *It's not just about staying skinny. It's about connecting with yourself, empowering yourself.*

Although if Staci dug into her conscience, it was all about being skinny. They ran on the back roads past red-clay drives that disappeared into thicket, and nameless mailboxes for neighbors they never saw.

Sooo, crazy week, right? Staci asked, panting.

Coral wasn't quite slender, but she was fast, and Staci worked to keep up.

Staci huffed between phrases. *I'd call Slash an experiment, okay? You bring in a wild thing, tamed by other human beings, but you have no fucking idea if he'll end up loving us.*

Coral managed to stare at Staci while running.

Okay, Staci said. *When you look at me like that, I have to straight-up ask: do you like me or hate me? I mean, sometimes I worry that you don't like me, and that's why you took the van that day, and all that.*

Coral tilted her head.

You're mysterious, Staci said, trying to laugh it off. *Just like let me know if I bother you, I guess.*

Beads of water formed above Coral's lip.

Because I hate when somebody just talks shit behind my back, or cuts me off. That has definitely happened to me. I've known some capital-c cunts over the years. Lot of people don't know how to be honest. But you can't make someone do what you want. They have to choose to do it. It's funny, I'm forty-two, and the whole thing about the more you learn the less you know is true.

Staci stopped to catch her breath in the shadow of juniper trees. Coral and Staci scanned the scrubland, catching a gray fleck of horse in a faraway field.

Trying to sound casual, Staci said: *Feels great to be out here, and not worrying what Ray's thinking and doing. Ray's been acting weird, but—*

Coral's eyes turned pale and old as the moon; it was a look beyond judgment, it was all-knowing. It tore a hole through Staci.

Anyway, never mind about that, she said feebly, once she could say anything.

Somehow Staci knew she'd get that look when she said his name, so she must have wanted it. Coral went back to seeming vaguely bored, and then bent to pick something up. It was the pelvis of a small animal, slightly gooey with guts and tendons, not cleaned and bleached yet. Staci watched as Coral scanned the ground, and picked up a hawk feather. In one hand, she held the offer, and in the other, the claim. Then she casually dropped them both.

SLASH PEERED OUT his arena through a twinkle of fireflies; fur shimmered in the shadows. Something about his posture, cringing, looking left and right, made him an accusatory presence on their land, creating tension. Staci and Ray and Ernie didn't feel united *against* the cat, but they did feel defensive together. They felt like assholes when they'd meant to be heroes.

And yet they went about washing the coffeepot or making broccoli casserole, they went about playing Monopoly and smoking cigarettes. They chatted about rainfall forecasts—they didn't really know what else to do. In the morning, Ray watered the garden, smoking, sun rising like a magenta bomb. He didn't even look toward Slash, thinking hard about happy things like drag racing or Long Island iced tea. This cat was bringing him down.

IN THE KITCHEN, Coral flipped through one of the library books while Ernie cooked beans and eggs. She tapped the page and looked to him with expectation, and Ernie licked the spatula.

Cool, he said. *I get it.*

At Kmart, he gave her some cash and she vanished into the store. *Nice work,* he said when she rolled the cart to the van. He put on the hard rock station as they drove back, and they both kept their windows down, the wind tossing their hair. *Yeah, nice work, Coral,* he said again, cleared his throat, trying to think of something else to say and failing. The van was sizzling with energy, so he focused on driving.

Back home, Ernie shouted to Ray and Staci to come outside as they carried the goods into the yard. Arms crossed, they watched Coral lob the big plastic balls, one yellow and one neon-pink and one teal, into the cage through the guillotine door.

Ernie said to Staci and Ray, with thinly veiled hope: *Her idea.*

The balls rolled to a stop in the grass and clover, and Slash looked at them for a good long while until he got up and dragged his feet to the yellow one. He ducked, coy, moved his chin, and batted the toy, and it bounced off the shed and came at him and he batted it again They all grinned, and Ray and Ernie high-fived.

Ray shouted: *Yeah, Slash! Get it!*

When a ball came to the fence, Coral reached in and pushed it back to him. Slash swaggered around the shed, knocking one ball into the other two like on a billiard table. Making infinity loops on the grass, crossing the cage, his body way more relaxed than they'd seen so far.

Staci smiled at the girl. *You did good, babe. That was really smart.*

It was early June in Texas, the sun like a switchblade. Ray hooked up the sprinkler in the yard and they packed a cooler with ice and Lone Star cans. In a bikini Staci ran through the arc of water and its rainbows like she was fifteen, and Coral sat in the grass, fat toes splayed, as Slash openly watched everyone. After a while the cheetah stretched out in a luxurious pose and slept in front of them all.

Ernie was a couple feet from Coral, and he could smell her wet hair, a whiff of bacon from breakfast, the chemical sweetness of orange soda, and sweat. He felt like he might pass out. The truth of her had broken through the membrane of his consciousness. She was real. He could sense the warmth of her blood, the pumping chambers of her heart, the heat in her throat, and he shuddered. Her head surrounded by clover flowers, she squinted at him like: What's wrong with you?

And he couldn't even meet her gaze—he knew it now—no more dodging—he was madly madly in love.

FULL MOON, HOT night. Coral got up around 3 a.m., put on sneakers, and left the house. She tapped a stick on the cage and waited, but he didn't come out and she moved into the purple-dark woods.

These low trees, with convoluted branches, held moonlight in circles and curves. Perhaps night was clearer than day because fewer human psyches were operating, and plants and insects and animals dominated.

Back at the house, she squinted but Slash was still hidden. From the void, he moaned with aggression but sounded like a whimpering infant. She slumped into the house but didn't lie down, she stood at her window. Coral put her hand to the glass as Slash stepped out into the pen, the white bits of his fur bright in the moonglow. The cat blinked, wary, as if waking up into the world for the first time. He pissed musky golden urine along where she'd walked.

The sun became a neon strip on the horizon.

Slash twisted to groom his back, and paused, as if he heard something.

Then he turned his majestic head to look right into the window at Coral.

She locked eyes with the animal, and stopped breathing for a moment.

THREE

Loving

DR PEPPER

ERNIE, RAY, AND Staci were watching NASCAR one afternoon when someone knocked on their front door. They turned off the TV and looked at one another.

Howdy! Anybody home? came a muffled voice.

Staci finally got up and opened the door. It was the nephew of that guy who rented them the land.

Um, hi? she said.

Remember me? he asked. *Jasper.*

I mean, yeah, she said, and finally invited him in, uncertainly waving her arm in an arc, because he wasn't budging.

Jasper's brown eyes were big and dopey, and his mannerisms were like bad imitations of Rock Hudson or Cary Grant. Sure, he'd worked in fields and driven tractors, but he still had the hands of a child.

Well, hey, he said. *My uncle just wanted me to make sure you got everything you need.* His eyes roved around the room.

What else, Ernie said, *would we need? Why would you ask that?*

Ray passed the kid on his way to the kitchen and smacked his back. *Don't mind Ernesto. He's a weirdo. Want a cold one?* he asked.

Hey, I'm not one to say no, said Jasper, smiling brilliantly and insincerely. *How y'all finding it here?* he asked as they drank on the couch.

Ray said: *Pretty good, since Ernie's a power gardener.*

Ernie smiled. *Thanks, man.*

Wanna give me a tour? Jasper said.

The room suddenly got stuffy. Was that why the kid came over, to poke around?

Maybe another time, when there's more to see, Ray said smoothly, *we just planted the garden so.*

I don't mind if it's incomplete.

No tour, Ray said.

A long uncomfortable silence.

Jasper knocked his class ring against the bottle and looked around, then draped one arm on the sofa back. *Where's your sister?*

Ernie took a moment to remember. *Oh you mean my sister.*

Jasper made a face. *Are there other sisters here?*

I have a sister, Staci said, because of the silence, *but she's in New Jersey. But you probably mean Coral, she's napping.*

Jasper nodded as if that made any sense. *Hey listen, there's a Sunday hoedown at the end of each month, at the Pentecostal church up there on River Ranch Road. Y'all should try it out. They roast a pig, and they know what they're doing when it comes to roasting a pig. It's a good town, I got to tell you, nice people.*

Sound like you're running for mayor, Ray said.

Jasper chuckled. *You're not the first person to suggest that.*

Suddenly Coral came out of her bedroom, rubbing her eyes.

There she is, Staci said cumbersomely.

Jasper jumped up and offered his hand. *Not sure if you remember me—*

She's deaf, Ray said.

Oh! Right. Then Jasper signed hello. *Good thing Boy Scouts taught me to sign when I was a kid.*

She doesn't do that either, Ernie said with disdain for the man. *Just speak slow and loud.*

Jas-per, he shouted, pointing at himself.

Coral nodded.

Great to see you, he shouted.

Coral had a luster, an iridescence, today—was it the long nap? an outsider coming into their house? the weather? Her corduroy shorts and black sleeveless T-shirt were not sexy, but her mouth was rosebud-pink and fat.

Ernie popped off the couch. *Listen, Jasper, we're sort of busy right now, but leave your number, maybe we can all meet up for barbecue one night?*

You bet. Jasper handed over a flimsy discount business card with his beeper number. *Only if Coral comes!*

Ernie smiled like he would kill the kid.

And Jeremiah wanted me to remind y'all rent's due in a couple weeks, Jasper added.

Of course, no problem, Staci said, and walked him out before anything happened, chomping her gum and giving him a toodle-oo wave and slamming the door.

Ray got up to watch him leave through the window, and he suddenly ran outside barefoot because the little fucker was peeking around the house.

Can I help you with something? Ray said in a certain tone.

Oh hey, I didn't mean to make you get up off the couch, Jasper said. *Just wanted to catch sight of that garden y'all are so proud of. But listen, I got to get home, so you take care, hear me?*

Ray didn't answer, and Jasper stumbled up into the truck cab and got the engine going, somehow, looking over his shoulder again and again. He drove over a clump of marigolds Ernie had just planted, and Ray went inside but didn't have the heart to tell him about the crushed flowers.

ERNIE GOT BUSY in the barn the next morning because it was that time again. The air hung, humid, dew dripping down windows. He wore a mask, he hated what he was doing, and was only at the Epsom-salt stage. As he worked, he had conversations with people who weren't there, like Vick or Cupid. Talking about anything, telling them how happy he was here but how he missed eating dinner with them too, especially missed Brandy's gumbo, or explaining what it's like having Coral under his wing, or apologizing about the times when he'd been in a really bad mood. He half spoke out loud but didn't hear himself. The shapes of those old friends—they *had* been friends, he sees it better now than he did then—echoed through the barn. He should have tried harder with them all, he should have been more open. Here one day, gone the next. When would he learn?

Around noon, Ray poked his head in. *Hey bud,* he said. *I'm going to make sandwiches, want one?*

Sure, whatcha got?

Ray suddenly forgot. *Wow. I must have a dent in the skull. I looked two seconds ago and now I can't remember.*

I'll take anything. Just no mayo.

Ray walked to the kitchen, trying to be amused. This morning too, when he opened his eyes, he was like—wait a sec—is this a motel room? Or am I at Beedle's apartment in Arkansas? He had these moments, at dawn, or waking at 4 a.m., or right after sex, when he was no one. He was awake but he didn't exist. A ding in the machine, he told himself, nothing more, but deep down, he wondered if it was possible to lose it all.

Ray ate lunch in the backyard, and caught Coral looking sideways at him, leaning on her rake. Her cheeks turned orange-peach when she did yard work. He made merry eyes to signify how's-it-going and set about rolling a smoke and cracking his post-lunch Dr Pepper. She stared, her brow furrowed.

He exhaled, surveying the vista just to avoid her, but she dropped the rake and walked toward him. He felt a sense of doom. She stepped too close and touched his vest button, which was done wrong. He laughed gruffly, smoke exploding around his face.

Ah shit. I'm all crooked today. He rebuttoned it with his cut-up stubby dark fingers. *Hey, thanks for watching out.*

And she didn't look smug. She looked at him—how could he explain this—with no familiar expression at all, but she was not blank either. She was telling him something by pointing out his wrong button, but he couldn't know what.

ERNIE FINISHED HIS work, then did jumping jacks in the yard to wear himself out, he had too much energy. He loved the ideas blooming like rabies upstairs in his psyche, and also deep-down knew they never led to good things. So he went out to the woods.

Ernie wandered, collecting a pebble of deer shit, a black-glitter rock, and an acorn. He added a Queen Anne's lace blossom. He arranged them in a clearing and stood, tall as Rasputin and spindly like the Tin Man, and put his hands together.

Lynn, I don't know where you are, brother. What sort of otherworld you're in. I want to remember you on a bike, riding into the dusk. Drinking whiskey at a bar, figuring out a place to sleep. I feel stupid for hating you the way I did.

He thought for a moment, cleared his throat.

I was just pissed you took my place. His eyes stung at the truth of that, and he closed them for a minute. Then he finally said: *Judy—I have no words that are good enough. I'm sorry I haven't been to visit.*

Ernie sat on the ground and picked up a dead moth, studying it. Held his pink Bic to the moth's wing and set it on fire, dropped it, and watched it burn. It upset him, even though logic said the thing was already dead. He wondered if Coral thought he was a bad person for not visiting Judy. He thought he should bake cupcakes tonight for everyone. He remembered hitchhiking, years ago, and the man had his radio tuned to a sermon about forgiveness, and it fucked Ernie up for months. Across his mind now suddenly scurried a fleet of baby mice that were turned out of a smokehouse—where and when did he see that?

He drew circles in the dust with a stick while notions wafted around his brain. Ernie let beautiful facts and ideas mingle and mix up there. Do as you like, he told them. He held his hands to the sun as he walked back to the house—the blood moving in his palms, the red illuminated by that strong light, that was God. You don't need to go hunting around in churches and crack houses. God is with you, in your face, in your mouth, all the time.

Okay, but let's not get super-crazy, he warned himself, then laughed out loud.

In moments like this, he couldn't help admiring the loose autonomy of his thoughts. The supremacy of letting things hang, unconnected!

He strolled through heat and trees and thought of Gloria. She was only in her thirties when he knew her, but she loved watching westerns and playing bingo. Two local men courted her. One fella was cordial, he had a groomed mustache and brought the boys Hershey's Kisses. But the kids worshipped the other guy, who was red-faced and muscular, who tripped to open doors for her, made jokes and laughed too often and did tricks with quarters. His eyes were wild— behind them was bedlam, lawlessness, love. Gloria always brightened up when he got there. He wore four dog tags, and he'd squat and let the boys read the names, but he was quiet when they did.

Ernie snapped a branch as the house became visible.

Only now did he understand those men and their patience, how they never forced Gloria to love them. Ernie wondered if one of them ever did win her over. Ernie knew he should let Coral take her time in realizing his worth too.

He'd always been a patient person—to a point. Like with the hollow plastic eggs Gloria gave out on Easter, each holding a nickel or Bazooka gum. He was the only boy to keep his egg closed for days even though he could see the shadow of the coin or the candy in there. The gift *was* the mystery, and as soon as he opened it, it would be something else—it would be a thing. So he joyfully hoarded his little yellow pellet for days, and when the time came, he really *really* loved breaking it open.

COCAINE

RAY DIDN'T WANT to make love, and they fought again. In the morning, Ray sat at the end of the bed, pulling on his boots, watching Staci sleep. A patch of sun crept over her shoulder, illuminating the lower half of her face. Her eyes were still in shadow. He smoked and looked at her—she was a tough lady.

Her teeth started grinding, and then her face was restful again, naked and clean and not braced against anything or anyone. She could have become a bitter old cur, considering what she'd been through and seen. She took pride in being the one to blame.

He'd known some pieces of work, he thought, taking a deep drag and exhaling. But this gal, who'd been pulled through the mud, who'd been high and lost, she stayed angelic, or maybe even got more angelic. Ray thought it was bullshit, her recovery talk, her self-esteem books, the lectures on cassette tapes she listened to over and over. But there was something beatific about the effort. He didn't always feel like this, the way he felt this morning, generous and able to give her credit where credit was due.

Sometimes these very things he was musing on and loving her for were the very things that made him sick of her. But aren't we strange, thought Ray, looking now out the window, aren't we all so strange. . . .

He eventually got her up with a cup of coffee, and they barely spoke. Staci was blow-drying her hair and hadn't even started on her makeup.

We don't have time for this, babe, Ray told her. *Just come as is.*

Wait a minute, she said testily.

A minute? It's gonna be fucking late afternoon before we hit the road. Come on.

I'm not leaving the house like a ragamuffin.

No one cares.

She took that like a slap. *Screw you!* she spat, tossing her compact on the floor, where it broke. *And now you owe me a blush.*

I don't owe you shit, Ray said, and started moving through the house, indelicate as a buffalo, collecting his vest, his smokes, making it clear he was definitely not waiting, and even if she was ready, he was not taking her. He came and stood in the bedroom door.

Staci's eyes filled with tears.

Ray gestured at her vaguely, without looking at her. *And I'm not doing drama today. No crybaby nonsense. I've got business in El Paso, and I'm gonna go do it. Capisce?*

Fine! Go. See if I'm here when you get back.

At this he grinned and laughed meanly. *You'll be here.*

He left. Staci moped around the house, and felt vaguely unwelcome in the world, like she wasn't invited to this day. Had he been innocent as a kid, or was he always mean, or was he just honest in a hypocritical world? In some ways Ray was simple. His back hurt when it rained because he fell out of a deer stand in a tree years ago.

He got shot with a BB gun when he stole a kid's bike and laughed and he kept riding and never gave the bike back. He'd taken Benzedrine all through ninth grade. He had a dog for five months who disappeared and he still couldn't say her name. He looked great in camouflage but silly in a tuxedo. He liked to soak in the present moment like it was a jacuzzi. He apologized for things he'd done but never, not once, for who he was. Staci used to pretend to share his bravado, she acted dumb numb and ready for fun, but lately she couldn't pull it off.

Over the course of an hour, she moved between the kitchen and the front door, unsure. She jotted tasks on a notepad. She made more coffee and took the mug into the car, knowing she would spill it. And that's how, on this gray menacing sad ordinary day, she found herself parking at the liquor store. Well hello, old friend, she said in her head, using her best Hollywood-diva voice. Even as she was paying for her Absolut Vanilla, she was mentally framing her relapse share for a meeting in the near future. With a Cherry Coke from the convenience store, she mixed a little bitty drink in the van and felt better.

Then she drove to the nearest strip club.

Meanwhile, Ray was grateful to be on the highway because it required all his consciousness to avoid trucks driving too close, or moms feeding backseat babies, or police, so he didn't have room to think. He passed a church with a playground, its slide a red tongue. Boarded-up fireworks stands, a deer carcass on the median with its head reared back, a hardware store surrounded by a dozen pickup trucks.

Maggot was somber today, his eyes pink. Nobody was playing pool. Death metal droned from a closed room, and huge aluminum pans held the leftover debris from grilled meat.

You want something? Beer or something? Maggot's new girlfriend asked, polite like a 1950s housewife hosting her husband's corporate boss for dinner. She wore a rockabilly headscarf, and lipliner that created an alternative mouth.

Hit me, Ray said.

Simultaneously Staci drank at a dark cool bar while an anemic woman with orange hair humped the stage. For some reason Staci decided to stew on the shitty "friends" she'd had along the way. The time the girls tiptoed out and left her in a hotel room post-bender in Vegas, probably giggling in the taxi, knowing she'd miss the plane; the next day they'd apologize and coo, *We just couldn't wake you up!* Realizing Charmaine was sleeping with her boyfriend by finding her goddamn nursing-school textbook by the bed, the bitch's name written in loops on the front page. When Laney sold her that stupid Acura, playing dumb about the transmission being ready to blow. These resentments circled her heart like hornets.

A dancer calling herself Sugarcane sat on the stool next to her, Staci bought her a Tanqueray greyhound, and they talked about Dallas clubs and the humidity today. The woman offered Staci a smoke and they sat there, pensive. Finally Staci asked her if she knew who had what, betting she could get what she wanted here, and the woman pointed to the DJ, a young scarecrow in a trucker hat and super-oversized clothes. He sold her a bag, and she did key bumps in the bathroom.

Walking through the club, she looked at the men in work T-shirts and Timberlands, all of them riveted by the dancer, eyes watering with desire that was one inch away from hatred. As a teen Staci's ears pricked up when a magazine outlined spellcasting on your man. She and her girlfriends would practice hypnotizing one another by the dry riverbed where kids met to smoke, make out, drink. But when things didn't go well with a guy, the dudes loved calling her a witch in a way that connected every little part of her—any element that was original intuitive sexual sovereign—to a voodoo power she'd supposedly hijacked to get some dick. Guys loved to be spellbound until they violently rejected it.

Staci ordered another white Russian, but when a man opened the front door, she remembered it was daytime. She shuddered, flashing back to a stranger's apartment somewhere somehow. A few bodies, men, guys moving around, investigating empty bottles in the dusty cloudy light of that nasty morning. How'd she always get herself into those living rooms, chambers that became silent and foreboding at a certain point when everyone was evaluating what was gone and then they were looking at her and evaluating what they still had left—

She jumped off the stool, crushed a half-smoked cigarette, left a twenty on the bar, and gave the bag to Sugarcane. Stace, she chastised herself fervently in her head, you can't come here anymore.

On Ray's ride back, the sun burning his arms, he did feel a little beat. He didn't like that Maggot at one point asked if he'd come to Texas straight from Florida, or if there'd been somewhere in between. What business is it of yours? Why would you care? But whatever, next stop, let's go, he didn't feel like being paranoid.

As he filled his tank with gas, Ray didn't think about Staci and why she was wrong, wrong and ridiculous about everything. But that idea would be waiting for him at home.

So he went drinking. He bought Jäger shots for every loser at Tomcat's Bar & Grille, got a blowjob in the parking lot, standing in broken glass, mud, and Indian paintbrush flowers. He couldn't stay hard. He jacked himself off onto her nose.

Well, then, she said, brushing off her knees as she stood.

After that, he really went drinking.

He rode his bike toward home hours later, blind drunk but a maestro at straight lines after decades of practice. He still got lost on the back roads, passing an RV park that looked familiar, German shepherds silent and alert in a junkyard, another RV park that looked really familiar — oh wait, same RV park, a cherry tree in bloom.

He hadn't sobered up while being lost. He'd poured liquor into his system so fast that it was still releasing into his brain. He found the house, kickstanded the bike, and wove to the bedroom, cursing, knocking a glass to the floor on his way. Staci jumped out of the bed before he fell into it. She stood in her nightie, her face unseeable in the dark. Such ragged desire she had for this idiot. Torn and shameful, so much love tied to so much anger. A sorrow fell over her when she realized now, as she often did during random moments at a cookout, or in the shower, driving together in the van, that he would never belong to her.

He snored and tossed on the bed like a rhinoceros. She was almost moved to tug off his boots, put a blanket over him, but why? Why would you do that, girl? They'd had a hundred nights like this, where they both did what they did, and came home. But this time, the fury in her was like a white flame. Curled up on the couch in the living room, part of her was burning away. It was impossible for her to understand at the time, but this was a good thing, this was the most beautiful thing that could happen tonight.

WHEN RAY SLAMMED the front door, he woke Coral up, and she left her bed and walked straight into the night. An owl swooped above, the shadow heavier than the bird. When she got to the pen, there was Slash, his eyes radiant. He wasn't lying back in the corner, with that blasé posture, biting goat's-head burrs from between the pads on his paws. He wasn't pacing with controlled aggression. He was sitting as if he'd been waiting for her, his head cocked, spine straight. A statue.

He rubbed his cheek against the cage, making a violent purr, and her face flushed pink as she walked toward him. His eyes flicked down as if it was wrong to keep eye contact, but he always returned to her gaze. Finally she crouched.

He tumbled, lying on his back, showing the downy circles of his stomach.

Her heartbeat made her shirt quiver, that's how hard it was thumping. The veins on the sides of her neck throbbed. He stood near her again, rubbed his cheek on the cage.

And she raised the little feeding door, and reached inside the cage, hand open and facing up. At first he just looked at her fingers, moving his head this way and that, leading with the jaw. Then he rubbed his brow against her hand, purr-growling, staring at her with big brown eyes. She breathed raggedly, and knelt on the other side of the wire, and they stayed like that, on different sides of the cage, but touching.

No one was in charge. There was no protocol. There was no rush. There was no etiquette, there was no small talk. No clichés. No referee. There was no history. There was no blueprint, no sequence, no expectations, no name for it.

The moment was lush and long, the sky winking with stars.

The sudden bond between Coral and Slash seemed to extend into the landscape itself. Trees and shadows and wheelbarrows and black snakes and sagebrush and shovels and vines of green tomatoes and clouds became united, everything was linked, synced, and loaded, including the house and the people sleeping in its dark rooms, all of it one piece for the hour. It's like Coral and Slash were the plug and socket for a vast environment.

IN THE MORNING, Ray found Staci sunbathing on the patio, and handed her a bouquet of Queen Anne's lace.

They're from the highway, Staci said dismissively, giving him a look.

Doesn't mean they're not pretty, Ray said, his voice destroyed by the night before.

She studied the bouquet for a spell. *It's got ants all over it,* she said suddenly as they crawled onto her hand, and she tossed the white flowers away. She stared at Ray as if the future was in his eyes.

Fuckin' A, you used to love me, she said, shooting a dart in his direction, and it landed pitifully.

Shut up, he told her, trying a jovial tone. *I do love you. I'm just old and I got a temper.*

That's a new one! She was genuinely surprised. *You're old?*

He hadn't known that was going to come out of his mouth. *We're old, yes, dearie.*

No, you are. Don't lump me into that.

You're forever young, he tried, grumbling with lust, running a coarse hand on her freshly depilated thigh.

She didn't react, and after a moment, he stopped. He let go and sighed, looked up at the sky.

Staci, you don't want to be alone, you don't want to die, you don't want to deal. I get it, you and me are made of the same stuff. And you think if you push me around enough, make enough trouble and chaos, you can slow time down or some crazy-ass magic trick like that.

She got the willies and turned away.

He kissed her forehead. *You're a beautiful woman,* he said, meaning it. *I love you more than all the others.* He waited for her to say something. *Hello?* he asked.

I'm tired of there being "others," she said, but in a calm tone.

It's a figure of speech, he said.

She looked away. He was expecting the drama, the slammed door, then the opened door, the shrieking speech, the breakdown, the tears, the last-word slap, then the kissing and the fucking. She pushed bangs from her eyes and really looked at him.

Aren't you tired? she asked.

Naw, he said, and went to make coffee, lighting a smoke on the way.

She looked at her foot, bright hot in the sun. Her soul felt restless in her body, panting, and she thought, for the first time (well, for the first time when she wasn't ODing in an ambulance): I'm not going to be Staci forever. I'm not going to live forever. This is *a* body, not *the* body, *one* life, *my* life. She'd never felt the freedom of that, only the fear.

Ray came back with two mugs, and then napped in the grass. He sagged, hefty, massive in muscle and bone, and the earth held him, and she listened to him snore, and the day's light kept changing. She had a flashback: she was eleven, hanging on monkey bars somewhere in Hackensack, and a teenager whistled at her, and she vaguely felt herself depart from being human and start down the path to being a woman. She didn't have words for it then, but she knew.

And she'd understand, months from now, that *this* afternoon, in this backyard in Texas, was another turning point. It's when she headed back to being human.

GLUE

RAY AND ERNIE counted the money from El Paso that week, and grinned. It was a lot of cash, and they weren't giving a dime to Tim. Although without Tim being the one to send the goods into the world, Ernie had a harder time blocking out the abstract vision of a street kid somewhere with black nubs for teeth who thought Navy SEALs were trying to get into his tent and kill him. He was their heartbreaking customer.

Ray looked at Ernie. *Let's have a party, man.*

Yeah?

Hell yes, dude. Whenever there was tension in a house, Ray's favorite thing to do was beat it to death like a piñata. *Staci's pissed at me, maybe this will cheer her up.*

You think Coral will like it?

Who doesn't like a party, Ray said.

And so—they partied.

The men grilled steaks in the heat, downing beers and swatting bugs from their calves, while Staci and Coral made coleslaw and corn bread in the kitchen. Ernie waved the ladies to come out, meat was ready, and they ate in lawn chairs, beers held upright between feet. Coral was drinking a Mexican Coke Ernie'd bought for her. He kept sneaking glances to see if she was having fun. Ray and Staci were formal with each other because they hadn't gone through their soap-opera fighting and makeup sex; sorrow hovered over them, trying to land.

Slash emerged from the shed like an uptight neighbor who relents and comes to the block party instead of staying home and calling the cops, but the cat wouldn't look at anyone, staring into the distance like a shy boy. Coral squatted near the pen, then she opened the guillotine door and put her hand into the cage. Slash studied it, twisting his head this way and that as if discerning what it was. And then he licked her, and he kept licking her. Languidly, powerfully. Over and over. Coral made a sound like a giggle, or a bird's chirp.

Staci was flabbergasted. *He's grooming you.*

Ernie's mouth was open.

Ray laughed. *Am I hallucinating? Or is she about to get her fucking fingers bit off?*

When Coral removed her hand slowly and gently, as if to tell Slash she meant no offense by retreating, Staci saw cuts on the girl's skin from his spiked tongue, tiny threads of red that Coral smeared on her shorts. Staci and the guys shared looks. Coral turned to them, and they grinned like parents trying to act cool after their daughter calmly explained she's joining a cult. Why was this unexpected, wasn't it exactly what they wanted?

Way to get the party started, Cor! Ray shouted.

Ernie gathered everyone's gristle and fat onto one plate. *This is a delicacy to him,* Ernie said to Staci. *Your turn.*

Staci stepped through the grass, barefoot in a baby-doll dress, carrying the bits. Slash's head tilted, amber eyes locked on her. She giggled and spastically threw the leftovers on the ground and ran. Slash sniffed at the glistening pile, looked at her, and went into his den.

You insulted him, Ernie said. *You should have put it in his bowl.*

I totally freaked, I'm so sorry!

Hey, Ray said sharply to Ernie. *She doesn't need to put her hand in the mouth of a fucking wild animal.*

Ray slyly looked to see if Staci was glad he defended her but she seemed oblivious.

WHEN THE GNATS came out in armies, they headed into the house. Ray sat at the table, his party appetite just getting going.

Strip poker, he announced.

Nobody looked directly at Coral, who had lingered outside to see if Slash would come out then took a chair when he didn't. But Coral looked at them.

Not sure that's a good idea, Staci said cryptically. And then made a *duh* face at Ray.

Ray shuffled cards half-heartedly. *I'm sure I've mentioned this already,* he said, *but you people are no fucking fun.*

They played Texas hold'em instead as the sun set, but Coral didn't know how to play this one, so she sat and watched. She perched near Ray to look at his cards. He could smell her: the hormones of innocence. Sounds like the worst punk-rock band ever, he smiled to himself, as he put down a five of spades.

He did not, repeat not, find her attractive in any way, but when her thigh touched his, he suddenly had the world's hardest hard-on, it was immediate and excruciating, a cross between vertigo and a toothache. And he had to get up, fumbling and mumbling about finding his lighter, which was in his back pocket. In the bathroom, he splashed his face with cold water, took a big breath, and went back to the table and moved his chair away from hers.

After a couple rounds, Ray made chocolate and marshmallow sundaes and whiskey shots, and Staci poured white zinfandel for herself. They all sprawled out in the living room and Ernie suddenly had an idea. Well, he'd had it before, but it seemed like a good time to get everyone on board.

Let's all get an S on our wrist, huh? For Slash?

Using a safety pin and ballpoint-pen ink, Ray did Ernie first, pricking a wobbly letter on his forearm. He did his own thigh after, and then Staci lay down on the couch and had it done on her shoulder.

Our blood oath, said Ernie.

Ray laughed and said, *Except we probably shouldn't combine blood since me and Staci have hep C.*

Why not tell everyone, Staci said.

I just did, Ray said, and grinned.

For a few of them, watching someone get a tattoo was not a new affair. They knew how to sit in a circle, partly uninterested, slightly excited about the artistic outcome, slightly malevolently enjoying the pain and torture of their friend. Ray wiped the blood with a damp paper towel as he worked, and Ernie was giddy, proud.

Cor, you want one too? Ray asked, rubbing the pin with alcohol.

She shrugged and opened her palm.

That's going to hurt if you put it there, sweetie, Staci told her.

Ernie looked away because she insisted on her hand. Ray did what she wanted; Coral's eyes watered but she didn't move an inch. Ray kept looking at her face, uncomfortable and impressed. They all put saran wrap over the tattoos: family! Ernie was dizzy with triumph.

They kept drinking as the moon rose, and Staci looked blearily at Coral in the smeared glimmer of night.

I can't believe I never knew you at the compound, Cor. I mean we— (indicating herself, Ray, Ernie)—*all sort of knew one another. But we didn't know you. And trust me, I could have used a girlfriend.*

To be honest? Ray said to Coral. *I thought you were a Goody Two-shoes.*

Ray. Stop, Staci said. *I think you're the sweetest, Cor. You don't even need to say anything, ever, and I can tell.*

I wasn't being mean, Ray told Staci. *Come on, look at us, the four us, partying together. This is hilarious.*

"La Grange" came on the radio and Staci turned it way up and beckoned Coral to dance. Coral bopped around, swinging her arms, eyes closed. No one looked at anybody else because they'd bust out laughing and they didn't want to hurt her feelings.

The disc jockey said: *You're listening to 103.5, Classic Rock out of San Angelo, in the good old Lone Star State. Here's a love letter for you, from the Rolling Stones.* It was "Love in Vain."

Slow dance o'clock, Ray said, pushing his creaking body out of the chair to take Staci.

Ernie awkwardly looked to Coral: there she was. Coral didn't look away so Ernie took her hands, barely holding the tattooed one. His hips were pulled away in a church hug, hands sweating, his arm muscles hard and twitching even though he tried with all his might to be gentle. They did a calculated slow waltz. He couldn't believe this was happening. He could hear some guardian from early childhood saying to him: *Careful, careful, easy now, don't drop it.*

The couples moved around each other, shuffling in the coppery-dusky-dark room, Ray smoking over Staci's shoulder, Ernie afraid to hold Coral too close but keeping one hand on her back in a show of tenderness. She was always off-step, but she grinned as he moved them, he couldn't even handle it. She felt ready, she felt hot to the touch. Was he dreaming?

When they pulled apart, Ernie didn't look at her. He just landed on the couch, popped a beer, and drank it in one gulp, his saran wrap crusted with maroon. Opened another. He watched Coral dance solo for a few more songs, dipping his eyes each time she turned his way, and he was unable to even imagine what he himself wanted. Eventually they all were strewn around the living room, and everyone was out of it, except Coral, who was just flushed from dancing. Ray smoked a joint, Staci curled into him, the two of them driving for oblivion so they didn't have to deal with their rift.

Ernie said: *I mean, if Tim could see this, he'd be blown away. For real. He would.*

No one would agree.

Tim, Tim, who gives a shit, Ray mumbled.

I'd say we did pretty good so far, Staci said, to say something.

It started drizzling. Coral kept looking outside but Slash stayed in the shed.

Our garden's getting more rain, Ernie said.

I so love our garden. I mean, it's nuts, Staci said. *You take a seed, which costs like five cents, you take sunshine, rain, dirt, you get this thing that didn't exist before.*

I wish we could just live off the land, Ernie mused, then he went into self-convincing mode, where he often went while drinking liquor. *But the bad business funds the good business, it is what it is. This country was founded on robber barons and pickpockets, criminals. That's capitalism. 'Kay?*

Everythingsss tainted, brother, Ray agreed, forgetting Ernie became a contrarian at this time of night.

We're not tainted, Ernie said, pissed. *Plants turn carbon dioxide into oxygen. Grapes turn to wine. Cow dung is a fertilizer. Everything in this world can be transformed. It's science, bro.*

Silence in the room. Ernie always said *bro* when he was drinking too.

Actually, in Landmark Forum they talk about change versus transformation, Staci said with a mild slur. *Remember, Ray?* To Coral: *We did Landmark a few years ago.* Then to everyone: *"Change" is becoming something different from what you are. It's past-based. It has to do with the past and all that. "Transformation," on the other hand, is creation. Invention. It's got nothing to do with anything.* She stared at her lap, thinking. *Or is it the other way around?*

Exactly what I'm fucking talking about! Ernie shouted.

I get it, babe, said Staci.

They sat in the dark, drinking, smoking, and a votive candle sputtered, a greasy napkin lay on the floor, empty bottles in clusters. Finally, Ray was passed out on the couch, Staci was close on his heels, her eyes slits. Coral finished another soda, looking at the stars beyond the curtains.

Ernie was talking fervently to no one. *Time to rise and shine, she'd say every morning.* She would muss their sleepy heads, her hands heavy with silver and turquoise rings, and the boys would look sideways up at her, their profiles deep in the pillow. They secretly wished she'd never move on to the next bed. It wasn't sexual, how Ernie adored her. *It's like how you love candy before you find out about drugs. It's all there is, you know?* he asked the room.

Glass prisms were hanging in her windows, and the boys would stand to get the rainbow—red orange yellow green blue violet—to land across their mouths and noses and eyes and chins. They walked barefoot. Fought in silence, prayed and almost meant it or almost knew why, and cried totally unexpectedly. *The soap was cheap and the toilet paper was thin and scratchy,* he remembered out loud. But it was heaven, the farmhouse with its carport, bird fountain, and sod grass.

Gloria, Staci murmured in a smudged voice.

In his mania, Ernie segued to a new topic. *Why did I sniff glue? Trust me, if I had a nickel for every counselor who asked me that. They wanted me to say I did it to belong, to bond, to be cool, to get numb. But I pretty much did it because it was there.* He liked watching the horses in the next-door meadow whenever he got high. They were a velvet painting, prancing in slow motion.

Ernie agreed with himself, since no one else was talking to him now. *We most certainly are alive. I feel more alive than ever. Today, I mean.*

Soon enough, Ernie was snoring, sitting up.

And that's when Coral went into the kitchen. She took off her shoes, careful and meticulous, and left them by the sink. Outside, she crossed the yard as she stared into the pen. He was right there, his white fur reflecting phosphorescence, the spots soaking up darkness. She took a breath, they kept eye contact, and she unlatched the door. She stepped inside and closed the door behind her. There was nothing between the girl and the cheetah.

In the dark, Slash's eyes glowed. She waited. The cat stood; he was about to attack. She closed her eyes, seemed to brace herself.

Instead, he lumbered up to her, sleek, he even came off as shy, and he licked her knee. He started to groom her; she sat on a milk crate and let him. She laughed and cringed but stayed there—he was tickling her and scraping her. He was slow and methodical. He gained momentum. She was trembling now.

FISH

WHEN ERNIE WOKE up, he couldn't remember how the night ended, but knew he danced with Coral. Elated, he watched his own hands crack eggs into a skillet. Wow, my hands are so old, he thought, scarred, calloused, the freckles, the reddish hair. But this egg, whoa, check it out, so pure, gooey, freshly made. The sun gushed through the window as he fried them up.

Coral came out of her room, hair messy. Shining.

Ernie was nervous as a teenage boy. *Well, hey there—good morning.*

Coral took her plate like she was sleepwalking.

I guess we danced last night?

Coral vaguely smiled.

All right then. He beamed, then realized he was burning the toast.

You guys! Staci rampaged into the kitchen and ate some eggs from the pan with a wooden spoon, then spoke with her mouth full. *You're not going to believe this. It's Ray's birthday, I almost forgot all about it.*

Ernie said: *Last night was his party then.*

It doesn't count because we didn't know it was his birthday while we were partying.

Ray blustered into the room, greasing his hair back into a rubber band with his big hands, and stinking to high hell, and coughing.

Dude, happy birthday, Ernie said.

Aw, thanks, man. What do you say we go fishing? Camp out for a night?

Ernie jumped on that. *Let's do it!*

Staci was not exactly excited to sleep outside, and Coral paled, looking out at Slash.

The cat'll be fine, Ray said. *He's a big boy.*

The way Ray smiled at them all left zero room for saying no. They got their stuff together, loaded it into the van, Slash watching suspiciously. And when they dumped extra meat into his dish, Slash made a bewildered meow that stopped everyone in their tracks. He sounded like a giant housecat mad they were leaving. Coral tilted her head as if asking a question.

Are you guys doing some kind of telepathy? Ernie joked.

She's letting him know we'll be back in a day, Staci said, as if she understood the intricacies of how girls and cheetahs communicate.

Before the van made it all the way down the drive, Coral jumped out and ran back into the house and got her pillow, jammed it into the cage with Slash. He sniffed it. He nuzzled and tasted it as the van pulled out.

THE MAN AT the tackle shop on the highway gave them directions to a good and little-known fishing spot.

Righteous, Ray said as they plowed deeper and deeper into the woods.

Parked on pine needles, they unloaded the cooler of beer and unfolded blankets on the bank. The sun fell in big glittery drops on their skin. Black butterflies, whose wings were like wet suede, moved between the trees as Ernie and Ray put rods together, while the women lay on long flat stones in the shade. Each line had a clear bobber and a lure, for bass or perch. The water was a milky green jade. There was no one nearby.

This is how it should be, Ray said. *I never liked the cold up north. I loved California, but California kicked me out.*

I didn't know you lived in Cali, Ernie said.

I've lived everywhere, man.

Colonnades of cypress lined the river, wood duck floating on the surface. The water was high after a rain, and it cut through limestone bluffs, the half-submerged tree roots making elegantly twisted cages, and it was hard to distinguish shadows from rocks. Coral squatted and peered into the water; did she see the fish, pale bodies that ran against the current?

After an hour with a couple bites but no luck, Ray pulled his line out and held it against the pole.

I think we should try farther up the river, he said. *Ern?*

Sure. The ladies will miss us but.

Neither Staci nor Coral noticed them leave. Ernie and Ray found a spot and fished in silence, shirtless, a Newport King in Ray's free hand, Newport Kings being his vacation brand, and beer bottles stood tilted on the stone. Short white feathers floated, their quills curved up, the downy fluff perfectly dry on the water. A frazzle of light shot off the surface with a force that could make the men blind.

Until he sat still in a place for a good while, Ernie was never able to see what was around him—there was just the ordinary landscape—and then—*bang*—a zillion things—the infinitesimal units of life and the universe being revealed in a rush. It made him panic about what he was missing the rest of the time. How could he fail at awareness! He was frantic for everything. The water was green, sliding, this was a cradle of a moment.

Coral was seventeen when she got to the compound, according to her sister, Ernie said, out of nowhere.

Okay.

Which means at some point, she's going to turn eighteen, Ernie said.

You got that right, buddy.

She could get married.

She could.

Think she would marry me?

Maybe. But Ernie, consider the facts—she doesn't really—talk, you know? Although maybe that's the dream! Ray started laughing and coughing.

I can tell what she means, so I don't need her to say it out loud, Ernie said in a solemn voice.

Well, okay, then.

It's not sex I'm interested in. You know me, I'm sort of the platonic type. But the more I think about it, we could make a good pair.

Ray lit a new smoke.

How come you don't marry Staci? Ernie asked.

I asked her a hundred times. She said she doesn't want me to feel like I have to. She wants to stay lovers forever. Go figure.

Ernie mulled this over.

Listen, man, Ray said. *You like how everything is right now, don't you?*

What are you asking?

Well, you get revved up about things. All I want to tell you is: when you love somebody, best thing, hardest fucking thing, is to leave them be. Let them come to you. If it's going to happen, let it happen.

But you chase *after what you want,* Ernie said after a while.

I'm different, Ray said.

They cast their lines.

Ernie couldn't let it go. *But don't you think me and Coral are sort of a natural pairing?*

Ray smiled wryly. *You're both freaking weird.*

Come on, Ray. I'm dead serious.

I think she's a good kid, Ernie.

She's not a kid.

I'm just saying, man. Don't force anything, okay?

Ernie looked mad. *Are you talking about that girl Jennifer? Did Tim tell you about her?*

I'm not talking about anything, Ernie.

She lied. I wrote her one letter, that's it.

Hey. Stop. I care about you. Don't lose touch with reality. That's all I'm saying.

Ray, I never felt better than I do now. I feel amazing.

Ray was about to say something but got a bite, and they started hauling in the fish, Ray's cigarette jammed between his lips, Ernie with the net out, cheering. They eventually strutted back to home base, sunburned, dangling their substantial catch and grinning like maniacs. They put the fish on the stone as the women clapped, and while Ray fetched his skillet and plates, Coral knelt.

With one finger in its mouth and her thumb under its jaw, she held each fish, cutting behind the side fin to the backbone. Then she angled the knife toward the tail and cut, the noise ragged as she severed the rib cage. Hints of gray and pink in the milky meat. When she was done, she rinsed the knife and her hands in the river.

From being on the road for years, Ray had a fine-tuned camp kit: mason jar of olive oil, a vial of premixed salt, pepper, cayenne, and dried oregano, and a sack of lemons. He folded the fillets into his homemade chicken-wire basket and put it on the fire. The fish's skin got browned by flame. The inside stayed juicy.

Ray was reminiscing. *Me and my older brother and my cousins, we used* to hitchhike to the Michigan lakes. *Hang hammocks and tell fucking ghost stories until somebody freaked out. One night, I swear to God, a gnome or some shit like that—*

A gnome? Ernie asked.

I'm serious, Ray said. *This little dude came out of a tree trunk.*

You were on peyote, Ernie told him.

Ray laughed. *Not yet, I was like seven. Everybody saw him. His face was yellow like he was sick, and his eyes were round like golf balls. He looked like he was gonna eat us, and finally he ran away, making noises like an airplane. He was like—straight out of a campfire story.*

That did not happen, said Ernie.

Ray laughed again. *Ask my brothers. They'll vouch.*

Staci said, *The lesson is, careful what stories you tell, because they just might come true.*

What kind of convoluted put-down was that? Ray asked.

She looked at him in the flickering firelight, deep long shadows under her eyes, and said nothing back. They all lay down on the dirt after dinner, towels rolled up under their heads, stars fizzing through the tree limbs. Ray tried to hold her, but she turned over.

DURING THE NIGHT, Ernie fantasized so relentlessly about Coral that he didn't even want to sleep. Nothing separated them, no bedroom walls. They were out under the moon with the nocturnal creatures and the incandescent clouds, and this would be the right place to kiss her. He pictured a spider or snake getting into her blanket, and she'd be scared and crawl over to him. He'd soothe her, he would hold her.

He drifted off, woke again in the pitch-black. His fantasy evolved into their new home somewhere someday: a chicken roasting in the oven, PBS on the television, front-yard rosebushes, leaves glossy and reddish. A vision of kissing her churned through his body like smoke, he couldn't handle it. He suddenly realized he was squatting over her—not in fantasy but in real life—and she was starting to stir. He rushed to slip under his blanket and lay frozen like a rock.

He watched the sun bleed orange into the woods, waiting for the first bird. The birdsong opened the day. Ernie got into the water in his skivvies, and he floated with his feet toward the current, and the water took his reddish hair up and away from his head as he closed his eyes. His skinny ass touched the rock below as an anchor.

The others woke and blearily ate donuts and drank cowboy coffee that Ray made in the pan, and Coral watched Ernie lying in the water. He was still while things were running by, running over, running under and through him. His body was stretched, arms reaching beyond his head and his bluish toes pointed. He looked like Jesus when they took him down from the cross. There was just a shadow in Ernie's white briefs but she didn't look at that longer than any other part of him. His black-edged fingernails were finally and slowly getting clean.

Coral leaned over the water, and everyone thought she was staring at her face. Until she grabbed—with lightning speed—a carp in both hands.

ERNIE DROVE UNDER a sky that stretched up into a tower of clouds, and everyone looked out the windows without talking. Coral was examining her tattoo, either bemused or confused or disgusted—she shifted her palm around like she'd caught a baby rattlesnake. When they reached the house, Coral slid open the van door with a bang and tore into the yard. Slash glared from the pen. The pillow was shredded, its contents like snow all over the grass, caught in the corners of the cage.

As Coral ran across the yard, Staci murmured: *I feel like we separated them,*

They'll get over it, Ray said. *Don't be dramatic.* But he looked away guiltily.

Coral plopped down like a sack of cement outside the cage, legs splayed awkwardly. She dropped her chin and gave the cat a look. Her eyes tilted up, their blue catching light like a gem, and who could stay angry with Coral? Slash slumped against the fence, as close to her as he could get. Coral stayed, fingers loosely clawed on the wire, hands hanging from the fence, her curved spine doleful like she was the prisoner.

The others unloaded the van, then Staci showered for a good hour. Ray was scouring the skillet, Ernie was filleting the rest of the fish, and Ray jerked his face toward the window, and they both blinked hard. The girl was in the cage with the cheetah.

Holy mother of God, Ray whispered.

Coral was tickling under Slash's chin. The fur was like corn tassels, or milkweed fluff still in the pod, silken threads pressed together. Under his jawbones was a triangular hollow. That spot, the tender and soft place of all cats. She rubbed him there, and he moved his chin aggressively, maybe to communicate that this is where he wanted to be rubbed, and she moved her fingers to scratch the chin bone—but she fell back to the hollow, over and over, as if to make sure it was there, or to make sure it was supple like the last time her fingers touched it, and then she scratched his neck, which had to be bristly and prickly in comparison, worldly and old and mean. She scratched his head, the bone plate between eyes, and then she found her way back to the hollow and suddenly—he nipped her.

She pulled away, face white, they stared at each other. His eyes were so much bigger than a man's eyes. He made a gesture with his head, slight, and she looked at her hand, but there was no blood. She waited. Did she feel small and dumb, having done what she wanted, and being snubbed for it? She sweated. He inhaled, he blinked, he seemed determined to look away, from coyness or shyness. The hay crackled.

Slash nudged her (roughly rudely), his wet nose against her hand, and then he found her fingers with the velveteen place under his jaw.

Incredible, Ernie whispered unsurely, and looked at Ray. *Right?*

Yeah, Ray said. *Right. Check it out. We cheered her up after all.*

To keep busy, Ernie went and found some cheap vodka under the sink to splash on his tattoo, which was red and puffy, probably from the river. But Ray couldn't keep his eyes off what was going down outside.

Ernie tossed in his sheets, sleepless, something bubbled like yeast in him, a sour rapture. Love was trying to dominate his mind, he couldn't think of anything else. He went to a few of his dog-eared faded bestseller daydreams for distraction. Like—the one where he gets rich and buys a white limousine with gold rims, a disco ball hanging inside it, purple velvet seats and twelve kinds of liquor and twelve kinds of cigarettes. He goes to his mother's house (in the dream he hired a private detective to find out her identity) and takes her shopping, buys her a new house with a hot tub, and she cries in gratitude. But this somehow morphed back to Coral, and the house was theirs, they had six kids, a yard, a pool, dogs and cats—and Tim stopped by on a road trip and was blown away by how well Ernie had done.

How it happened, he would never know, he was sure he was lying in his own bed, but someone tapped him on the shoulder—it was Staci. And it turned out he was standing on Coral's dark threshold.

Staci yawned and whispered: *What're you doing, old man?*

Um, I heard her cry out, must have been a nightmare, he lied on the spot. *Just wanted to check, I'm headed back to bed.*

Mm-kay. That's strange. Have to pee. She moved past him, bouncing off the wall, lazy and half-asleep.

STACI SAT IN the backyard, reading *People*, wearing a robe with lavender hearts, and black sunglasses. The morning sun was still pretty low on the horizon. When Ray came out, the way she moved her mug gave her up.

Day drinking? he asked.

Staci made a face—relax already, she wasn't coked up, wasn't drinking hard liquor. It was just a sip of wine. *What happened to "good morning"?*

Give it to me.

Are you telling me what to do? she asked.

He said in a quieter and more sincere tone: *Give.*

She crossed her arms. *Look at you, up on your high horse.*

He reached his hand out and wiggled his fingers.

If you treat me like a child, we're never getting anywhere, Staci said.

He snatched her mug, dumped pink wine on the grass. *You'll thank me.*

Her eyes brimmed with tears. She stared at him a long time, and she summoned all the hours he'd wasted looking out windows or spacing out while she talked, or falling asleep before they had sex, and now she was making him nervous.

What? he said in a dull voice.

And she said it: *Whoever it is, go to them, Ray. Whatever you need, go find it. Ride with your boys. Get a hotel with some tramp. Go on whatever fucking bender you can't stop dreaming about. I don't care anymore.*

The quick way he looked down made her sure she was right.

I— he started.

I don't want to know, actually, she said. *Just go.*

He stood there and then finally turned, and walked into the house, and after about twenty minutes, she heard his bike grumble down the drive.

STRANGE TO BE headed in this direction, Ray thought. When the highway traffic slowed to a stop, he wove between trucks and cars. He was shining, skin wet with sweat, he rode like he was a robot with the destination typed into him. All the cars were sealed with ACs blasting, except landscape crews riding in truck beds, the guys in front smoking out windows.

Six hot long hours later, when he got close, he cruised the main street for a florist and picked up a yellow bouquet, tucked it in his vest, and drove the final mile. The hospital was on a frontage road, a giant beige cube of a building, its lot shaded by big old elm trees. He parked the bike and went inside to the front desk, and everything was abruptly cool, pale, and quiet.

I'm dropping these off for a friend of a friend, name is—let me remember— Judy Sanders? he said, not wanting to say he knew her. It wasn't wise to be here at all.

All righty, let's see. The nurse looked in a big logbook. *Room 304, elevator's to your right, sir.*

Thanks.

Riding up with a man in periwinkle scrubs and a hamper of sheets, Ray got woozy. He looked down, tried to stabilize. What the fuck, why did he feel like he was going to faint? Nervous as a groom meeting his bride at the altar? That's not what was happening, this wasn't about love. So why was he shaking? At the desk on the third floor, a nurse covered the phone receiver and looked at him, and so he said Judy's name again.

Are you with her mother? the nurse said.

Ray made a confused face. *With her mom? No.*

Oh, Judy's family is taking her home tomorrow. Thought you were one of them. Go ahead in, she should be awake, she just ate.

He stopped outside the door but forced himself to enter. The room smelled plastic and mentholated, and was dimly lit by machines. Her face was bandaged, and her eyes looked at him. He sat heavily in the chair, the flowers across his thighs, and he couldn't say a word at first. Nothing. Not even bullshit. His mouth felt welded shut.

Finally he croaked: *Hi Judy.*

The machine beeped and something whirred. She looked out the window, far past the landscape.

Hey Judy, what can I get for you, can I get you anything? He opened his hands up to give it more sincerity. *I'll do whatever you need.*

Judy didn't smile, but she also didn't look forlorn. She had a new way. Ray fidgeted with the bandanna on his forehead. He wished he could tell her a joke or a secret but couldn't think of any. Instead he popped a cherry lozenge and crunched it into a hundred glass splinters.

Everyone sends their love. We were all so worried— He stopped, because seeing her now didn't make the worrying go away.

She seemed vacant, done, tragic, and also above it. He tapped the bouquet in its cellophane on his legs, like playing the drums. Looking at her, he felt a great weight in his rib cage, he was remembering how she used to be, what kind of girl she'd been. She had never been full of herself. She was more like someone handed a script and pushed onto the stage to play a part she didn't understand. She'd try out sayings and gestures, shaking her hair back like Staci, clicking the table with her nails like she was impatient, and she wasn't impatient. He saw with clarity that sleeping with him was also desperate acting.

He'd invited her onto his bike one morning, when they were in the throes of sneaking around and fucking, it was February, the sky blue and sharp. He decided to give her the ride of her life and revved it up to one-thirty. Kept going. She clung to him and he howled in the wind. When they finally got back, his body was pumping testosterone and endorphins and adrenaline, he felt like a fucking warlord, nothing could break him. She got off the seat clumsily, and he watched her struggle to stand. She worked to compose the right face—it was barely coming together, the quivering lips the eyebrows the cheeks—she forced a happy expression. But he'd terrified her to the bone. She stumbled off, with a pseudo-sexy wave, and what did he do, he thought now. He'd laughed at her, hard and loud, laughed until she'd vanished into her room, but he was sure she could still hear him.

He stood and approached her bed. Laid the flowers at the foot and held up a grimy envelope of cash with her name written on it. This he tucked into her nightstand. He stood, hands clasped, like one does at funerals. *Judy, I'm so sorry.* He said it like he meant it.

She pulled her gaze from the window and looked at him. Time seemed to stop. Her eyes moved around his face and settled.

And that's when she said it: *You're an animal.*

He stared, he would never know for how long. Then he eventually nodded like a child who'd just been told his father was dead, and he walked backward out of the room.

All the way home he heard it, replayed it. It was like a bad psychedelic movie from the early 1970s, close-up on the woman's face, the mouth and the words morphing and pulsating through cheap camera effects. But here's what was crazy: the tone meant too many things to understand. Was she just breaking bad news to him? Telling him the truth, which he had to finally confront? Or did he hear pure moral disgust in her voice? What's bizarre is it also sounded like a real-time realization, like someone winning a round of charades: Oh you're an *animal*, that's what you are! But the version that distracted him so much that he almost crashed into a Greyhound bus was when he finally heard it as a blessing.

It was 4 a.m. when he got back to the house. He sat on his bike, the engine turned off and cooling, and stared at a half-rotted cactus for a long time in the shadows of the predawn sky. Oh my god, he thought, and looked up, searching, seeing stars but no moon. She didn't say anything. I made it up.

STEAKHOUSE

THE NEXT DAY, Ray woke up late on the couch. He groaned and rose, in jeans, shirtless and showing sunburned arms and a scarlet neck, and walked barefoot into the kitchen. Staci looked at him, protective of herself, holding on to her disappointment.

Coffee? she said in a stiff stranger's voice.

It was Judy, he said softly.

She stared at him, searching his face, and almost smiled—out of nerves, or shock. *No.*

He nodded almost imperceptibly.

They sat in the yard, and she absorbed this information. Judy. Why hadn't she known? He told her that Judy was also hanging out with Tim on the side, and this just broke her heart harder. It was pitiful, and nonthreatening, but also real, and so hurtful. She had to think through hours here and there when Ray disappeared at the compound, and Staci had been suspicious, or when Judy was weird to Staci, trying too hard to be friends with her, or when Lynn came on to Staci—maybe he knew? And then the rest of it, Lynn gone, Judy alone. Damaged. Staci felt sick.

Wow, she said, looking at the grass.

Ray took a big breath. *From now on, no more lying on my end, and nobody in my life except you. Take that as you want. You don't owe me the same thing in return.*

She looked at him, amused in a bitter way.

I'll prove it if you give me a shot.

This was new. Neither of them was shouting or throwing ashtrays at mirrors or tearing off in vehicles or crying in the shower. They were talking. How odd.

Really? she asked, skeptical.

Really.

They both looked at the yard, the sky, the barn.

She looked at him again. *Really really?* she said.

He nodded, and sighed, and shook his head, and nodded. It was a big promise, and he was making it, and it was hard to do but genuine.

THEY DECIDED TO hit the town for a fancy dinner, feed their hankering for rib eyes and air-conditioning. Half of Staci was not willing, but the other half was very curious. She did a hundred lunges in the bedroom in a panic to feel fit before putting on the red dress. Decided on smoky eyes and fuchsia lipstick. When she got on the bike, and he pulled onto the highway, they knew they looked good. She could feel Ray's spine straighten; showing off was their aphrodisiac.

He walked her into Stegner's Steak House like he'd built her from scratch, his pride was so immense. Her dress shimmered as they crossed the room. Ray smoothed their white tablecloth with his ring-heavy hands, shifting the glasses and silver and candles as if he'd set the table himself.

Welcome, we're glad you could join us, said the waiter.

From his cart, he picked up and displayed a New York strip, filet mignon, porterhouse, a brined pork chop, and then a Maine lobster, its rubber-banded claw waving sluggishly. They ordered gin martinis, and Ray didn't even look judgmental—it was a celebration! She sipped and nibbled like a beauty-pageant contestant on a stage. A table of businessmen with giant guts and ridiculous ties couldn't stop gawping at her, and Ray and Staci talked like they were on a blind date, self-conscious and earnest.

Ernie's got the hots for the girl, Ray said. *Maybe it would be good for them.*

Staci turned the glass in her hands. *I doubt it.*

Why?

Coral doesn't like him.

But I've seen her hang with him in the garden and whatever.

Yeah but that's not love.

They shared calamari, dipping the scraggly little medusa heads into tomato sauce.

I guess I knew that, Ray conceded. *He asked me about her when we were fishing, and I tried to tone him down.*

You guys were so cute fishing, you were like a little kid, Staci said.

Fishing is my best memories. Me and Johnny with our jelly sandwiches and beers we stole. Bringing the fish home, making my mom happy, that was the best part. Does that sound sentimental as fuck?

She reached over and ruffled his hair. *Yeah,* she said.

She cooked like an angel. Those were nights my mom and dad even danced in the kitchen to the radio.

BACK AT THE house, Ernie and Coral stayed in their own rooms all evening. Ernie kept racking his brain for things to suggest, reasons to knock on her door, but failed. It was like a beach motel in the dead of winter with two sole guests who could hear each other's televisions but never spoke or interacted.

He had a moment in the kitchen filling a glass with water. Thinking about how stupid he was, why couldn't he just rap on her bedroom door, offer to make dinner, be cool, do what everyone else in the world seemed to know how to do. Why. He only realized he'd been knocking his head with his fist when she opened the fridge and he turned at the noise. He smiled, the blood draining to his knees as he realized she'd seen him beat himself up. Ugh. It made him want to die.

The way she straightened her back and gazed at him, softly—he was sure it was not with pity but with sudden understanding—only made it worse. And then she quietly padded back to her room with a slice of Velveeta and locked the door.

RAY AND STACI almost let their food get cold because they were yakking so much. They talked and talked, remembering their favorite bartender in Miami who watched boxing on TV and took five-minute naps with his head on the bar. Reliving a Key West hurricane. A wet T-shirt contest in Daytona that she won. They talked about Slash.

I mean, how cool, Staci said, eating creamed spinach. *We own a cheetah. We have a cheetah in our backyard.*

Yeah, and the girl is a cat whisperer, turns out, he said, attacking his steak.

Staci brought up opening a salon.

I thought you never wanted to do that again, Ray said.

No, I don't want to work for a bitch like Leasa again. But if I could run my own place, and make people feel good and feel pretty, that would be awesome. I could almost do it in Bandera, there's enough tourists to make money. I mean, if we stay in Texas.

Staci recrossed her legs, toes wedged into the platform spike heels.

Yeah, if we stay in Texas, Ray said, and flagged the waiter.

Two brownie sundaes and two tequilas later, they settled the bill. They left leisurely, arm in arm, walking and giggling past a group of oil-man cowboys who were waiting for cars at the valet. One of the men belched, drunker than Ray and Staci put together, and gave Staci a look as she and Ray headed to the bike.

Whasss your rate, honey? the guy lewdly shouted. *I coul' pay you better than him.*

Staci saw Ray's face turn scarlet in five seconds. A pale line around his lips. This was the mask of violence. She knew it well and reached for his hand with her long acrylic-nailed fingers, bracelets clanging on her wrist.

Hey baby do you have a smoke, she said to distract him. If she told him not to fight, he'd fight harder.

It didn't work. Ray pulled his hand from hers and strutted over. He swung his mallet of a fist, and the guy swung back, it happened too fast to track, grunts of effort, someone's nose was bleeding, but whose? Everyone shouted, the valets stepped in and held the fighters from each other, and that's when Ray clutched his chest and sat down in slow motion.

Ray? Staci said, anxious. *Ray, what's happening?*

Good question. Ray saw a fun-house-mirror world of random memories, kissing a girl with a middle part in a school bathroom, his grandmother hitting him with a pot of tomato sauce, red on the walls and the floor, what could he have done? A deer in the woods. A church bell ringing. The smoke above the compound. His drunk dad kicking his mom. His brother showing him a *Playboy* hidden in a comic book. Coral pointing to the wrong button on his vest, prophesizing this moment.

We'll call an ambulance, said the manager, kneeling with Staci by Ray.

Staci was scanning Ray's eyes, and he looked at her, shook his head.

N-n-o, don't do that, Staci stuttered. *He's got pills at home,* she lied, *this is just a blood-sugar thing, I'll take him home—*

Well, I don't know, the manager said.

Ray tried to get up, but Staci kept him down.

He just needs to sit and—can you grab us a root beer or something? she asked.

A valet guy ran off like an Olympic sprinter. Ray sipped the soda and Staci convinced them Ray would be fine on the bike behind her. He was able to stand, he looked down the whole time, but he somehow got on the bike. Adrenaline had flooded her system and she somehow made it around the block and pulled over in the shadows.

Ray, you got to help, she said.

He grumbled, she could feel him trying. His left arm wasn't holding her tight enough, so she took a bungee cord and bound his wrists together around her waist. She went thirty-five on the back roads, knees bleeding from the parking lot, barefoot. Somewhere along the way, she'd lost her shoes.

ERNIE WAS HALF-ASLEEP when he heard Staci yell his name. He ran out, and together they guided Ray to bed, laid him in the sheets. Ernie desperately tore through the Yellow Pages and called a medical hotline for information about what Staci kept calling a "baby stroke." Her stepdad had a few over the years, she knew the signs. Staci sat on the bed and dabbed hydrogen peroxide on Ray's cut hand while Coral knelt on the floor and refilled his water glass when needed. The left side of his face drooped, and his left arm was weak.

Ernie hung up. *Look, they said it would be safer to take you to the hospital, Ray. Sometimes little ones lead up to big ones.*

Ray wanted to say no but only managed to convey, with the ferocity in his eyes, that he'd kill them if they took him to the ER. Ernie and Staci sat up and watched him snore for hours, not knowing what on earth else they could do, and eventually fell asleep on the floor.

In the morning, Ray was wide-awake and grinning. *I'm alive!* he roared.

Staci groggily hugged him. *That was so insane,* she said, pulling away.

She came tearing in here like a goddamn soldier, Ernie told Ray.

I know, dude, I was there, Ray said.

You seemed out of it, is all.

I was out of it, but I was there, he said, laughing hoarsely.

They made grilled cheeses and sat around and smoked. Dragged the TV into his dark bedroom with the AC unit cranked and dripping. They watched a show Staci loved about haunted houses—not the old mansions with spirits speaking ancient poetry, but regular houses. A two-bedroom ranch in a Denver suburb, or a duplex in Queens. These houses were haunted by ghosts Staci would actually recognize. Teen girls who ODed, suicidal dads, car-accident brothers who would walk into the kitchen, looking for pretzels.

Staci was having trouble though; Ray's body parts worked, he remembered the year and who was president, but something made his shadow darker. He tried joking and smoking and farting it away as they watched *The Simpsons,* but it crept through him—rust after a storm.

You look good, daddy, Staci lied.

She was sitting on the bed, legs crossed, kicking one foot viciously into the air as she ashed into the coffee cup. She was pissed, disappointed, like a kid who didn't get what she'd been promised for her birthday. He had pledged himself, and then fallen apart. Things between them had been real—for one night.

I look like hell, he said, laughing.

She gave him a hundred-watt smile, but Ray knew: he was weak and she didn't want him. After dinner, she crept away and slept on the couch, leaving Ernie and Ray to drink and smoke, listen to country songs on the radio. Ernie saved Ray's ass that night simply by entertaining him.

This thing has tripped me up, Ray finally admitted. *I'm kind of shaky now.*

Shaky makes sense. You know what they say about security, Ernie said.

Ray blew smoke. *I don't know what they say, Ernie.*

Humans are the only creatures who believe in security. It's a freaking myth and yet it's how we build cities and stuff, because we're not just always occupied thinking about survival. Your security has been messed with.

Calm down, Ernesto.

Do you believe in God?

Why not.

I personally think God is in flowers and starlight and disgusting things too, like horseshit.

Fascinating, Ray said with sarcasm and also affection.

When somebody has a near-death experience like you did, it can give you this superpower, like—you can see where God is, you can fully feel that time is of the essence.

I didn't have a fucking heart attack, so there was no near death.

You came close. Ernie was quiet a moment. *Coral gets it, what I'm talking about.*

Did she tell you that? Ray asked sarcastically.

I can see it in her eyes.

Man, you're fucking crazy.

Ernie felt embarrassed, stubbed out his smoke. *I'll let you get some sleep—*

Ray sighed. *Wait. Get us another beer, would you?*

But Ray didn't drink it, which meant he just wanted to hang and had used the beer as a prop. Ernie suppressed his pleasure about this as they talked into the early morning. Basically, Ray felt like he'd gotten a knock on his door: some celestial loan shark was coming to collect. You owe the father, pay up. That's why he'd been losing his memory, piece by piece. It felt like the wealth and property of his being, of his life, were due back, and it scared him to the marrow of his bones, and it also felt like an unburdening.

For some reason, Ray said, his mouth dry after talking for hours, *I do feel more—I don't know—peaceful, even though I feel like shit. It's weird.*

They both watched the milky blue morning mist rolling and curling in the yard. The heat was coming, but not there yet.

I don't think it's weird at all, Ernie said.

TOMATO

STACI MADE CORAL come with her to the supermarket because she felt so low, she couldn't imagine being alone for five minutes. The lights at HEB shined luridly as Staci grabbed foil-wrapped burritos and moodily threw them in the cart. Her plan was to binge-eat the minute she got home. They were staring at cereal boxes when Staci felt an ominous presence and turned around.

Coincidence? I don't think so, Jasper said, imitating a movie.

It's you again, Staci said glumly.

He held his hand out to Coral and shouted: *Jasper. Jeremiah's nephew.*

Staci said, *We know.*

But do you really? he asked like he was James Bond. He cracked a smile to show he was being funny. *Doing a little shoppy-woppy, huh?*

The cart was piled high with meat and bones from the butcher, boxes of pseudoephedrine and aspirin, vitamins for blood pressure. And burritos.

Jasper whistled. *That's some barbecue.*

Staci laughed fake and loud, realizing how bizarre it looked. *Barbecuing is the best.*

I mean, what have you got here? Jasper started pawing through their haul. *Can you just explain to me—*

Hey, wasn't there something fun happening in town? Staci said, panicked, leaning on the cart. *Something about a pig and a church, maybe?*

Actually, now that you mention it. Coral, I've been meaning to ask—want to go dancing sometime?

Staci made a face. *Are you asking Coral out?*

Sure I am. It's the gracious thing to do.

Coral's eyes roamed around his body, and he pretended it wasn't happening.

Well. She is sick of hanging out with us old people, Staci confided to Jasper.

Tonight? I'll pick you up.

Coral didn't shake her head no, so that meant yes to him.

That was easy, he said, and held his hand up for a high five from Staci, then swaggered away.

Staci was flooded with guilt and couldn't look Coral in the eyes. After a while she spoke. *Look. You need to hang with people your age, that wasn't a lie. He's not like, a match. But listen, you practice on the losers and get your game up for when Mister Right walks in. Okay?*

When she could finally bear to peek at the girl, to see if she was livid, or crying, or something awful, Coral was tearing open a corner of a marshmallow bag to pop one into her mouth.

THAT EVENING, STACI pulled together some outfits and knocked on Coral's door. The girl was in a towel, her skin pink from the shower. Staci was laying options out on the bed when Coral dropped her towel, stepped into black shorts with no underwear, her bush like a squirrel's tail stuck between her legs. Staci's eyes widened but the girl didn't flinch.

Do you—I brought a few— she gamely tried.

Coral pulled a white Hanes shirt over her head, and combed her wet hair, water droplets flicking off the tips.

Okay . . . Staci nodded slowly. *Perfume? Lip gloss?*

She hawked makeup like a department-store saleslady, and Coral didn't sneer, she just didn't take anything.

Listen. You don't need to go if you don't want to, Staci finally said, her voice high with a bad feeling. *You know that, right?*

Coral was tying her black sneakers as the truck pulled up. Coral looked out her window as if she might signal Slash that she'd be back in a jiffy, but he was in the shed. Jasper knocked, and when Ernie opened the front door, Jasper smiled, holding carnations.

Howdy, Jasper said.

Can we help you?

I'm taking your sister dancing.

Ernie's eyes popped. *Really. Does she know that?*

Staci hurried out. *Yeah, Ernie, um, Jasper has great plans for the night. Right?*

Sure do. Two-stepping down at the Midnight Fox. Jerry Warrens and his band, doesn't get any better.

Coral walked into the room and a shiver ran through the group. She didn't look at Jasper in a particular way, not in any way a person could describe at least. She certainly didn't look nervous. As Jasper opened the truck door for the girl, Ernie busted into Ray's bedroom to watch from his window.

Did you hear that shit? What the hell?

Ray was drinking milk and rubbing a knot out of his own hairy shoulder. *He's a loser. It's nothing, Ernie, just a night out with someone her own age.*

Staci hovered at the threshold of the room. *He saw us at the super-market and we had like a cart of expired rib eyes and twenty pill bottles*

So? Ernie said.

I had to do something so he didn't ask questions.

Why didn't you tell me he was coming? Ernie asked her.

Why would you want to know, Ernie?

Because.

Tell me why exactly, Ernie, Staci pushed back. *Come on, everyone knows. Say it.*

Whatever, Ernie said, getting flustered.

Staci sighed. *She'll have a terrible time, trust me.*

He turned away. Staci really was sorry. Oh Ernie! she thought. Look at him. His convoluted grandeur. His hair was always tangled and pulled, but the dark redness was lovely. And his eyes—the lids curved like glass or ceramic, shaped by an artist. And if she tried to tell him he was beautiful, he'd hear it as pity. She knew men too well.

THE TRUCK BOUNCED over the road.

Life is good? Jasper asked.

They passed swatches of farm, golden lights indicating a farm-house. Coral nodded, her face and body jittering as the truck rattled. They drove for a while.

So all that land there to your right, my family owns it. My family used to have three hundred and eighteen people working for them, when the mines were open. Jasper tried to hand her a flask. *This is the best agave tequila you ever had.*

Coral looked at it and away.

See that barn? That was my granddad's. Rodeo champion, even though he had a bad leg from the war. And that farm we're about to pass up here? Tornado came and picked up one of their cows and put it down in the next county. It was still chewing cud like nothing was wrong.

Jasper swigged and handed her the flask again, but she didn't take it. She faced him while he drove, she seemed to be casually inventorying him. Looking at the slight bulge between his legs. Looking at his mouth, then at his hands. Looking at his chest. He shifted his weight, uncomfortable; he decided to be flattered and made an awkward laugh-noise and winked at her. But she just turned back to the road.

Coral jumped down from the passenger seat before Jasper could give her a hand, and they walked up to the old dance hall where a bouncer waited. He wrote a red X for drinking on Jasper's hand, but Coral was too young to get one.

I meant to mention you look great, Jasper said without looking at her, as they walked in.

The space had a high ceiling and a worn pine floor, packed with two-steppers and beer-drinkers, white folks and Mexican folks, young and old, terrible dancers and breathtaking dancers. Cheap crooked slanted tables perched on the margin, covered in gingham. Jasper was glad-handing everyone, but forgot to introduce Coral. They sat down.

See that girl over there with the pink boots? Her brother fell off a roof when he was eight and died.

As he gave her a rundown of the general public, Coral seemed to fixate on the drums. The drummer's powder-blue cowboy shirt was dark at the pits. He swung his head around to the lazy snappy beat, and couples turned in circles, and his eyes were closed but his grin was loopy and lavish and real. Coral stared. Jasper tried to get her to dance but she wouldn't budge, so he fetched her another ginger ale. He danced with a couple family friends, formal waltzers.

Okay, enough of this, right? he asked Coral during the second set when she was on her fourth soda.

She leaned in like she was going to go up there and try the drum set herself. He rolled his eyes when she wasn't looking. They left. Jasper pulled the truck into a random field on the way home. He smoked out the window.

So he's really your big brother? I thought he must be your dad, he's so old.

Coral watched him take a drag off his Marlboro. He glanced at her big round breasts in that T-shirt, trying to stare just like she was doing, but he couldn't hold it and had to look away.

Your crew's got a pretty strange vibe. You ever wonder about finding a new posse? My buddy Gunner always says we are the company we keep. Y'all have a little ex-con energy going on—I mean, not you. You're quiet and sweet, which is why I like you. He grinned and showed all his teeth.

Coral kept looking at him.

Jasper said, *My uncle thinks I should leave you all alone. But I'm sort of like, well, it's our property, isn't it our duty to know what goes on there? I'm proud of our community, I like to keep it the way it is. Not afraid to say so, even if it makes me look old-fashioned.*

You understand? he said, and stared with penetrating attention. He seemed to think she might start talking, like she'd just been waiting for a real man to ask a real question. After the long silence, he said: *And—I hope you'd tell me if you need help, if you need out of that house, understand?*

I'm being too serious, huh? He chewed his gum, grinning, then took it out of his mouth and put it in a soda bottle.

You want to make out? he asked.

Coral looked curious. She really did. And so he sloped over and kissed her.

He pulled away, her eyes were open. She licked her lips, then she reached out and tugged his cowlick, like a baby with a mother's earring. Jasper laughed uneasily. She half-closed her eyes and abruptly tilted toward him for another kiss. This seemed to be quite a surprise to him. He pulled away, like he'd been cornered by her, like he wasn't sure about a girl initiating kiss number two, wetter than the first. It set something off in him, and after she sat back, his heart pounded. With lust, perhaps, or in addition to it.

He moved in before she could come at him again, grinding his mouth against hers, his tongue probing deep, and he thrust his hand up her shirt, squeezed her tits like punishment. And suddenly he got three right hooks to his jaw and eye socket that left him stunned for the next ten minutes, blood running into his collar, his eye closing. Her fist had been a rock.

Her breath was ragged as she stared at him. Then she tried to switch places with him and drive herself home. He pushed her away, his eyes giant with a what-the-hell expression, and he started the truck with his free hand, holding a rag from the glove box to his head.

They were silent passing starlit clearings of yucca and cactus. Jasper got out of the truck and walked with Coral to the house. Ernie, pacing in the living room, saw the headlights and opened the front door, and couldn't hide his surprise.

Jasper said acidly: *I wouldn't be a gentleman if I didn't deliver her to the door.*

Oh boy. Drama at the dance hall. Did someone look at her wrong, Jasper?

Jasper managed to say: *This injury is care of your sister. And for the record, I did nothing to deserve this. Okay? She's insane. In case you didn't know, and I'm not real sure how you could miss something as obvious as her being INSANE. You might want to give her a little talk on men and women before letting her out in the world. I could have done so much more than what I did and still been within my rights.* Jasper's nostrils were flared.

Ernie was almost too delighted to think straight. Ray had gotten up to see about the noise, and was trying not to laugh. Ernie pulled himself together and gave the guy a small wad of cash from his pocket.

Buy some whiskey, or get some boots. And don't mind her. Forget this happened, man.

Jasper wasn't about to forget. *You better watch your ass. Asses. Don't you be fooled by my niceness. You won't see it coming, I play cool until I go bust.*

Thanks for sharing all the details of your personality, Ray said with a lazy fuck-you smile.

But the silence after Jasper left the house, and they heard his truck door slam, wasn't as confident. His tires spewed dirt as he reversed. Coral stood there in the living room, knuckles on one hand bleeding. Even if Jasper left them uneasy, Ernie's eyes were misty as he smiled at Coral.

You're amazing, he said, hand to heart. *For punching him in the face.* She smiled back.

Oh, wow. Was this the moment? he wondered to himself. The way she kept standing there, looking at him—like she wanted something. He got hot around the neck, and played with his hair, stroking it over his shoulder.

Want a bandage, or some— he started, reaching for her hand, but she put it behind her back.

A lemonade? he said.

She gave him that mystery face, so he made the be-right-back gesture with his finger. In the kitchen he poured Country Time powder into a glass of water, then twisted the ice tray, one cube twirling across the linoleum. He let it go, didn't care, he mixed the drink, and came back—

The back door slapped closed, and he watched her cross the yard. He thought: Well hell, she's home, she came home, and that's what matters. He placed the lemonade by her bed for when she turned in, and he was giddy the family was intact. He'd been giddy before, oh yes he had. And tonight he just ignored the nearly inaudible creak in his heart of a hundred possible institutions opening their doors to welcome him back, with a guard or a nurse smiling on the threshold and saying, *Come on in, Ernie! We missed you.* Ernie's power was to spit on the inevitable.

CORAL BEELINED TO the pen, and Slash drowsily greeted her. His ears twitched, he must have sniffed Jasper on her. He looked to be on alert, inhaling her clothes. She raked his neck with her undamaged hand. When he smelled the blood on her other hand, he hissed, lips pulled away, the architecture of teeth on display. Then he rubbed his cheek to hers.

MORNING LIGHT PIERCED the room as Staci lay in bed. Every once in a while, she'd blurt out a sound of disgust and despair as she thought about Ray and their inevitable separation. When she dragged her ass out to make coffee, she found Coral eating Froot Loops with a bruised hand. Well, fuck me harder.

How you doing, sweetie? Staci finally said.

Coral glanced up from her Technicolor breakfast, and Staci slumped into a chair.

I can't believe I let you go to town with that guy. I'm such a douchebag.

Coral looked out the window.

Hey, Staci said. *I got something that will make you feel better.*

An injection of self-esteem, right? A brilliant idea, she thought. She rolled the TV cart into Coral's bedroom, Staci skidding in her velour Dallas Cowboys slippers. She popped a tape into the VCR, and she and Coral leaned back in bed.

Okay, here we go. Ready set enlightenment, she said. Footage dissolved from palm trees to diamond-and-gold necklaces, to lovers holding hands, a yacht. A voice droned on and on. *Step Four, be specific with your vision, what do you really want?* said the narrator. The woman sat alone on a beach, eyes closed, and a black Mercedes hovered on the blue horizon, then the woman opened her eyes, nodding and grinning. *Step Five, don't expect it to be easy.*

Staci was distracted. The sky had become not cloudy but completely gray, and the yard was lightless and flat, except for flowers nodding as they got visited by bees, and nodding when the bee left. Staci sipped her vanilla-vodka-and-Pepsi and reminisced about her home-movie collection left behind at the compound. ATV-racing in the Everglades; her and Ray making love in a field with their bikes staged in the background; club members wishing Ray a happy birthday one gnarly rambunctious night in Michigan as Staci roamed the party with the camera and got pinched and spanked. All that footage gone.

Staci looked at Coral, who was dutifully watching the TV. Was she a little sister, which made Staci the big sister? Not sure I fit that bill, Staci thought with some self-loathing. She sometimes used Sharon, her real little sister, as a bookmark for what she could have been if she hadn't become herself. The sisters came from the same womb and sperm, grew up in the same apartment, played the same games with the same neighbor kids. But even as a toddler, Staci had night terrors and constantly lied, while her sister loved the flute and made papier-mâché sculptures. And what do you know, Staci turned into a middle-aged outlaw and retired stripper, and Sharon was a mother, a wife, a citizen. They'd been out of touch for years, Staci just wasn't up to par, she wasn't good enough—but wait, if Staci really thought about it, didn't she get a letter from Sharon forwarded through three addresses a few years ago, and Staci never replied?

Lately, her memory kept overturning verdicts. She'd been thinking Sharon had shunned her, but if that one letter reached her against all odds, how many others did Sharon probably put in the mailbox?

THE VIDEO WAS scrolling credits and Coral was still sitting up in Staci's bed but snoring when Ernie called them to the garden.

Look! he was shouting, elated. *Come out here.*

The tomatoes were scarlet, juicy, heavy on the fuzzy stalks. Ernie handed a few to the ladies, and Coral ate hers like an apple. Staci held one, sun-warmed, pleated at the stem, a dark seam down its side, to her nose and inhaled, and a zillion micro-cells of joy busted open inside her. She snuck into the house.

Ray, say there was a tomato, she yelled toward his room. *How would you want it?*

If it's good and ripe, nothing but salt.

On the counter, she cut a big one, the fruit collapsing, seeds and gel blobbing onto the plate. She sprinkled salt on the thick slices. In the bedroom doorway, she looked like an angel delivering summer-time itself.

Well well, he said. *Get over here.*

They sat close, both leaning over the plate to eat, but juice fell on the sheets anyway. Ray looked at her, and suddenly took her hand with his meaty damp slick fingers, and gripped it to his cheek, and then let go. He had tears in his eyes—was she tripping? He wasn't even trying to hide it, he just looked at her.

I love you, Staci, and I know you're going to leave.

She looked down.

I mean it when I say I'll be okay, he assured her. *We'll always be good in my heart. All right?*

She realized she was ugly-crying.

Hey, did you hear me?

Y-y-yes.

He kind of laughed. *Just don't tell me where you're going so I don't come looking for you.* He said the last part gently, and this made it worse. He started messing with his cigarette pack, and so she left the room, snot running from her red nose, and cried in the kitchen, standing up, holding the plate.

Ernie found her there. *Hey, what's wrong?*

She shook her head, trying to smile.

You don't like the tomatoes after all? he said, trying to be funny.

This got a yolky snorty laugh out of her. *I loved them. Ray loved them too.*

This brought on new tears, and he hugged her clumsily.

It's okay, he said softly, *it'll be all right.*

She could feel it, in Ernie's skinny brutal arms, how badly he wanted to comfort her, and it just wasn't something he knew how to do. But he patted her on the back, and he tried, he tried.

YOGURT

AFTER DINNER, THE horizon dripping with sunset, Coral went outside and opened the door to the pen, but she didn't step in. Instead she held the door wide open. Slash looked alert because this was different. She gazed at him and he just kept on gazing at her. He put a paw down on the outside grass, as if monitoring her. The motion was smooth and slow, then he leapt out, and sprinted in a golden blur, making an arc in the dusk, and crouched by the tree, staring back.

She sauntered toward the woods beyond the barn, and looked to see if he was following. Padding along, he had a lightness and deftness never seen in the cage, of course. He was loose. How did she know he wouldn't run off? Was it control, or obedience, or something else entirely? Once they got on the trail, he'd run fifty feet, then return to her, trotting. She always crouched to rub his cheeks, to scratch behind his tufted ears. He'd stalk, slinking along the ground, or lope. They meandered through the backwoods.

Coral took Slash to the creek where he sniffed at the wildflowers, their petals still dripping with the sun's heat in the dimming night, pissed on the bank, and followed her in, ankle-deep. She lay on her back, half underwater, and he slapped his reflection, splashing her. Coral laughed, hiccupping, and splashed back. A water moccasin nearby traced its S on the surface, disturbed by them, and they watched until it moved away. Slash was strong and lustrous, alive in the wild, and Coral's arms were gleaming too. They were caught like the dark star and the white star in a binary system, locked in orbit, driven in loops.

When they got back, the moon high and full, Coral stepped into the cage but then crawled into the shed with him. She'd never come into this inner sanctum, and she latched the door behind her. In the inky darkness, her eyes adjusted. She was kneeling, and his purr rocked the air as he licked her thigh, her other thigh, and he rolled back on the dusty earth, with an indolent grace. She lay on her side, and they were suddenly parallel.

And then—there were only glints of gold fur, teeth, skin, and the whir of purring, the rustle crush and rank perfume of hay, as they fell asleep. Heat as they breathed in tandem. So still, so motionless, for an hour or more, not even turning over. Toward dawn, he bared his teeth, eyes shut, his lips quivering, his legs twitching, hunting, in some kind of dream.

LYING IN BED, a fan blowing night heat around his room, Ernie was consumed with visions that wouldn't stop. He wanted a carousel for the backyard, maybe they could buy one off a defunct amusement park somewhere. Then he started thinking about organizing a hot-air balloon ride for Coral's birthday, the four of them floating over the Texas hills. Or! What about making this farmette into a goat dairy? They could sell cheese and yogurt. He thought in bundles, possibilities launching and bursting and falling like cheap fireworks. Half-asleep, he conjured a crowded post office. A madman barges in, and Ernie talks the man down. Ernie tells the shooter about his own self-hate, his desire to kill himself, he might even talk about getting molested at five by someone's brother. The shooter can't believe a man this tough can talk this honestly. The shooter falls to his knees and gives the weapon to Ernie. And the girl in the background, in the mustard-yellow shorts and black shirt, who stares in awe at Ernie the hero—it's Coral!

HE WALKED OUT to the yard—the sunrise so hot, it fried dew off the grass. As if cosmically timed, Coral came out of the pen into the milky heat. She must have gotten up early to give Slash breakfast, Ernie thought. Hair tousled, she walked to the garden, sort of limping, languidly. He decided to let her be for the moment, she seemed solitary and thoughtful. Before heading into the house, he watched her squat at a squash blossom, and saw the claw-punctures on her back and fresh scratches down her arm. That's wild! he thought. They must have been playing for real.

FOUR

Telling

WILD STRAWBERRIES

WHEN STACI FOUND Ernie later that morning, he'd weeded the front yard, showered, finished one pot of coffee, and was making a new one, staring at the machine dripping. His hair was wet and dark, dampening his shirt.

What am I going to do? he said, agitated. *I can't take it.*

She turned a chair backward, cabaret-style. *I bet I can guess what this is about, babe.*

He looked at her, eyes half-lidded with desperation, then he took the pot to pour her a cup. The coffee dripped onto the hot plate and sizzled, but he didn't care.

I'm in love with her, he said, *obviously.*

She held the mug with both hands, nails up like a castle turret, took a delicate slurp. *Oh my god, delicious. The first sip, always so good.* Shaking back her blond hair, she sighed. *Ern, everyone knew you were in love with her, like, before the fire.*

Everyone but me.

Well, yeah.

What should I do? he asked point-blank. *Get her a present?*

Staci nodded slowly. *You could get her a present.*

Will you help me find one?

Of course, babe.

Should I get her a ring? Ernie asked in a hoarse whisper even though Coral's door was closed.

That's sort of loaded, you know?

Oh yeah, was just saying.

What about an anklet?

They got in the van whose dashboard held a lavender sprig, a matchbook, and three spent cherry-red shotgun shells. The college radio station played Ray Price as they bumped along the road. The van gently leaned as they turned past the two things in every village that made Staci feel wonder and hope: a ballet studio and a martial arts joint. What's more innocent than the bubblegum-pink tights of a ten-year-old? A little kid in karate pants, the sole of a foot meeting a cheap floor? If scientists wanted data on the goodness of humans, they shouldn't look in the chapel or the mayor's office, they should go find these studios on any frontage road in America, embedded between a no-name pizza spot and the shady insurance office.

Staci and Ernie slammed the van's heavy doors shut with a clunk. They walked to the store, where a pair of gray kittens slept in the window among watches and signet rings and diamond pendants.

Your AC feels good, Ernie nervously told the woman behind the counter.

Summer's truly arrived, the woman said.

We're just looking for something cute, Staci said, *nothing too fancy. Do you have anklets?*

Sure do. The woman's purple polyester kaftan swung, and Staci followed.

As the women looked at another case, Ernie was frozen, dumb-struck by a string of baby pearls. Like the one he stole from Gloria's dresser when he was thirteen, on a dare, when she was helping Brad with his homework downstairs. Ernie'd taken the necklace from its tiny Macy's box and hid it. He'd been furious, but he could never re-member why. He just had fury in him. Ernie wanted to ruin every-thing, he wanted it to be over, and he did ruin it. And it was over. Troy told on him to their counselor, and Gloria promised they could work it out, but Ernie had a ton of demerits and the counselor said it was out of his hands, it was the last straw. So a social worker moved Ernie out the next month, and he never told anyone where to find the pearls. Never apologized either.

Ernesto, check it out, Staci said, dangling a gold anklet from her fin-ger. *It's an angel charm, and Coral's an angel, so this is perfect.*

Okay, he said, uncomfortable in the shop. *How much?*

The shop owner seemed surprised it was so easy, but she took his cash, and he and Staci emerged into the oven of the parking lot. They rolled down the van windows, sitting on the baked-black hot pleather. Neither spoke, they just watched the clouds hang in the hot sky.

I'm going to leave, Ernie, Staci said softly. *By myself, without him.*

Ernie gaped at her, at her eyes lined with sapphire, eyebrows drawn high and thin.

Why? he finally asked.

She shook her head, helpless. *I have to. My heart is telling me to go.*

Stunned, Ernie looked down the road. *I didn't think you were going to leave first. You, out of everyone.*

I'm sorry, babe.

She studied him; he was disconsolate.

I'm raining on your present-buying field trip, she said.

Naw, he said, and looked farther away. *I've just had insomnia lately, can't sleep at all.*

That's the worst, she said softly. *Hey, aren't we near that swimming hole you talked about?*

You only swim in hotel pools, I thought, Ernie said.

I was joking when I said that, she said, but she hadn't been joking.

Heading to the spot, they detoured briefly at a cardboard sign reading WILD STRAWBERRIES. It took them down a dirt lane, the van rocking over the bumps. The manufactured home was shady and quiet. Lace in the windows, no one there, just a card table out front. Two dollars a sack, honor system. They stuffed bills into the Folgers can, not speaking, feeling the hush of the place. While they drove, they ate the sweet tart juicy super-ripe berries and it practically got them high.

They parked and hiked through scrub, under a formation of rock with a damp ceiling, ferns growing upside down, bats sleeping in the crevices. The bat shit on the ground smelled like nothing that nature made.

Trailing her hand through the grasses, Staci pointed out starflowers. *Truthfully, I never gave a shit about the countryside before, but I've been really looking around,* she said, picking her way down the hardscrabble path. *I'm noticing flowers like everywhere, and those spiderwebs that only show up at a certain hour. I must have walked through them before, I never saw them.*

I know what you mean, Ernie said.

He looked down as they walked because she wore teenager shorts on a woman's ass. Faded tattoos on her back showed through the tank top, including *8-13-1985* written in a gothic font, with *clean & serene* below it. When they arrived at the deep lake, it was silent. The surface still as honey. And they were alone. Ernie tore off his T-shirt and boots, and waded into the cold water, yelping and swinging his arms.

Come in! he shouted.

But she sat in the grass, knees up, arms stretched behind her, unexpectedly shy. *I'm just going to chill, Ern, you have fun. I'm enjoying this shade.*

Ernie floated for a while, then walked up toward her, dripping, bony, beat up, glistening with water. Here was a man with almost no self-regard, Staci thought, and yet he was way more comfortable in his own skin than her.

She'd lived with a dual-body sensation forever, but noticed it now, sitting in the spiky grass. Staci was a pair of bodies, her actual body (imperfect and mortal) followed night and day by a ghost body that had no scars, no lumps, no zits on her ass, no razor burn where she shaved her pubic hair. This slick plastic doll had been trailing her since eighth grade.

She'd always worked out. People told her she looked fit, beautiful, it didn't mean shit. She put her puppet self out into the world, trussed, painted, aggressively available, but deep down, she wasn't good enough. Even at twenty-five, Staci technically knew how badass she could come off, dancing under neon lights, on a glossy black stage, and simultaneously she thought of herself as all wrong. Two truths.

Her entire life she sucked in her tummy even when she was alone. Yet here was Ernie, sprawled on his stomach, napping in nature, sunburned, flabby at the hip, stringy at the calf, his hair ablaze, magnificent in his way. His trust in her made it easy for him to lie there. Why couldn't she lie there too?

Quietly she stripped off her clothes, everything, and tiptoed to the lake. Wading in, her skin got goose bumps from thighs to neck, but not from the cold. She let her feet find the rocky bottom, breasts floating on the water, head above the surface, and she grinned like a crazy person because it felt so fresh and unknown. This moment was for no one else, there was no audience.

That phantom body dissolved in the water, and she dove under, and came up, hair slicked to the skull, eyes closed, makeup draining down her face, and she dipped down again and again. She floated on her back and the sun outlined her in gold, the ripples around her body shining in loopy brilliance. Her face dried and got hot and pink while the rest of her became waterlogged, the lake itself holding her gently toward the sky.

All week she'd been obsessing over who to call to borrow money, who to glom on to and meet up with, who would be the next partner after Ray. Who would be the next crib for her soul? Never once, until now, did she think it could be herself.

She felt something like a blush take her body by storm. A pale-red blessing that moved through her. This was how flowers, they age.

FEAST

YESTERDAY ERNIE AND Staci got home, sun-frazzled and slap-happy, and he just couldn't get up the courage to give Coral her present. So he steeled himself today and drove to town to get her breakfast, and *then* he was going to do it, no matter what.

Ernie passed a work crew doing a job on the road's shoulder, a woman flagger on the team. This stranger in her hard hat and vest made him think about feminism, which he agreed with, but he was old-fashioned about a man taking charge when it came to love. His gut said Coral was in the same rosy smoky haze of love as him, and she was waiting (and waiting!) for him to kick it off.

He parked in the empty lot. The Greek god looking over this morning was Colonel Sanders, the guy in suspenders, on a sign streaked with rust. The sunlight was a mess of cross-stitching and blooming spots, filtering down through trees and landing. He stared at it.

A soda cup in a puddle, a shopping cart turned over. He was blinking compulsively, smoking out the van window, smoothing the wrinkles on his forehead, trying to handle his emotions. He put both hands on the steering wheel, the cig between his fingers, and shook his head blearily, almost smiling. He addressed someone: What are you doing to me? I can't handle her. I can't handle this.

Inside he knew the oil was sizzling in the metal basket, aprons were tied, registers stocked with faded soft money, which seemed to be the only kind around here. The sky was dark as Satan's mind. Ernie planned on getting her a chocolate milkshake in addition to a chicken sandwich, and he was nervous about it.

Ernie, sometimes you stop making sense, he said, and loped to the front of the place, flicked his smoke as he pulled open the glass door.

Let me have the best chocolate milkshake you got, he heard himself say.

He drove back to the house, a Styrofoam cup between his legs, a white paper bag on the dash, getting himself ready mentally, no procrastinating, no delay. He had trouble getting out of the van, wondering if this was the stupidest thing he'd ever done. No, sitting here thinking about it as the shake melted was the stupidest thing. And yet his body was refusing to get off the cracked seat and walk into the house and hand the girl the goddamn motherfucking milkshake.

Okay that's it, he said, and went in.

At her door, heart fluttering, he cleared his throat. This was what she wanted him to do, girls just don't always show it. He knocked, silence, then knocked again. He heard the bedsprings creak, and he prepared a smile. His hair was tightly braided down his back, his fingernails cleaned.

She opened the door.

Heyyy, he said, licking his lips shyly, *so I got you a—*

Her face was puffy from lying down, the Motorhead shirt untucked from those hideous yellow shorts. Her eyes looked pale but wicked, taking him in without politeness, staring with no apology.

And he couldn't speak.

Because lounging on her bed, like a king, was the cat. The animal maintained a relaxed posture while preparing to tear Ernie's throat out. The cat's eyes narrowed, his purr turned to a hiss.

Do you want to—go somewhere else? Ernie asked the girl.

Coral looked back, and she and the cat seemed to decide something because Coral faced Ernie again and the cat started licking his paw even though his paw didn't need licking. But she didn't budge.

Okay, then. Ernie robotically handed her the chocolate shake.

She took it.

Chocolate shake, he said.

She didn't try it.

And I got you a present. He gave her the red box.

She opened it: the angel on the gold chain.

Because you're an angel, he said dully.

He moved to kiss her cheek, she pulled away. Coral's expression put the last nail in his dream.

Do—do you want me to put it on you? he asked anyway.

He knelt to fasten it around her ankle, and Coral looked at him squatting.

You hate it, he said, standing.

She looked at him. He wanted her to spit on him, to disrespect him, he wanted a reason to hit her. But she did that *thing*, she stared with a thousand universes glowing behind her eyes. That's the only way he could describe it. And she left the anklet on, and gently closed the door. Staci poked her head into the hall, and the look on Ernie's face made her retreat. Ernie slammed his own bedroom door so hard the house shook.

Both the girl and the cheetah glanced up at the *whack*, as if listening for more commotion, and then, when none happened, they went back to reclining, permanent like royalty. Coral was brushing his fur with her pink plastic hairbrush. He purred, eyes half-closed.

SLASH MOVED INTO the house full-time, sitting in the living-room armchair or lying in the patch of sun by the sliding glass doors, the bronze fur along his spine shining. He wandered from the kitchen to Coral's room to the living room like someone waiting for a phone call. He even nipped Staci's dangling slipper one morning, took it off her foot with his teeth, and she let him.

No really, I want you to have it, Staci told the cat retroactively, half joking, but she said it gently, hoping not to set the animal off.

It was like hanging out with a hand grenade. Everyone knew that if they reeked of fear, the animal could attack. How does a person decide not to be afraid? Ernie refused to come out of his room. He'd regressed to a pimply scrawny twelve-year-old, with hormones like antifreeze slugging through his bloodstream, and that prepubescent drive to make sure everyone knew they were wrong about absolutely everything while he was right about everything with there being nothing specific on the table to argue about. He'd been holed up for three days, and his room was stinky with the cheese of self-pity and longing, the dirty hand towel of shame. Staci talked to him through his cracked door, which was all he allowed.

Ern, she said. *We miss you.*

She used me was his despondent answer.

Go for a walk with me, Staci tried.

I'm humiliated.

Let's go for a drive.

After a moment, Ernie said: *Please leave me alone.*

He wanted the anklet back. He thought about barging into her room and tearing it off her ankle. Let the cat kill him, who cares. He smoked cigarettes back-to-back, lighting one off the last, plummeting into the void. He was livid, he was furious, but mainly he was at square one, a well-known place he never should have left.

ERNIE WAS SPIRALING in his bed. Between these seasons of the soul, he forgot what it felt like, forgot that this part wasn't sadness—it was more the draining of meaning, like ticks or leeches had sucked the blood out of everything. And happiness, he remembered, was forgetting that this state of being was even possible. Happiness in fact was being sure that it was *not* possible. This specific stupidity was his favorite place to live, and he'd been evicted.

When the sun rose, he sat up, no point trying to sleep anymore. The garden went unwatered, the plants wilting, browning. He didn't go swimming, he didn't read books. He smoked in his sheets, staring at the wall. Ashing toward the ashtray. Shaking his head every now and then, rubbing his bleary eyes.

To no one, he'd mutter: *The least she could fucking do is explain herself.*

They all lived like this for about a week, barely speaking, Staci now and then packing something into a suitcase and then taking it out, trying to decide where she was going and how to get there. Ray watched hot clouds roll over each other, re-forming, blocking the sun for a minute so the world could catch its breath. Ernie threw bottle caps at the wall. And Coral and Slash lounged inside and out, roaming, floating, playing with the pink plastic ball like it was a psychedelic cherry on the cake of their every moment together.

THE POOR GARDEN. Planted just to die? That seemed unforgivable, so Staci and Coral put on hats and spent an hour salvaging fruits and vegetables. Ray's idea was to cook it all for dinner, and cheer up Ernesto. Tomatoes, spinach, basil, zucchini, none of it perfect, all of it with bug bites or brown spots, but edible.

Here, put it on the counter, he said. *I'll take care of it.*

Coral and Staci sat at the table, playing cards while Ray cooked. The cheetah lay on the floor by Coral's feet, nuzzling a teddy bear and then ripping its insides out. The cat's appearance of being loose and calm only made Ray and Staci more terrified. He could slit their sternum in a hot second, tear their stomach out with his teeth—they made no sudden moves. Every now and then, Coral absentmindedly rubbed Slash behind his ear or fed him a Ritz cracker, and Slash licked water from the bowl into his giant gothic mouth. Ray found himself just staring.

Does he let us know when he's got to go out, I wonder? Ray asked the room.

I'm sure he could like, scratch at the door, Staci said.

The air conditioner noisily battled the Texas heat. The machine leaked outside, and Ernie had planted mint under it to take advantage of the dampness, and the mint was thriving, even though Ernie wasn't.

How's it coming, babe? Staci asked Ray. Her tone was cute, the opposite of the taunting, resentful, sexual way she used to talk to him.

Good, he said. *The soup's got to cook awhile.*

Ray spoke in an easygoing tone, determined not to show his real self. How did he get to fifty-two without having his heart broken till now? He couldn't even look at Staci. It was like someone poured battery acid on his soul. So many things made sense: how people acted after heartache, what they'd do for revenge. He never fully got it before. Now he was stuffing his face with Parmesan sliced off the wedge and torn bread as he cooked, sautéing zucchini and baking stuffed tomatoes, eating his sadness away.

Slash got up and padded through the room, and Ray and Staci

jumped in their skin. He moved with stealth when there was nothing to stalk. And even though he had dominance, he cowered like he loathed ceilings. He suddenly sprawled on his back and took a couch cushion in his claws, tossing it and catching it, holding and nibbling at it. Then he nosed open Coral's door, leapt onto her bed in one motion. She followed him.

Life around here, Staci said, with no one to finish the card game, *never gets boring.*

WHEN DINNER WAS almost ready, Staci set the table. She opened the sliding door to get a breeze in the room. Every burner on the stove was used, steaming the fragrance of garlicky herby ratatouille and a green soup and other things Ray made from a fifty-cent cookbook bought at the Salvation Army.

Come out, Staci yelled to Ernie. *Ray whipped up a feast for you.*

Ernie poked his head out, saw that Coral and Slash weren't there, and emerged.

Man, Ray said to him as he passed, never one to mince words. *You smell like ass.*

I know, he said, and he did know. The filth, that feral layer, would become a protective film soon enough, the way it always did. Ernie sat and turned the lazy Susan, which had been barren when they got here, but now held soy sauce, sugar, habanero sauce, a pepper grinder, Cracker Jack toys, a ceramic cup of coins, McDonald's napkins, a honey bear. Ernie stopped it from spinning because it made him dizzy.

Everything is from the garden, Ray said, as he delivered platters and bowls. Sweating, he finally sat and tucked a napkin in his shirt. *Dig in.*

You want to say one of your grace things? Staci asked Ernie.

Ernie shrugged. *What's there to be thankful for?*

You could tell Ray you're grateful for this meal.

So could you

Silence, stalemate.

Staci looked at Ray: *You know I'm grateful.*

Look, I'm going to start eating, I'm not waiting on you two while my food gets cold, Ray said, unable to meet her eyes, his hands already greasy.

This is cool, Ernie said with gravity. *Thank you.*

Slash strutted out of the bedroom, head low, eyes tilted up; he stopped in the hall and—as if he'd been planning this for weeks—pissed on Ernie's door, the hot gold urine sinking into the carpet pocked with cigarette burns. Everyone was silent, watching. Slash waited as Coral filled two plates, and then he followed her outside.

Are you joking? Ernie said. *Are. You. Joking.*

Out the window, the pair sat in the grass and ate their picnic.

She's a kid, Ray tried.

Why am I not enough? Ernie said.

He looked at Ray, and then at Staci, as if they might know.

She should tell me to my face, Ernie said.

After an awkwardly long moment, Staci mumbled: *I don't see her telling you anything, really.*

IT WASN'T DAWN yet, the darkness was thick. Ernie sat up in his sheets, he'd heard something. Nothing audible. Something he could feel, coming from Coral's bedroom. He put an ear to the wall. It was like catching sputtering static from a ham radio, and he knew he'd underestimated and misunderstood everything. He just knew it. Had he assumed that the girl tried to think like most people did, and just failed? Ha. That was a joke on him. On them all.

He saw when she arrived at the compound that she was driven by something—maybe not an agenda, but she had will. Coral didn't lie around in those early days flirting and stealing from people's rooms and sleeping till afternoon and trying to score, like other characters who showed up over time. Some force pulled her into the world every day. Ernie clucked his tongue, remembering now and putting the pieces together. Everyone thought of her as childlike. Ha! Ha ha ha! Ha ha! Childlike.

No, the very opposite, he mused smoothly, deliriously. She got to the stuff of life before it was sterilized into concepts and alphabets, she took it when it was raw. If his thoughts were cut like lumber, hers were happening before there was even a tree, or before the tree was a seed. What comes before a seed? She knew! But she would never tell him.

He was feverish now as he "eavesdropped," trembling with one cheek mushed against the wall. He could sense the bond between those two in there, it was foreign. They didn't communicate with humans but why would that mean they weren't communicating? What was happening in the other room was fundamentally different. He started laughing. He threw himself back onto the bed, numb.

These two didn't talk, or gesture, or repeat what they'd heard. Ernie almost fell off his bed when finally, with a whack across the soul, he understood:

They traded light.

And that was the end. The jealousy was almost liberating. But not quite. It shut him down, no appetite, no hope. Just sent him marching to a darkness he'd met before, but darker this time.

TWO DAYS LATER came the call in the middle of the night. Staci woke up on the couch, cleared her sleepy throat, and answered the phone, a T-shirt hanging off one shoulder.

Yeah? she groaned.

A female voice—somehow familiar—said: *You guys need to get out of there, the cops are coming.*

Staci was wide-awake. *Who is this?*

Click.

Staci couldn't breathe, she opened Ernie's bedroom door without knocking.

Babe, she said heavily. *Police.*

Electricity through his bones. *Now? Right now?*

Someone called. I don't know, Ern, police might be on their way. They might come tomorrow. I don't know.

He got up, shirtless, staggering. Staci woke Ray, with a tender kiss, like a mother to a son. When he opened his eyes, he knew. She pushed in Coral's door, the girl and the cat were already upright, lights off, eyes gleaming.

Cor, I don't know what to tell you, Staci said. She was looking at Slash, afraid he'd pick up on the panic. *We have to jet.*

Ernie grabbed books, shoved them in a bag. His shave cream, an apple, what else? He knew he wasn't thinking straight. Money! That's right. He grabbed whatever he could find. He was forgetting something. No time. He could hear Ray scrambling in his room to put things in a duffel bag, moving around, disordered. Not talking.

What made Ernie so distraught was being in the yard and facing the garden he'd planted and loved and then neglected. He looked into the sky, and all around, he kept turning and turning. No! No. All the flowers and vegetables, ruined by sun, their edges sad and crispy in the night. How could they abandon the garden without making it right?

It was so clear all of a sudden. Ernie had just always thought too much, trying to make things happen out of thin air, what's wrong with me, why do I do that? Always wanting what he didn't have. Life was a series of situations, you find the good in each one, that's all you can do, because none will last—now that was obvious. Man, he was just so tired of being Ernie. He stood, hands on hips, his back hunched.

Then Slash streaked from house to pen, ducked into the cage door. Staci and Ray stood with luggage in the yard, like newborns pushed into the world, and Coral came out with her pillowcase of clothes and the Discman. Slash made a noise that stopped even her. The cheetah was pacing, now and then looking into her eyes, scary like when he first landed here and refused to connect.

Ray spoke: *Coral, we need to leave.*

The cat screamed. The sound ripped through the darkness. His teeth, his black lips—pink tongue—the threads of sorrow staining his face—he crept close to the ground, this way ten feet then that way ten feet coming back. Coral squatted. She was shaking. The cat screeched again and pounced toward her, threatening. Coral stood, she didn't back up but everyone knew she should, the door was open, the cat was in attack mode.

Cor, Ernie said softly. He left his knapsack in the grass and moved toward her. *This time there's no playing. You've got to come.*

Her eyes were blood-red and slit. Ray stepped back and pulled Staci, but Ernie kept moving forward. Slash's pacing got faster and his loop shorter.

Coral, come with us, Ernie murmured. *You can go your own way once we're out of here, but—*

Coral took the pistol out of her waistband. It was a dull cheap gleam of a gun, and loaded. Ernie thought Ray had it, Ray thought Ernie had it. She had it. The cat screamed again. Coral didn't budge. Her eyes were wet, and she turned back to look at Ernie.

I'll leave you alone after we get somewhere, if that's what you want, Ernie said. *Please just come.*

Slash bared his teeth. Frothing. That's when Ernie realized what she wanted to do.

He finally said: *No one will judge, Coral. We understand. The cops'll shoot him if you don't do it first. Or best case, he'll get locked up somewhere, no control of his life.*

Coral looked back at Slash, she was blubbering like a kid.

Have mercy, Ernie said.

Ray knew, in slow-motion terror, that what was about to happen wasn't an accident. It was the dark side of her law, and she had to do it.

She wiped her wet face with her wrist, gripped the handle—took a huge breath—pulled the trigger. If anyone had been able to see straight, they might have caught love in her eyes.

A single gunshot.

The dark plants shivered. The moon hung. A coyote yipped far away.

VULTURE AND DOVE

BY THE TIME police cars arrived, sending blue-and-red light over the driveway, the front door was wide open, and it was pretty clear someone had tipped off the household. Officers swarmed the house anyway, moving through the rooms, shouting directions, emptying drawers and slamming open closets. No one was there. No one in the yard. No one in the barn. No one in the cage.

DAYLIGHT. A DIRTY sky became the palest mauve expanse, the clumps of trees silhouetted in the early hour. The town woke up the way it always did, shopkeepers turning their CLOSED signs to OPEN. The gas station's sign dimming as the morning brightened, the prices staying the same. In groves of mesquite stood cows who started off at dawn being sinkholes of energy in the topography, and then shined in the brutal light, but hardly moved. A bald lawyer looked down from a billboard. An old red Buick Riviera without tires rotted in front of a florist shop. An armadillo crossed the road.

THREE DAYS WENT by.

Morning. The moon and the sun were both up, the sky black on one side, crimson on the other. The van was parked deep in the woods. Coral stretched in the back of it. She'd slept again with the doors open. Peach pits were strewn on the ground under the bumper. She got out and took her clothes off, crouched in the creek and used handfuls of water to take a bath. Rubbed between her legs and scooped water into her armpits. Then sat in the first dashes of sunlight to dry.

Above her, a vine was living off a tree, or the tree was kept upright by the vine. Yellow trumpet flowers yawned, too high to notice unless someone looked straight up. There had been an electric storm at midnight, cracking and zapping, but no rain. Everything still trembled from the lightning. She'd driven around last night, as she'd been doing, past streetlamps dropping cones of loneliness into empty lots, past a custard-taupe motel, past moonlit acres of beebrush and persimmon and purple sage.

She got dressed now, and put the keys in the ignition. She drove on back roads, never strayed far from their house. Saw a teen couple making out against a dumpster. A man in a mechanic's suit got into a truck with his blue heeler puppy. In a trailer's window hung a faux-brass lamp, unlit.

At the Dairy Queen drive-through, Coral pointed at the burger on the board, then waited for it with her head down. She had money. When everyone was running in circles that night, she took what she'd need. The gun was still in the glove box. After she ate, she parked the van in a different part of the same woods, got out and roamed in circles, covering new territory. Coral's sweat soaked her clothes. She rested in the shade of live oaks, slapped bugs on her thighs. Her hair was greasy enough that she could smooth it behind her ear and it would stay.

At dusk, she crept to a family farm, twisted zucchini and melon off their stems, sat in a copse of juniper with a knife and ate her raw dinner. And that's when she saw them, five or six vultures. She didn't move but just watched, pupils dilating. Then she stood up, wiped her wet hands on her shorts, and walked in the direction of the birds orbiting in lean brutal curves around something, over something. She stumbled because she was looking up. She could have been a zombie. Getting closer, she could see black wings as birds fought on the ground.

She squinted, breath shortened, and ran to it.

It was a young deer, taken down by the neck, and eviscerated. The flesh that was left was still magenta, the tendons white and fresh yellow. This just happened. Coral's eyes got misty, and she smiled. She looked around as if congratulating the trees and the bushes and the sky. Even the birds. Even the deer's remains. Hands in pockets, she had a radiance.

She followed the deer path into a ravine, where a thin stream ran between wildflowers. And there he was, Slash, alone, half-heartedly pawing the water. He turned to look at her, and tiny birds scattered into the air then descended as a group onto the grass. Majesty in the moment.

She tripped down the brush-tangled decline, and he ducked as she put her arms around him. His tongue scraped her face. She buried her face in his thick stinky fur while his purring got louder and rattled.

They stayed there, wet and shining in the water. Lying in half-sun. She'd break a stalk of hay and tickle him, he'd bat it away, and they'd sigh. These two souls were hooked up to the cells of every living thing around them, and life surged through the network in a sacred way. Ecstasy, triumph!

At nightfall, the pair walked through undergrowth to the van. She opened the back, and he jumped in. They went to sleep on its plastic floor with no food. The van was so hot, so small, but the night unfurled backward and forward in an opulently different reality.

In the morning, he sniffed around, shoulders working as he strolled, tagged a bush, the stems bouncing under the force of his stream. He came to a pool of sun, and closed his eyes, soaking it in. Then he set about pulling pine needles and sap from between his paw pads with his teeth. She perched with her legs hanging from the back of the van. They looked at each other. He ate a dove and a squirrel that day, but nothing else. She ate a dozen peaches. They both shat in the brush.

HARD TO SAY if it was naivete or arrogance or just hunger that made Coral drive them to the grocery store after a couple days. Parked, she shoved cash deep into her pocket. She gave Slash a look and locked the hot van, then ran-walked into the electric sliding doors, whose glass was papered with ninety-nine-cent deals. He stared out the driver's-side window.

She threw stuff on the conveyer belt, and the cashier talked to another cashier while she ran Coral's items, not curious about the powdered donuts, three dozen flank steaks on sale, and a six-pack of grape soda.

On her way out, Coral saw the *Menard Gazette's* front page: three blurry pictures of a cheetah by an aboveground pool in someone's yard. The article's sidebar read: *Cheetah Sighting! If seen, call Maddie at the Exotic Cat Ranch at 1-800-SAVE-CAT.* She ran-walked back to the van, unwrapped the plastic-sealed meat, and tossed it all into the back. Slash jumped over the seats and snarled, hidden as he devoured the beef, loud enough to make a family getting out of a station wagon exchange looks.

The woman who reported her was named Ginny Manner, and she would do a dozen news interviews about seeing Slash "trapped" in the van. Coral was driving west on US-190, rubbing Slash's chin, when sirens came from behind. For a few minutes, she kept driving, but the cops stayed on her bumper. She finally pulled into a bank parking lot, the van humid with stress and fear.

A cop approached her window with gun drawn. *License and registration.*

Coral stared at him but didn't roll down her window.

Step out of the vehicle.

Suddenly Slash reared up and snarled, scraping the glass, and the officer cringed like a child.

What in god's name? Frank, come here. Frank! It's the cat, I swear.

No frigging way, said Frank.

The two cops stood at the van, and Coral kept her hands on the steering wheel. Slash looked malevolently from one cop to the other, his eyes going shy if they looked back. The men conferred. Backup units arrived, but they didn't know what to do either.

Johnston said to take it to the exotic ranch place, one guy pronounced, after getting off the radio. *Outside Killeen.*

They looked at Coral for a long time, then at Slash, then at one another, then at Coral. The cops seemed to be waiting to suddenly remember what their training taught them about this situation: a cheetah in a van.

Finally, an officer stood two feet from Coral and shouted: *We're going to drive you to the refuge, okay? You're going to follow us, okay? And we'll have someone behind you too. So no shenanigans. Okay?*

Their caravan was broadcast on local TVs that night. One cop car leading Coral, one trailing her, lights churning but no sirens. Drivers pointed and gawked. The parade moved through small town after small town, past dead porcupines on the road, a radio-station building, a wedding storefront full of polyester lace. Jeez, the solemnity of the procession made it look like a bigwig politician was in town or someone beloved had died.

The caravan drove through miles of undeveloped land, arriving at a sign for the Exotic Cat Ranch. The leading police car spoke through an intercom, and the electronic gate opened. Coral drove over the cattle guard and up the long drive. The property unfolded: emerald, heavenly, dusty. A woman with a long white braid waited.

It was Maddie, in jeans and a collared shirt, walking with authority toward the approaching vehicles. When Coral put the van in park, Maddie moved in, her volunteers following in pastel scrubs like otherworldly apprentices. Coral stared out, her face framed in the dirty window, then looked at Slash, who scanned everything at warp speed. He was showing panic. Maddie stood three feet away.

My team here is going to sedate him, she said loudly. *It's not going to hurt. Got it? We will take care of him. I promise.*

Coral pressed her face into his fur, massaging the top of his neck where his mother would have picked him up with her teeth, where the nerves coalesce to feel love. But he jerked and nipped her hand. She clutched his fur anyway, and he submitted, clucking. He kept his eyes down but they slid side to side in a slow and steady dread. Coral and Slash were so hot, both bodies like furnaces turned to high. The blue sky an empty dome.

And while Coral had her face buried in his neck, Maddie sveltely jerked open the passenger door and injected the cat, the needle sinking into his flesh, and his body slumped. He was gone. Not dead but gone.

Everyone stared. His shape, the thing of him, the nails and teeth of him, the paws and ears, these elements, these parts, they seemed to make him what he was. He was a cheetah. But the second the tranquilizer knocked him out, he was nothing, the weight of his soul missing, and oddly, this made his body in Coral's lap so much heavier, just so heavy, and slack. His mouth hung open and she looked confused and she tried to hold it closed but it wouldn't stay, and she touched the fur under his chin one more time, her fingers rubbing frantically. She peered into his empty eyes, tilting her head, then straightening it, then tilting it another way. She started to bawl, she squeezed his front paw as if to rouse him, now shaking it and shaking it, frantically—

It took three policemen to restrain Coral so the animal could be removed from the van, arranged on a stretcher, and rolled up the drive. The girl needed oxygen, and she fought that too, until she couldn't anymore and gave in and breathed hoarsely from the cup.

FIVE

Tail End

AND SO. THE gang that had escaped a fire, set up a new house, and planted a garden, they were scattered, they were divided, flung, like dandelion seeds in the wind, fish into the shadows, embers to the rain, birds across a northern sky. Destruction, re-formation. It's only natural.

Staci and Ray broke from the pack but not from each other. In fact, on this chilly day in October, they're getting hitched by a justice of the peace on an Oregon beach. Staci's freezing because she's wearing a minidress with a vintage Madonna veil and white booties to match, but it's worth it. Ray's got on a leather blazer, faded jeans, and boots, and his beard is combed.

Do you, Raymond Aggatello, take Staci Jozowski, to be your . . .

When Staci realized back in Texas that she could live without him, that's when she started to really love him. Their witness this afternoon, of all people, is Mister Plenty, wearing a pistachio-green Nudie Suit rhinestoned and embroidered with peacocks. He doesn't even live here; he was passing through, ran into them at a Thai restaurant. Because that's his magical way. He also told them Brandy was the one who called. She'd been living with Tim—she was the last holdout—hiding with him and Luther in a Flagstaff duplex.

Tim heard where they were through the El Paso people and couldn't resist making trouble. He called the law anonymously, which could have backfired on him but he just wanted so badly for them to suffer. Brandy went behind his back, finally done with him, and took off to find Trick.

Mister Plenty probably leaves out a few things on purpose. Shayna's seeing some Aryan Brotherhood freak sprung from the Florence complex, leaving Tim to be a single dad. Sherry-Ann and Ashleigh are living in their car somewhere. Cupid moved in with a sugar daddy in New Orleans. Vick and Jared and Carlos are in the wind. Judy's parents take care of her, and no one's heard anything more. He doesn't bring Staci and Ray down with reports from the past. They luxuriate in this beautiful day together.

You may now kiss your bride.

They make out, Staci cheers and shrieks, the sand flying as she does a crazy dance, and they head to the chowder shack down the street where they'll celebrate with Mister Plenty and some strangers, with cheap champagne for everyone and ginger ale with a cherry for Staci, and it will be a good night. Riding there on the bike, Staci's arm wrapped around Ray's waist, she hollers down a crowded block and everyone stops, smiling at this woman whose veil blows psychotically in the wind, and she throws her bouquet into the sky and doesn't look back to see who catches it.

SLASH IS IN a large fenced area at the Exotic Cat Ranch, trees spreading their wide and low branches to shade a jungle gym. Two cheetahs are in there with him. The mangy old male is Sinatra, and he dreams in the sun and farts in his sleep. Victory is a three-year-old female from a black-market baby-cub petting operation in Louisiana; she got feisty at the end of her run and clawed a toddler in the back of the head and was thrown out. She's lucky to be alive.

She weighs 108 pounds, and her eyes are dark as obsidian. She'll attack a human if they scratch behind her ears, and two of her teeth are broken, which tells a story. Slash hissed at her in the beginning whenever she circled him. But today, it's been raining for hours and hours, it shows no sign of letting up, and they both retire to the rock den. He wakes up at a certain point and she's sleeping next to him, and they're purring in sync.

CORAL WEARS A white jumpsuit like all the incarcerated women at Gatesville, and when the guard finishes doing count, she and her bunkie, Tasha, shuffle back into the cell. On her metal desk is Coral's first letter from the Exotic Cat Ranch, which she hands to Tasha to read out loud. Maddie writes that Coral can come volunteer when she serves her term, *if* she stays in touch. Maddie promises to make recommendations with the parole board, and even offers room and board *if* Coral takes the opportunity seriously.

This is an investment that Maddie is making in Coral, and she wants Coral to study animal welfare and biology while inside, and to write and mail her regular updates. She signs the letter: *Sincerely, Maddie Gibbs.* Coral stares at the wall for hours after Tasha folds it into the envelope.

Tasha's half-asleep on her bunk when Coral looms above her. Tasha smiles lopsided. Then Coral holds up loose-leaf and a pencil.

You want me to write it? Tasha asks.

Coral's blue eyes move around Tasha's face. Apparently not. Coral puts the paper on the desk and draws an *A*, slowly, crooked, unsteady, and she sneers at her own hand moving as if disgusted by what she's doing. Tasha stands to look.

Yeah, that's an A.

Then Coral puts Tasha's hand on her own, her eyes transmitting something Tasha can't name. It's not a demand, or desperation, or manipulation. But it's absolute. Tasha teaches her to write a *B*, half-amused, half-alarmed. Then a *C*.

The page fills with the alphabet. And a cosmos of magnificent impossible chaotic raw life is reduced to ink marks.

WHERE DID ERNIE go? To know this means going back to the night they all ran, the night they separated, when he rode the bike alone through rosy dust and cool darkness. He didn't even understand how the machine was finding its way. He peeled off the main road and onto this back road then that one, and yes, blood was slick down his left chest and arm, the bullet went clean through him, the wound was matte with the chalky film of riding. His eyes dull but that didn't mean he wasn't awestruck, downright floored, by where he was going. It was to her house. Fuck, he almost smiled, having zero energy left, except what was keeping him in the seat, but here's her cattle gate, a live oak on each side, wide as sentinels, ashen in the full moon's light. Oh my god, there's the shrubs in the front, the carport, the bird fountain, her car!

He squints, the bike moves, and he might feel tears in his eyes, hot liquid that drops like pearls down his cheeks. He sputters a laugh that might have blood in it. The door opens, he's close enough now, a trail of dust in his past, he's close enough to see. Oh my god, his heart works hard, it's her. No one else has that silhouette in a doorway, lamp behind her. A denim skirt, silver and turquoise on her neck, cowboy shirt. The thick waves and waves of black hair with white streaks on both sides. She hasn't changed. Not one bit. He rolls the bike up, he gets off, he staggers to her, the bike falls but who cares, and she comes to him. Wind shifts the heavy tops of trees in an unearthly way, and just as he falls, she also goes down to the ground, to catch him. She holds him like she did when he was eight, dear and gentle, his lanky legs splayed, his head in the crook of her arm, and he looks up, looks at her face, the sky and its fast clouds beyond, and he breaks wide, his feelings so pure so fierce, he can't, my god he can't even think. All he finally knows, desperately knows, from the look in her eyes—is that she missed him as bad as he missed her. He panics and she soothes him, running her fingers on his cheek.

Why had he never thought of that? How could that be?

He's been loved this whole time.

Acknowledgments

Thanks from the heart to the amazing editors who helped bring this book to fruition: Alexis Washam, for believing in it to begin with, Jillian Buckley for helping me see and sculpt the map of it all, and Kaeli Subberwal for distilling the dimensions of the story into meaning. To David Ebershoff, and also to everyone at Hogarth and Penguin Random House who worked on marketing and publicity and cover design—thank you! So much gratitude to my incredible agent, Sally Wofford-Girand, for always being there and for offering such true support. To the dear sweet friends who read this manuscript and helped make something coherent out of it, I can't thank you enough: Alyson Richman, Jason Crawford, Melissa Tullos, Jim Lewis, Amanda Eyre Ward, Hellin Kay, and my beloved parents (and fellow bookworms) Jack and Debbie Libaire. A million thanks to my fabulous partner in crime, Neil Little, who encourages pushing the envelope in the best way. Thank you to the women who both participated in and facilitated Truth Be Told at the Lockhart Correctional Facility, for reminding me that telling stories is at the core of life, and for teaching me about how people heal themselves and heal each other. And deep thanks forever to my Texas family, who showed me two-stepping at the Broken Spoke and blues at the Continental, hot rod rallies, desert road trips, the bionic book group, a dove flying around the dining room, Frito pie, the joy of Texas rainstorms, brisket and Fredericksburg peaches and Cisco's huevos rancheros, the wild west spirit at its best, late nights at TC's, salade niçoise in a Spartan trailer in a backyard overgrown with grass and wildflowers, Mr. Novak & Conway, ocotillo, loops around the lake, grackles, pomegranate trees, and a thousand other revelations. Lastly, a nod to epic storytellers Boyd Elder and Dave Fry, R.I.P.

About the Author

JARDINE LIBAIRE is the author of *White Fur* and *Here Kitty Kitty*. She is a graduate of the University of Michigan MFA program and lives between Joshua Tree, California, and Austin, Texas.

Instagram: @jardinelibaireprojects

About the Type

This book was set in Albertina, a typeface created by Dutch calligrapher and designer Chris Brand (1921–98). Brand's original drawings, based on calligraphic principles, were modified considerably to conform to the technological limitations of typesetting in the early 1960s. The development of digital technology later allowed Frank E. Blokland (b. 1959) of the Dutch Type Library to restore the typeface to its creator's original intentions.